To

Best wishes.

2023

SLEUTH

OF

BEARS

ANNE LOISELLE

SLEUTH OF BEARS

iUniverse books may be ordered through booksellers or by contacting:

iUniverse
1663 Liberty Drive
Bloomington, IN 47403
www.iuniverse.com
844-349-9409

Because of the dynamic nature of the internet, any web addresses or links contained in this book may have changed since publication and may no longer be valid. The views expressed in this work are solely those of the author and do not necessarily reflect the views of the publisher, and the publisher hereby disclaims any responsibility for them.

Any people depicted in stock imagery provided by Getty Images are models, and such images are being used for illustrative purposes only. Certain stock imagery © Getty Images.

ISBN: 978-1-6632-5272-2 (sc)
ISBN: 978-1-6632-5273-9 (hc)
ISBN: 978-1-6632-5271-5 (e)

Library of Congress Control Number: 2023907640

Print information available on the last page.

iUniverse rev. date: 07/06/2023

For Ron

For Ron.

CONTENTS

Sleuth /sluθ/ *noun*
1. A person who investigates crimes
   Synonyms: detective, investigator, private eye
2. (rare, collective) A group of bears

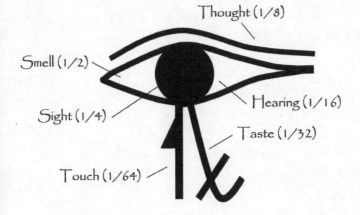

The Six Components of the Eye of Horus

Thought (1/8)

Smell (1/2)

Sight (1/4)

Hearing (1/16)

Taste (1/32)

Touch (1/64)

$(1/2) + (1/4) + (1/8) + (1/16) + (1/32) + (1/64) = 63/64$

PROLOGUE

Lily

This morning heavy fog lifts off the water, which at sixty-three degrees Fahrenheit is still warmer than the air. Last year? I would have thought this was crazy, unthinkable and unfathomable. How could I? And why on earth? But now it's my favorite place, my favorite time, my favorite thing. I look forward to it and then, when the morning has come and it's time to go, I almost chicken out every time. It's going to be so cold. But I can't stand not to get in. I want to go. I slide carefully and oh so slowly into the pool, breathing out hard to fight the urge to gasp as the chill seems to burn my hands and feet. I swim hard for two lengths, surrounded by mist and trees as sunrise begins to make its way up over the old diving well. I change from freestyle to breaststroke just so I can watch it. From there the sensations are familiar, exhilarating. A spark of energy from deep inside gathers and intensifies, emanating outward until the pain subsides. Now the water is glorious. When I finally climb out, I feel no cold at all, only a sense of complete satisfaction, a subtle high. I don't think it consciously, but I feel it: there is no place I'd rather be at this moment. Life is good.

Margaret

The water is freezing, and Margaret's heartbeat revs to its maximum. It is too much for her, and she is already out of breath as she gasps for oxygen under the pelting flow.

"Tell me everything! I won't leave until you tell me!" She hears the hysterical demand.

There can be no secrets now; she must reveal all and save herself. But it's too late. She can't breathe, she can't talk, she can't answer. *No! This can't be happening!* She tries to free her hands, to signal that she wants to speak, but she is unable to move at all. *What else can I do? Will nothing stop this!* Her mind rebels as the horror of it hits her: there will be no respite from the flood, and she will never breathe again.

CHAPTER
ONE

I t's funny how the most mundane events can turn out to be cataclysmic, while a truly extraordinary occurrence barely makes a ripple. Today, for example, started out just a normal day, really, with no premonition whatsoever of what was to come. It's early in October but bright and warm, verging on hot, this midafternoon as I stand and survey the lunchtime assemblage. We can accommodate as many as eighteen, and I note with satisfaction that we're almost full.

My name is Lily Piper. I am twenty-five and a yoga instructor at an Eye of Horus studio in Bethesda, Maryland (one of the tonier suburbs of Washington, DC). For the past two years, I've been clawing my way back to a semblance of normalcy. Each day, when I venture forth and do my thing and it's all okay, it's like a tiny miracle. While true happiness still eludes me, I have at least found balance and a sense of peace. I think that I am on the path to wellness, and I keep at it even though, to be perfectly honest, something is still missing—something big, but I can't put my finger on exactly what. I try not to dwell on that too much and instead take heart in knowing that I am healthy now, even fit, although not exactly what you'd expect in a yoga instructor. I'm short and stocky, perpetually fighting the extra pounds that come so easily and then refuse to budge. Hair that is currently short and curly is beginning to fall irritatingly over hazel eyes because I'm growing it out. When it's longer, the curls turn into waves, which really shows off my one secret vanity: a few naturally caramel-colored strands that beautifully highlight what would otherwise be a rather ordinary head of light brown hair.

"Hello, everyone. Ready to begin? Let's make a circle." Anyone who's ever been to other yoga studios will notice a difference at Eye of Horus right away. We usually start class in a circle. Everyone taps rhythmically with both hands just below the belly button. This is a simple exercise, but it warms the core and gently gets the blood pumping. I like it because we start the class looking at each other. When we see each other, we make a connection, albeit a subtle one. The more we make these connections, the more we strengthen our ability to connect to a higher and more universal energy. It takes barely a minute, and then we spread out into the room to begin our flow. We are still together but are now solely focused on our own bodies.

Looking around the room, it dawns on me that I know them all—their names, their levels of ability, even some of their quirks. When did this happen? I don't remember exactly. I began as a student with some of them, and others came on board after I became an instructor, but it always felt like a struggle to remember each of their names. Now it seems so obvious, and this realization, too, feels satisfying. Progress has a way of being invisible except in rare moments like this one, when you encounter stark proof of improvement. I lead the class through exercises that open our hearts and inspire creativity, and I myself finish up feeling energized and primed for action, for adventure, for anything new and exciting. They say that if you're open to it, opportunity will find you, but that always seemed so nebulous to me. I have to say, though, after today, I can't help wondering.

At the end of each class, we invite everyone to come back into a circle for a cup of tea. We instructors prepare it ahead of time in one of those big thermoses with the spout, and we have a tray ready with small Japanese-style cups. Those who choose to stay park themselves on the floor in the middle of the room, sipping and chatting for just a few minutes. Once again, it is connective, a way to finish as a community, a group together, not individuals alone.

In truth, most people head immediately back to the changing rooms to get on with the rest of their days, but there are always a few who stay. Sure enough, while the rest of the class bustles quickly out into the sunshine, this afternoon my four "regulars"—the ones who never skip the tea circle—congregate in our usual spot, waiting patiently for me to join them. These are the clients I feel I know best, so I guess in a way they're my favorites. It's always funny to me when I look back later at this tenuous beginning, but that's the way it goes—you rarely know it was a beginning except in hindsight.

I sit down in the space they've left for me, next to Miller Nguyen, who is short like me, with a hint of pudge beginning to spread over her fortysomething frame. Miller is Vietnamese by birth and still speaks with a distinctive melodic accent. She always seems to be in a hurry and does not suffer fools, gladly or otherwise. I used to be terrified of her, but she has always been friendly to me and lately I'm finding her bluntness to be enlightening rather than intimidating. You know exactly where you stand with Miller.

By now they're all familiar with each other, so no one is shy, but even so it's usually I who starts the conversation, breaking the ice by describing that day's tea and why I chose it. The nuances among different types of tea is an interest of mine, so it's an easy topic to share. Today, of course, is different. Today Karen Ellsworth plunges right in. She's the newest of the regulars, and although in her midthirties, she feels to me most like my kindred spirit. When Karen first came in, she was heavy and sluggish, but just six months after joining us, she has firmed up noticeably, and she's had her sandy blond hair trimmed to sport youthful bangs and a bouncy ponytail. At the moment, she is clearly troubled, the sparkle missing from her eyes.

"Something came up at work," she says. "I keep trying to decide what the right thing to do is, but every time I look at it from a different angle, I change my mind. I don't know if I've mentioned this before, but I'm an administrator at Austin Hill Hospital. I was reviewing paperwork from the morgue today, and I'm pretty sure we've performed an autopsy on someone we shouldn't have."

The circle lets out a laugh. We're not insensitive, but such a statement coming out of the blue does sound comical. She certainly has our attention, though, and she knows we're not laughing at her or her dilemma.

Haisley, who is about my age and a graduate student, is the first to respond. She is slender and toned, pretty but with a little bit of geekiness that can come across as ditzy sometimes. It's as if her brain is moving in a million directions that she doesn't have time to explain before she makes some comment that, at first glance, doesn't quite seem to make sense. Then again, sometimes she says exactly what I'm thinking.

"The person was dead, right? Don't they autopsy everyone who dies at the hospital?"

Miller adds, "Does it even matter? I mean, it's not like operating on the wrong person. They can't suffer, right?"

"No, that's true, and in a way that's my quandary." Karen shakes her head ruefully. "Actually," she turns toward Haisley, "not everyone gets autopsied. Suspicious deaths do, of course, but in cases where it's clearly a death by natural causes, there usually isn't one unless the family requests it. Even if for some reason the hospital wants to perform one, like for research or some community health scare, the family must give permission. A lot of families don't want an autopsy to take place. They may have religious objections, or they want the body to be preserved for viewing at the funeral. They don't really need a reason; it's horrible for almost anyone to think of a loved one's body being cut up."

Normally the circle disbands after finishing their tea, but this time everyone helps themselves to a second cup. We're riveted on Karen, but I sense that she's mostly thinking to herself even though she's talking aloud to us.

"We're very careful. We log all arrivals; paperwork follows each body as it goes through our facility and then gets sent to a funeral home or wherever the family requests. The medical examiners are pretty busy, so an extra, unwarranted, autopsy would only exacerbate the backlog. I mean, a mistake like this is really extraordinary. I don't believe it's ever happened before at our morgue, and I can't quite see how it could happen at all. But I think maybe it did. The paperwork states that the person—it's a woman named Margaret—suffered from COPD and congenital heart failure and died about midafternoon on Monday. There is no accompanying request for a postmortem by the family or any presiding doctor, and no permission form signed by next of kin. But the record has a flag stating that the medical examiner's report is pending, so he must have performed an autopsy. The family requested that the deceased be delivered to Yeates Funeral Home, but now we can't release the body until the report is in."

Karen looks up at the ceiling, shuts her eyes, then brings them down to look at us. She sighs, but if that was an attempt to release tension, it doesn't look like it worked. "I'm hoping the report will come in quickly and we can just send the body on with no one noticing the delay. But … should they know? Would it be upsetting for no reason? Or is it the right thing to do to tell the family? Suppose I just file the medical examiner's report when it comes and have the body sent on. Am I kidding myself and making it complicated when really I just don't want to let this screwup get known? Maybe they'll sue. Maybe someone will get fired."

We're quiet for a minute, feeling sympathetic but not sure what to say. What a position. Redd is watching Karen, and I can see from his expression that it pains him to see her so upset. Redd is tall and thin with graying hair. In his sixties, he's one of our oldest clients, quiet but popular. While he's a bit of an anomaly among us because of his age, because he is male, and because he is African American, Redd himself is wonderfully unfazed by all of this, so comfortable is he in his own skin.

"We can't tell you what to do, Karen," he says. "But we can sure tell how stressed this is making you. I'm thinking that old adage 'The truth will set you free' might be something to consider. If you have a boss, or if there is someone else in charge at the hospital, it will probably set your mind at ease to let that person know the truth. One step at a time, you know?"

The others debate the merits of this statement for a few minutes, but we don't come to an absolute answer before we really do need to break up and be on our way. We all wonder about it, though, and want to know how it turned out. Karen doesn't appear for the rest of the week, and our curiosity mounts. Also, I'm starting to worry about her, as she so rarely misses a class. I have a closer relationship to Karen than I do any of the others, mainly because she was enjoying the classes so much she was considering going for instructor certification. Sometimes after class she and I would sit in the reception area and talk about how she might approach the training, and occasionally we'd drift onto other topics too. We didn't see each other outside the studio, but I started to think of her as a friend, and I have a feeling she'd say the same about me. Should I give her a call and check in on her? Maybe she's sick; maybe there was a family emergency. I don't want to intrude, but I don't want to abandon her either.

If I'm honest, I have to admit that what I really want to know is whether her absence is related to the hospital snafu that she described to us. Such a strange thing to happen, a puzzle to figure out, and one with high stakes for Karen and her job at the hospital. Did it all get resolved, or is Karen in trouble? I can't stop thinking about it, and I'm not the only one. The other four of us keep asking the same questions whenever we see each other: "Have you heard from Karen? Did you ever find out what happened?"

CHAPTER
TWO

B efore I can decide what to do, Karen herself appears back in
class. I see her talking to Redd rather animatedly before the
start. Redd would be my choice too. He comes across as something
of a wise professor—even-keeled, unflappable. I'm glad and relieved
that Karen is back; I'm also dying to know how things turned out
at the hospital. But this day's tea circle is one of our larger crowds,
and while Karen stays for it, she doesn't speak. However, she, Redd,
and Miller stay behind to help clear up. We always request a few
volunteers to Swiffer the bamboo floors and wash the cups after
each class. It's helpful for us instructors, but it is also Eye of Horus
philosophy that performing routine menial tasks is part of the
practice, as it helps maintain mental equilibrium. Not so for today's
volunteers though. Today is more about assuaging Miller's curiosity
and defusing Karen's palpable dismay. The two of them and Redd
end up all together in our backroom kitchen, nattering away. They
spill out the door to include me in the conversation.

"The medical examiner called me the day after I told you guys
about the accidental autopsy," Karen explains to bring me up to
speed. "In fact, I was about to call him myself and tell him about
the accident, and just, you know… maybe see if he'd help me out. I
mean, I'm responsible for the paperwork, so he might blame me for
being the one who wasted his time, but I've talked to him before;
he's super nice. His name is Benjamin Benton, but, not surprisingly,
everyone calls him Dr. Ben." She's rambling a little, and I'm starting

to wonder where all this is going. But it's interesting, too, like watching big drama on TV—you're invested because you know the characters, but you're safe because none of it is your problem.

"Before I had a chance to say anything, he told *me* that his report was in, and that he'd deemed it a homicide by drowning."

Redd whistles. "Whoo boy. Didn't you say this death was due to natural causes? Nothing suspicious, so there was no need for an autopsy? And now that they did this autopsy, they're saying it's a murder? Mm mm mm." He shakes his head. "That's messed up."

"Is he really sure?" I add. "Did you see the report? How is he so sure? This does sound pretty messed up."

"Oh my God," says Karen, squinching her eyes shut and reliving the horror. "I couldn't believe it. I mean—how could this be? Here I was, thinking it might all just wash out, or at least that we just deal with it quietly, and then that call. Even over the phone Dr. Ben could tell something was wrong."

Haisley suddenly appears. I didn't know it, but she lives in the apartment complex just down the street from the studio. Miller, apparently, did know this and texted her to let her know that Karen had shown up and was talking. The things you find out. I had no idea Miller and Haisley knew each other so well, or that Miller even had Haisley's phone number. Turns out Miller has everyone's phone number. She's an inveterate networker (gossip?) and collects contact information like virtual challenge awards. I still can't decide if that is more creepy or more entrepreneurially astute, but it does come in handy sometimes.

"I just blurted out, asking him if he was sure we were talking about the right body. That was probably the rudest thing I could have done, and he could have taken serious umbrage, but he just asked me why the question. He was so nice, I, well, I told him everything."

"Ah ha!" says Redd with a nod.

"Oh, good" and "Oh no!" say Haisley and Miller, respectively, at the same time. This gets us laughing, and Karen wobbles her head side to side as if agreeing with them both.

"I did. I told him the family didn't know about the autopsy and the hospital didn't know it was done by accident. There wasn't a whiff of suspicious death or any reason to think Margaret's passing wasn't completely natural. I guess I was kind of hoping he would help me de-escalate the situation [her words, very administrative sounding to me, but a lot of us revert to job-speak when we're thinking and talking about our jobs], or maybe I was just hoping it would turn out to be the wrong body. But of course, it wasn't. Oh yeah. Dr. Ben's turn to be stunned."

"So ... what happened? What did he do?" asks Miller.

"At first he was completely taken aback. But he was still pretty calm and just asked if maybe I could come down to his office so we could talk this through. He didn't get angry; he just had me go over everything I knew again as he pulled up the paperwork to make certain we really were talking about the same body. It sure was. Her name is Margaret Crawford, and the number on her tag matched the one for a body reported to be a suspicious death, but her description did not. You should have seen his face—white as a sheet, huge eyes—but he didn't freak out or anything. He went back to the morgue and checked all the bodies and their paperwork. She had the wrong tag."

"What? How? What does that mean? What happened?" This basically came from all of us, a discordant chorus.

"I don't know how yet; that will be a whole separate investigation. But somehow she ended up with the number tag of a suspicious death, while that person's body ended up with Margaret's. Thank God the other body was still there when we had this conversation. So while, yes, there was this whole hullabaloo going on at the hospital, they were still able to perform the autopsy on the real suspicious death. It had nearly been sent to the funeral parlor for cremation as Margaret. That would have been ... jeez ... I don't even know.

What's a word worse than 'horrendous'? As it is, this is a calamity for the hospital, but that would have been beyond disastrous ..." At this, Karen closes her eyes and brings her fists to her forehead, a classic pose of someone in the throes of imagining the worst. For an instant, it strikes me as interesting that we all perform this same mannerism when catastrophe strikes. Why? How did we learn it? But just as quickly, I'm back, listening intently again to Karen.

"Even after all this, Dr. Ben isn't changing his report. He's convinced that her death was not of natural causes. When he first examined the body, he concluded death by homicidal drowning. He's standing by that."

CHAPTER
THREE

"**A**ny of you feel like going over to the Iguana? I'm thinking an adult beverage would go down pretty good right now," says Redd.

The Tijuana Iguana is a bar and grill in the same shopping center as our studio. It's fine as far as it goes—standard bar fare, fun-ish decor, caters to the lunch and happy hour crowd. Its greatest attraction is its proximity, although Redd's suggestion was pretty unusual. In fact, I've never been to the Iguana or anywhere else with any class members. Normally everyone is hurrying home or to pick up kids or walk the dog or whatever. But it suddenly seems very appealing to me, and clearly, I'm not alone.

"I'd love to!" says Karen immediately.

"Sure, why not," says Miller.

"I have to get to class," says Haisley, somewhat unhappily pointing to the backpack lying at her feet.

"Maybe next time," sympathizes Miller. "I just have to let my husband know." Karen and Redd are already on it for themselves, one on the phone, the other texting. I give Haisley a rueful grin and promise to catch her up soon. The rest of us collect our things and head out the door and down the sidewalk. We're already inside, scoping out where to sit, when Haisley comes rushing in. "I changed my mind!" she says, laughing. "I'm officially skipping class in favor of drunkenness and debauchery!" We cheer her decision, find a table, and give our order. Turns out they have a pretty good happy hour deal.

"So tell us more," Miller starts in. "Why homicide? And what are they doing now?"

"This is such a mess," Karen answers. "Of course, Margaret Crawford's family is confused and aghast; they're threatening to sue, calling us incompetent, wondering if the report is yet another mistake. And of course, the hospital is horrified at the possibility of a lawsuit, but they're also bending over backward to be helpful to the police, since that original suspicious death was mislabeled and nearly destroyed without being examined. Speaking of which, it's kind of ironic; in the end, that one was ruled an accidental death, not a homicide. So ... we're kinda sorta in the clear for that one. I mean, at least in this case there won't be a criminal investigation that gets thrown out and the bad guys go free because we don't know what we're doing. The Margaret thing is another whole can of worms though." She stops talking as our order arrives, drinks get distributed, and appetizers are placed on the table. We all take little plates and start helping ourselves, passing the apps around.

"Margaret's family is kind of interesting," Karen continues, just before taking a bite of a hot wing.

"To Margaret!" says Redd, and we toast. "Now, why do you say the family is interesting?"

"She was divorced, with one grown son with disabilities. Her sister flew in to organize the funeral and close out the estate, and she's been our main contact. I'm not sure what's wrong with the son exactly. His name is Nico, and he can talk and engage, but you can just tell he's not fully operating on an adult mental level. He also has severe epilepsy and has issues with balance, so he wears a bicycle helmet everywhere he goes and walks with a cane even though he's only in his twenties. He lives in a special-needs housing development called Sherwood Independent Living, so he's in a group house with other adults with disabilities and a house captain. The house captain—a guy named Geoff—has been helpful. He's very patient, as Nico's questions tend to be a little bizarre, but Geoff seems to have a knack for bringing him back to earth and getting to what he's really asking and why." Here Karen pauses for a few more bites and a sip before continuing.

"The sister's name is Alice Munney. She's feisty, and she's the one adding the firepower. That is, she hasn't hired a lawyer yet—at least not that we've heard from—but she did go storming to the chief administrator about the autopsy, threatening to sue and wanting the body left in peace. But then when she heard the medical examiner wasn't backing down from homicide, I have to say she quieted down. Maybe she's thinking that her sister was murdered and she wants the killer to be found, or maybe she's involved and is worried. I can't tell; everything I hear is secondhand, as the family deals directly with our chief administrator at this point. Damage control, you know?"

"Hmm," says Miller. "Maybe she wanted to rush this through and now she's afraid someone is onto her so she's laying low!"

"Could be." I nod. "But anyone would be angry about an unrequested autopsy, especially since you said she flew in from out of town, right? She probably wanted to settle as many affairs for Nico as possible and get home quickly, so at a minimum this is probably an unwanted delay for her. Then, when she learned her sister was actually murdered, the fact that she's making less fuss about the autopsy could mean she's not so angry about that anymore. Maybe she wants Margaret to be avenged." I'm thinking about my best friend Tessa. My guardian angel, my salvation when I was at rock bottom, Tessa is the closest thing I have to a big sister. I would want her to rest in peace; I would be defensive about her body being cut open and measured and mauled because of some administrative accident. But if it turned out someone had murdered her ... just the thought brings my hackles up, and I'm ready to fight. No way would I want anyone to take her life and get away with it. I'd want them to pay, all right.

"Yeah yeah." Miller snags the remains of the zucchini fries. "But you say her son is disabled? Maybe the sister thought she could take advantage and steal Margaret's money or something."

Miller comes across as a little cynical, and maybe she is, but mostly she is just very outspoken. If it enters her head, she says it out loud—good or bad. She once told me, "You sure don't look like a yoga instructor, but you're good at this! I come to your classes whenever I can. They're really different." I remember feeling flattered, affronted, and bemused all at the same time. But ultimately it was this frankness that really made me warm to her. I think she's honest and she's bold. Also, she probably doesn't mean to be, but I find her very funny.

"Maybe she thinks it's the son who did it; his name is Nico, right? Maybe he's not just disabled, maybe he's, like, a dual personality or something and has a violent side! Maybe she wants to protect him." This contribution is from Haisley.

"What I want to know," interjects Redd, "is why Dr. Ben thinks this wasn't just a natural causes death, and are the police taking it on?"

"That's getting interesting too," Karen starts in again. The appetizers are gone, but we've all ordered a second round of drinks. I'm not a big drinker, and for some reason I don't think the others are either, although I don't know them well enough to say. But happy hour three-dollar beer and five-dollar house wine—that's quite compelling. It feels so cozy, as if we're all in on something together. No doubt about it, I'm starting to feel the pull of socializing again, after a very long dry spell. *Enjoy it*, I tell myself. This is probably therapeutic for me.

"I think I told you guys before that I know Dr. Ben a little from around the hospital—he's nice, he's friendly, and he's always in the line early for taco Tuesday lunch day, as am I. So, we've talked, and he always seems so mild mannered. But I'm starting to think he has some 'umph' to him too."

"Umph?" Haisley looks at me, probably because we're the closest in age. "Is that some kind of old-timey slang?"

"Umph," says Karen. "Spirit! Guts! Fortitude! Something. Maybe it's a sense of justice, but he doesn't want someone to get away with murder. He's getting questions and pushback, and he's always calm, but he won't let his findings get discounted.

"He's taken to stopping at my table when he sees me in the cafeteria, I think just to talk to someone who is in the know but not in a position of authority—at least, not someone who is determined to convince him what to do, one way or the other."

According to Dr. Ben, Karen tells us, a homicidal drowning is largely determined by circumstances surrounding the death, such as previous threats or abuse, a big new life insurance policy—stuff like that—and by the absence of obvious natural causes rather than the types of things that turn up in an autopsy. He confessed that he took special care with Margaret only because she was tagged as a suspicious death; he assumed that meant that there were other factors that indicated something was amiss, and someone wanted to see whether an autopsy could confirm that suspicion.

"So it's a little bit chicken-eggy how he made his determination," says Karen, taking another break to sip more wine.

We're quiet, also enjoying our drinks but engrossed in the details as Karen tells us more of what she learned from Dr. Ben. It turns out that while Margaret did have COPD and indications of congenital heart failure, these did not appear to him advanced enough to have caused her death now. While either of these diseases could have eventually progressed enough to cause her demise, that was not at all likely to happen this year, and maybe not even this decade. So what else could have caused her death? During the autopsy, Dr. Ben found a bruise near the top of her head, a little to one side and covered by her hair. It was in the shape of a circle with faint dots inside, like a drain. Karen stops here and peers at us as if over imaginary glasses.

"That's a pretty strange bruise, but it's what would happen if someone grabbed you by the neck and pushed your head down into a bathtub. Dr. Ben said that if you turned on the faucet full blast, it wouldn't even require a lot of water to accumulate; you could drown in the flow."

I glance over at Miller, who mouths "Oh, man," and then at Redd, who is again shaking his head sadly.

"Doesn't sound good," he says.

"No, it doesn't," agrees Karen, "and he found other things that back up that scenario." She tells us Margaret had froth inside her mouth and nostrils, water came out of her mouth when Dr. Ben pushed on her abdomen, and her lungs were abnormally distended. These, he told her, are what one would expect to see in a drowning victim, not someone who just died naturally.

"Uh huh," Redd says, nodding. "So that's conclusive?"

Karen shakes her head. "Not completely. There's almost no such thing as conclusive autopsy evidence of homicide by drowning. But Dr. Ben told me that he was convinced there's something here, since it's so rare to see all these things together. He also told me that the only way to ensure further investigation was to write 'homicide' in the report. He says that to prove it, and then hopefully find out who did it and get them convicted, there has to be a real police investigation, and he thinks that needs to happen. That's why he's not backing down on his conclusion. Like I said, he's a quiet but determined defender of justice." Karen says this last sentence with a smile and her eyebrows raised meaningfully at us. I interpret this as approbation for Dr. Ben's stance, mixed with wonderment that he's putting himself on the line in this way.

Karen's phone buzzes, and after glancing down at the message she looks back at us and shrugs. "This was really nice, but I'd better get going. My daughter wants to know what's for dinner and when is it."

As Karen gathers her things, Miller says, "Tell us more next class!"

Redd follows that with, "Oh yeah! Keep us informed! This is getting interesting!"

Soon after Karen's departure, we all start to make our moves to leave. Haisley and I are the last ones out the door, and she turns to me with a joyful smile and says, "This *was* really nice. So much better than taking notes in class. We should do it again! For us uninvolved observers, Karen's little mystery is the best entertainment in town. I hope we do learn more." I grin and nod back. I think so too.

I'm not callous, but now that I know Karen is fine and still has her job, I have to admit that I leave the Iguana filled with a general sense of bonhomie and good cheer rather than anything akin to sadness, and certainly not unease. Of course, I can't help thinking about Margaret on the way home. What was she like in life, and does she have someone to fight for her now? That fleeting notion from the Iguana has stuck with me—that I would be outraged if I found out that someone had murdered Tessa. My mind shifts back and forth between Tessa and Margaret, my emotions merging them together. I would want to know who and why, and I would want that person to spend the rest of his life regretting such an abomination. Yes, I would be there for her after death if necessary. Tessa gave me a restart at life; she opened the door to a way for me to heal and guided me through it. Guid*ing*, I should say, as she has never stopped.

CHAPTER
FOUR

Tessa Corbin is my babysitter. Well, I mean, not anymore of course, but that's how we met. I was six and she was seventeen, in her last year of high school. My parents trusted her completely; they knew they never had to worry when I was in her care. She was wonderful—easy to be around, guided by the rules but not absolutely strict with them, somehow always able to talk to me like an equal but maintain her status in my mind as the one in charge. We'd play games and do crafts, and time would fly. Our association continued for years, as Tessa remained at home after graduation, taking her time deciding what to do next. I often went to visit her even after I was old enough to look after myself, and she always welcomed me. For some reason, the vast age difference between us never kept us from being close friends.

Now Tessa lives with her husband Frank and their four kids. And I live in their pool house, converted years ago into a guest house. We live our separate lives, with many days going by when we barely see each other, but it's turned out to be a wonderfully convenient solution, a win-win, as they say. I don't pay rent—Tessa and Frank won't hear of it. They love a full house, and I love their kids, and Tessa and Frank know I'm always happy to watch them if they want to get away for a while. I'm the perfect fallback; it's a rare evening indeed when I'm not at home.

My life is very simple now, stripped to the bare essentials. This is not by choice, but how many of the really big changes in life come to us by choice? It doesn't feel like a bad thing though—quite the opposite. Maybe it's a state of preparation, the way to start from nothing to begin the process of re-creation. Maybe this is where I need to be in order to take the next big step; maybe this is the only way I'll be able to figure out what that step is. I feel on the verge of being happy, but I'm not quite there yet. I don't know what it's going to take to make it over that final hump. Sometimes it feels so close; sometimes it feels like a chasm that I divide infinitely in half, so the gap gets smaller and smaller but never disappears. When I'm not relieved about my current state, I'm vexed by it.

I started life an optimist, a lover of fun, a giggler, an extrovert. I was ambitious and competitive, and although I hated losing, that was still an acceptable outcome for the sheer pleasure of being in the game. I was not a worrier. I was confident, enthusiastic, fearless. I was a bit of a brainiac but loved playing sports and being on the team. Any team.

Before the accident, I was on a kind of career frenzy. After graduating early from high school, I started on full scholarship to the University of Maryland at seventeen. I was determined to be head of the class, determined to get the best graduate fellowship, determined to discover something that would change the world. I dreamed of winning the Nobel Prize or something like it, imagining myself at the forefront of dramatic breakthroughs. I knew exactly where I was and was in a hurry to get where I was going: I was going to the top.

Driving back to the dorm one night after attending a guest lecture series at American U., I didn't check my blind spot and merged straight into a truck. My car was totaled; the truck didn't come out too badly. The same could be said of the drivers. The truck driver walked away essentially unscathed. I was in a coma for two days and had breaks and cracks and tears all over. I was in the hospital for almost three weeks, and I spent many months after that still recuperating. Everything went into a tailspin.

The things that were torn or broken eventually did heal up. But my head, my brain, didn't go back to normal. I became depressed, pessimistic, anxious, and utterly asocial. I couldn't stand to be around other people, but I also couldn't stand myself. There was nothing to look forward to, nothing that was stimulating or interesting. Old pastimes that used to keep me active, or even simple pleasures like watching movies, could not hold my attention. I became preoccupied with ending it all by ending my life, more as the only comfort I could find to cling to than as a real intent. Sports? Exercise? Oh, hell no. Movement produced aches and pains that hadn't been there before and that I didn't feel motivated to overcome. Instead, I slept during the day, lay awake at night, and ate—mostly junk food, to alleviate the boredom that led me back to the path of that one fixation: making it all stop, somehow, some way. I imagined shooting myself, jumping off a building, going to any extreme to end forever my ability to think and so to be unhappy. I was never a pixie, but in college I was in pretty good shape and wore normal-sized clothes. After the accident, I gained sixty pounds. At least. I stopped getting on the scale. I felt lackluster and woolly. I wore enormous baggy clothes or crammed myself unforgivingly into ones that had become much too tight. Either way, I looked terrible. My despair grew deeper.

The first ray of possibility came from out of nowhere, on another day like so many since the accident: wintery cold, gloomy, a weekday—but I was not at work. Once again, I had called in sick for no reason. I was still in bed in late afternoon, disgusted with myself and slightly panicked at the passage of time. This had happened too many times. My stopgap job as an office assistant, such as it was, was in jeopardy. I was living in a run-down room in a run-down townhouse with three other students—well, with three students, as I was no longer enrolled anywhere. While they were friendly, I knew they felt as much as I that I was the odd one out. But this was all I could afford—and if I lost my job, well, I had no plan for that. A year after the accident, I was fully recovered in every way. Except that I wasn't—not nearly. I was going backward.

That day, I felt as if I just had to get myself up and out. I was terrified I would end up spending the entire day in bed and wake up in the morning to ... knowing that. This was my perpetual paradigm: I was afraid to move and afraid not to. Finally I decided to go to McDonald's. The motivation of french fries and greasy food was just enough. I bundled myself into a big winter coat and walked down the sidewalk toward my destination.

I felt a lot better almost immediately. It was cold, but with patchy sun amid the clouds, it was not nearly as gloomy as it had seemed from inside. So when I saw Tessa, I was happy; I had bumped into the one person on earth I actually wanted to see. She was the Tessa I remembered of old: quiet, gentle, nurturing, protective. She'd been for a run in Rock Creek Park but now was starting to feel chilled so on the spur of the moment had decided to get some hot coffee and a croissant. When she invited me to join her, I said yes right away. We've never needed small talk, and we didn't here. I was genuinely interested to hear about her life with Frank and her kids; I was at her wedding and at her first baby shower, and I had even babysat her kids a few times before the accident, but we hadn't seen each other for a couple of years. None of that mattered. She broke the ice with her own news but knew, as she always does, what I really needed at that moment. She said I seemed sad and asked what was wrong, and out it poured. I didn't say everything was great or that I was just recuperating but would go back to college next semester or any of the things I would say when I ran into other people I knew. I told her what was going on for real and how I felt for real. That's how it's always been for me with Tessa.

"Lily," she said, "I'm so sorry. I wish I'd known earlier; I would have come over! You know, maybe you just need some time and space to either heal more or figure out how to move on with who you are now. You know the guest house is empty now. Why don't you come stay there with us, and we can take care of each other a bit? The kids love you, and Frank would love to have someone bring the guest house to life. Just the other day he mentioned how it seems so forlorn with no one there. You can swim in the pool too; maybe it'll help you start moving more without being in pain."

And that was it: a lifeline, a way out, the first possibility of a move that I didn't dread. It wasn't the end, of course; I proceeded through all the phases of guilt, fear of failing even this unencumbered gift, fear of destroying Tessa's love for the old Lily by showing her the new one. Yes, there was all of that. But that was mostly later. This day I ate a small, healthy-ish meal instead of those french fries, walked home with a sense of hope and motivation, and sorted and packed long into the night. Out of the blue, the day had ended better than it began.

CHAPTER
FIVE

Today seems to be ending well too. I'm on a little high from the ad hoc trip to the Iguana, socializing with friends for the first time in months, the intrigue of Karen's hospital conundrum, and that extra glass of wine. Instead of going straight home to what has become my usual routine of some simple but healthy dinner, more often than not followed up with way too many miniature cookies, I knock on Tessa's door. She and Frank are in the kitchen; Frank is making loaves of bread (Frank loves baking bread) and Tessa is "supervising" while sipping peppermint tea. They both seem happy to see me, so I pull up a chair, help myself to a mug of tea, and tell them about the mystery. They find it intriguing, too, and ask some good questions, to which I have no answers. Then Frank, who is a realtor, asks where Margaret lived. This is a new one, as it hadn't occurred to me to wonder, but it's a very Frank kind of question.

Talking about Margaret makes me want to know more about her, so when Frank grabs his laptop and starts searching, I wait and watch expectantly. While there are many Margaret Crawfords in the world, there aren't all that many older ladies in town here with that name, so we narrow it down quickly to the likely correct one. Frank then finds not one but two addresses; Margaret had apparently downsized recently. He uncovers that she had owned a house near Old Georgetown Road for many years but sold it in April and bought a townhouse only a few miles away. We're on a roll, so we check out both properties on his realtor site to see whether there are

23

any photographs. Frank can't help himself when it comes to houses, and I'm just enjoying the hunt.

Margaret's first house turns out to be nice enough on the outside, not huge by suburban DC standards, but with a pretty good-sized yard and screened-in side porch. It had been built some sixty years ago, with a full basement and an attic. The first floor comprised a living room, separate dining room, and updated kitchen, along with the master bedroom and master bath. A vaulted ceiling over the foyer and living room robbed the upstairs of space, but even so it accommodated two bedrooms side by side with a full bathroom at the end of the hall. The basement wasn't finished, the photos showing a concrete floor and old-fashioned drop-down ceiling with those long fluorescent lights you see in workshops. Sliding glass doors led out back. It sounds voyeuristic, but there's something gripping about seeing the living quarters of a person who has recently died.

Of course, Margaret was long gone from here and in her new place, but these photos show how she left it when she sold it. She is suddenly very alive and real to me—someone who packed up the house where she lived so much of her adult life and moved to a new one. Was she looking forward to starting fresh? Was she happy? This brings me immediately to thinking about the day she died. What was Margaret doing? How did she drown? Did she suffer?

Frank clicks next on the townhouse where Margaret moved, which is a much more recently built two-bedroom, two-bath unit. The primary suite takes up the entire second floor and includes a huge bathroom and a separate laundry area. The first floor is open-concept living/dining room and kitchen, with a second bedroom and hall bathroom off to the side.

"Both bathrooms have a bathtub," notes Frank. I nod my head but don't say anything. All the pictures of the townhouse would have been taken before Margaret moved in, so we don't really know what she had done with it, but even so, seeing where she lived, where she died, is starting to feel ever so slightly macabre to me.

"I can't believe it. Someone almost got away with her murder. Maybe still will get away with it."

"Hopefully not, now that the medical examiner has weighed in," says Frank. "Makes you wonder though. He only examined her by mistake. Are accidents really accidents, or is it fate?"

Fate. Margaret's murder should never have been discovered, but by a fluke of fate, it was. And me? I was looking for adventure, and here it is, opportunity knocking. The ME has got the police investigating, but will they find her killer? Or will she languish forever as undetermined, eventually relegated to an eternal cold-case file? My eyes swivel between Tessa, now collecting the mugs and putting them in the sink, and the laptop, with Margaret's townhouse still displayed, and something of my old drive and determination kicks in. If it were Tessa, I wouldn't let it drop. I'd follow the case, press the police for answers, even see what I could find out on my own. I could do that for Margaret. I feel a surge of excitement at the very idea.

Not wanting to alarm my hosts with my newfound intent, I start making moves to leave. It's getting late anyway, and Tessa needs to get the kids ready for bed.

"Let us know if you hear anything more," she says.

"Sure thing!" I promise as I head out the door. With a quick wink, Frank hands me a warm, fresh loaf of sourdough to take along. Heaven.

Back in my own place, I turn on the TV and sit on the couch with my laptop, surfing aimlessly as I'm wide awake but not quite sure where to start. At some point I notice that Karen is online too. After hesitating for a moment, I risk opening up a chat with her. I don't do this as a rule—my current state of introversion finds the idea of online chatting as abhorrent as other forms of interaction— but as I say, I'm feeling loose and garrulous this evening. Anyway, she responds, and I tell her about the houses. She tells me I'm a weirdo (but with laughing emojis!) and that I should find myself a real hobby. She's right, of course. I send her a thumbs-up and a smiley face, and with that we close our chat.

Houses—I can start there.

I look up Sherwood Independent Living, where Margaret's son Nico lives. Score! The address is a bikeable distance away, which is good because I don't own a car. I haven't developed any particular phobias about them; it's just that I have so little money now that I can't afford the payments, the gas, and the insurance that owning would require. But my bike is an e-bike, which means it has an electric motor that provides extra speed and allows me to pedal easily over hills, and I enjoy how it wakes me up and warms my muscles. Not only is going over to take a look doable, but it will make for a pleasant ride.

CHAPTER
SIX

With a plan in place, I'm done for the day, so after an exciting evening contemplating death and murder, I find myself snugly tucked up in bed by 10:00 p.m., thinking about life. The process of life changes you; it changes your body, it changes your brain, it changes your outlook and your beliefs. Sometimes the change is an obvious course, expected and unremarkable. Sometimes it is calamitous, comes out of nowhere, and is unfair. "My life is ruined," we may think, or "changed forever," or others may say, "She was never the same again." This is when things change dramatically, with the changes being unplanned and often unwanted. But really, these things, too, are just the process of living; if you've ever aged a day, a year, or a decade, you've changed forever, never to be the same again. As for ruined, well, that is in the eye of the beholder. To look back on what used to be, on what was promise and potential, can provide a bleak contrast to what you are today. Promise is no promise; it is a glimpse of one possibility out of millions for the future you, should you remain on earth to see it. Everyone knows this, but not everyone *knows* it, consciously reflecting each day as it goes by, "Okay, here we are. This is me today. Now what am I going to do with it?" I know it now. I take nothing for granted.

Tessa was the first big thing that started me on my path back to this semblance of health and contentment. Eye of Horus yoga was the second. In both cases, I was desperate but not sure where to look for help, and I just came upon them. Is this accident? Fate? Luck?

Coincidence? I've thought about these questions often, but they're unanswerable. It's one of those times when asking questions doesn't help; you just go with it and allow your life to reap the benefits.

Tessa gave me shelter and a reprieve from the loneliness of being literally all alone. Living in her guest house, I always knew she was there. She'd swing by just to say hello or send the kids over to see if I wanted to "play." Even if I didn't feel like it at first, they were so cute and innocent that I always roused myself to do something with them for a while, and I always did feel a bit better afterward.

Then there was the pool.

Tessa and Frank's pool is no run-of-the-mill backyard basin. Theirs is the real deal and then some. Frank's father, Emil Corbin, was a real estate developer, and back in the '70s he came upon what was once the Mattaponi community pool, which had been closed down and was for sale. He bought it intending to use the grounds to build housing. Mattaponi is an unincorporated area of Montgomery County that looks down over the Potomac River, and it is high-value real estate. Even though it's near Washington, DC, the grounds are well hidden, with only the gravel drive visible off the main parkway. At the top of the drive, you would come to the parking lot with the pool on one side and tennis courts on the other. The entire complex is completely surrounded by trees, with a hill of pines rising up above the pool deck.

Emil did put two lavish houses where the parking lot and tennis courts used to sit, but he found he couldn't bear to part with the pool. So he kept it: full size, with six competition lanes and a diving well. Then he completely renovated it. He smoothed the edges so that instead of a hard "L" shape, it became more rounded, more natural in formation. The old concrete deck is now a curvy paved patio that slowly morphs from hardscape by the pool into grass, then flowers and bushes, and then, behind a tall fence, those trees. The far side is lined with huge rocks along the fence, just below the trees, with a trickling waterfall that feeds and circulates the pool, which is saltwater now, minimizing the once pungent smell of chlorine.

Finally, the bottom is painted so that instead of the usual light blue color of a swimming pool, the water has a deep green tint. The whole effect is that of a tranquil mountain lake hidden in a forest.

The back of the house Emil built for himself faces the front of the pool. It's not a luxurious house by Mattaponi standards; it sits where the old office building and locker rooms used to be, with a footprint not much bigger than that. But it is warm and beautiful inside, with a big laundry/mud room and bathroom to one side (where the old boys' locker room once sat), and a kids' play room to the other (the girls' locker room side). A huge brick-floored dine-in kitchen and living room is at the center, and a spiral staircase leads up to an added second floor and down to a finished basement.

The original complex included a baby pool and a snack bar, but those were replaced by an enclosed cabana and a hot tub. About ten years ago, Emil ceded the house to Frank and Tessa, after first renovating the cabana to turn it into a mother-in-law flat for himself and his second wife, Phyllis. They lived happily but not for long there. Emil passed away from a sudden stroke, and a few years after that, Phyllis decided to move closer to her own son and daughter-in-law in Florida. So there it was, ready for me. It's a small but fully functional house, with full bath and kitchen, a gas fireplace, and its own little patio out the back, looking up to the stars and out to the forest. It is beautiful, comfortable, ideal.

After I moved in, I quit my job and for weeks did almost nothing but sleep, eat, and feel the relief of not having to worry about work—or about anything. Of course, Tessa—being Tessa—kept an eye on me but didn't hover. The Saturday before St. Patrick's Day, she and Frank did a Leprechaun 5K fun run with the two oldest kids, twins Julie and Christopher, who at the time were six years old. I went along to watch the "littles" (then two-year-old Brielle and almost-five Charlie) while they ran. Everyone there was decked out in green, and Tessa gave me her race T-shirt, so I looked festive too. We went for cupcakes after the race, and while being out and about was stressful for me at that point, I was glad I went. I took a few pictures and posted them, showing me surrounded by smiling faces doing something enjoyable on a holiday. Online my life looked happy and carefree.

One morning not long after the 5K, I suddenly felt like getting up and out of bed early. Unheard of, I was actually making coffee by 7:00 a.m. I looked out the window and was astonished to see Tessa swimming laps. It's not a heated pool, and this was late March. I was horrified—and enthralled. How could she stand it? Just the thought of getting into the water gave me the heebie-jeebies. But she looked strong and graceful out there, mist from the water almost hiding her at the far end of the pool and obscuring the trees as the morning sun was just starting to light the world. When she finished her laps, she hopped up onto the deck and made her way over to the hot tub, where she sat for a long while with her head back, eyes closed. She looked utterly serene. I was captivated. My first thought: *Can I even dream of emulating such a magnificent morning routine?* My next thought: *It's totally crazy, so why would I want to?* I went on to wonder, *Hmm, which questioner is the real me?*

CHAPTER

SEVEN

The day after our happy hour at the Iguana, I'm off from work but still out of bed early, feeling unusually energetic. You'd think that after a good night's sleep and the always more rational light of day I would have reconsidered my impulsive resolve the night before and set aside my plan as wine-induced folly. Not so. Maybe some part of me wants to keep alive the excitement of feeling part of a group, involved in a mystery, but for whatever reason, I'm eager to be on my way.

It's bright and sunny again, more like spring than fall, which is my favorite time to be on a bicycle. Part of my route is along the bike path, and part of it takes me through quiet side streets. Around ten thirty I find myself turning into the parking lot of a set of neat three-story buildings, each with a stairway in the middle and elevators on either end. I walk toward the landing of the nearest building and notice sets of two first names and last initials on each of the mailboxes. The same protocol reigns at the landing of the next building, where there is a "Nico D. / Erik G." on mailbox 204. Well. This seems almost too easy. I'm seized with a feeling of elation at my detective skills and nervousness at the scheme my mind appears to be forming. Refusing to be daunted by success, I get back on my bike and pedal to the end of the road, where there is a small shopping center with a supermarket at one corner and an auto parts store at the other. I head for the supermarket and buy a bouquet of flowers and a box of chocolates. Since I use my bike for pretty much all my transportation needs, it is perpetually outfitted for spontaneous shopping such as this, with a trunk bag affixed to my rear wheel rack that has two large side compartments that zip open into pannier bags. I place the bouquet into one of the panniers, stick the chocolates into the trunk bag, and return to Nico's building. Before I have a chance to chicken out, I race up the stairs and press the bell to number 204. As I stand there, it hits me: Nico D.? not C. for Crawford? Did I get this wrong? How many Nicos could there be in this home? Damn. What to do? My mind is a jumbled mess, but my feet stay frozen in place, so when the door opens, I really have no choice but to stay the course.

"Hello, can I help you?" says the tall, skinny man wearing a bicycle helmet now standing in front of me.

"Oh, hello," I say in return, trying not to stare at his helmet. "I was told Margaret Crawford's son lived here. My, umm, my mother was a friend of Ms. Crawford's and we, aah, we heard she passed away." I'm losing my nerve and starting to stammer, so I hold out the bouquet and chocolates to distract him. "These are ... well ... please accept our condolences," I finally squeak out.

"Oh! Hello. That's right, I'm Nico. Thank you very much. Would you like to come in?" He opens the door wider and steps aside a little unsteadily. I remember that Karen said he normally walks with a cane, so I decide the polite thing to do would be to put the chocolates and flowers down somewhere so he won't have to carry them. I can already see what Karen meant about his mental disability. He is very polite, but there is something about his high-pitched, somewhat stuttery delivery that projects simpleness. I'm regretting getting myself into this, as I don't know how I'm going to get out without looking the fool or, worse, raising Nico's suspicions about me. For the moment, though, I'm trapped in the charade, so I just keep going.

The apartment decor is a little worn-looking, but everything is clean and orderly. I put the chocolates and bouquet on the kitchen counter and look around as Nico carefully makes his way over to a chair in the living room and sits down. Two mugs hang on hooks over the sink; one is blue with the Superman symbol, but with an *E* instead of an *S* (for "Erik," presumably), the other black with a yellow batman symbol and "Nico" written across the bat. The wall next to the kitchen is filled with every one of their old school photographs, each one's grade side by side, framed and hung in neat rows. I'm looking at the earliest ones as Nico asks, "Your mother was a friend of my mom's? from where?"

"Oakton," I say with a big smile and a nod toward one of the class pictures. "She was an administrator at your Montessori school."

"Oh wow!" says Nico. "That was a long time ago! It's nice she remembered. Is she still there? Will she be at the funeral service?"

"Aaah. No. No, unfortunately, she's living in, umm, Arizona now. But she, um, she saw it on Facebook and of course, you know, remembered your mom. Since I'm still here in the area, she asked me to, ahh, you know, drop by on her behalf."

Not smooth, no, but believable, I hope. Nico doesn't really seem to notice. I watch him as he reaches for something in a cabinet next to his chair, noting again his extreme thinness. He's young, in his mid- to late twenties, and has a wiry musculature that implies more strength in his arms than I originally thought. When he turns back to me, black hair has escaped his helmet and drooped into dark eyes that seem darker against exceedingly pale skin, and he is holding a vase.

"That's really nice of you. Would you mind putting the flowers in this?"

"Sure," I say, coming over to take the vase. I go back into the kitchen and start clipping the ends of the stems and arranging them in their new container. I used to be pretty good at small talk, and feeling elated again at having gotten away with things thus far, I decide to give it a go. He is looking over at me now, and the silence feels a little awkward.

"Are you ... have you ... do you have other family nearby?"

"Not really," he says. "My parents got divorced when I was still a kid, and my dad moved to Italy, so I almost never see him. My aunt Alice is here now, but she lives in Boston, so she'll have to go home soon. I'm expecting her to come by any minute. I thought it was her at the door when you rang the bell."

Before I can respond, that very door opens and a youngish man with glasses walks in. He is wearing a sweater with pockets that seems more suitable for someone's grandfather, and he's chubby, with the facial manifestations of Down syndrome.

"Hi," he says.

"Hi, Erik," Nico replies. "Erik, this is … oh, you didn't tell me your name."

"Lily." I beam at him. "My mom's name is, um, Valerie." My mom's name really is Valerie. Why bother to think up something else? Keep it simple when you're lying; everyone knows that's the cardinal rule. Of course, my mom and dad live over in Laurel, Maryland, not Arizona, but I don't want Nico to think her stingy for not wanting to make the half-hour drive to her old pal's funeral.

"Oh, okay. Erik this is Lily, her mom was a friend of my mom's when I was in Montessori school. This is Erik, my roommate."

We say our hellos, and Erik admires the flowers. He asks if the chocolates have nuts and caramel and looks overjoyed when I tell him I think they do. I figure this is a good time to make a break for it, and with a few parting words of sympathy I'm outside again and back on my bike. My heart is beating hard at my own audacity, and I'm not paying attention to what I'm doing, so I have to brake suddenly to avoid colliding with a woman coming up the path. She also hasn't been paying attention, walking along looking down at her phone, so we both start apologizing to each other at the same time. This makes us laugh, and as we are collecting ourselves, I have a brainwave.

"Are you by any chance Nico's aunt Alice?"

"Yes, I am," she replies in surprise. "Do you know Nico?"

Her face betrays confusion and a little astonishment, which is understandable. I'm not handicapped, and if she is familiar with the place, she probably knows I don't work here. This time I'm ready, though, and I go through the whole spiel about my mom and the Montessori school as if it is real. No umms or aahs this time. Having tested out the story and found it sound a few moments ago with Nico, I could now deliver with confidence.

"Oh, that's so nice," says Alice. "And amazing. I guess Facebook can be a marvel when it comes to circulating family news like this. Yes, I'm Alice Munney, Margaret's sister, a.k.a. Aunt Alice."

We smile at each other, and I tell her my name is Lily and that I'm Valerie Piper's daughter. Alice Munney is a petite woman, about my height, which is five foot two first thing in the morning, but Alice is birdlike and probably a size two to my size ten. She looks to me to be in her late fifties or early sixties and well preserved; either she dyes her hair or her natural color has lasted longer than most, as it is dark and thick with subtle highlights. She is dressed professionally with nice shoes, slacks, and a cowl-necked sweater. I have a general sense of a high-achieving go-getter, although today she looks very tired. Or sad. Or both. I feel a sudden rush of sympathy for her, and when I give the stock "I'm sorry for your loss" line, it is sincere, and I think Alice can tell that.

"Thank you," she says. "This has been very difficult, and Nico needs help, but he's difficult too. He doesn't really understand how things work, and can get very paranoid. This is so unexpected; it never dawned on us that she wouldn't be around for a long time to come. She was just always there, always reliable. Did you know her yourself, or just your mom?"

"Oh, ahh, no, just my mom," I manage to reply. The stammer is back, but I hadn't been expecting the question.

Alice, though, just nods. "Of course, that makes sense. You look about Nico's age, so you were probably just a toddler when they met."

We both start walking slowly back up the path toward the building, me pushing my bike, as I have now realized that I left my own helmet sitting on a bench where I'd parked it to visit Nico. This is somewhat serendipitous, as it allows me the chance to elicit a little more information.

"I'm an only child, but I can't imagine what it would be like to have a sister and then lose her. Were you close?"

Under other circumstances, this might be considered an intrusive question, but here—two people meeting because of the death of a family member—it feels perfectly natural to me, and Alice takes it in stride.

"Margaret and I were really close growing up, even though she's three years older, which can be a lot when you're little. But I didn't like her husband much, and we sort of drifted apart. We kept in touch by phone occasionally, but that was about it. When they got divorced, Margaret and I got closer again. Unfortunately, Nico was very upset by the divorce and resented me suddenly being in the picture. He blamed Margaret for his dad leaving and somehow conflates me being around more with Margaret kicking him out. That's part of his paranoia. Of course, it wasn't like that at all; their marriage had been disintegrating for years, and his dad finally up and left one day. Margaret turned to me in part because she was at her wit's end building up her consulting business while caring for Nico on her own."

I nod sympathetically. "That does sound like a lot. You know, he didn't seem unhappy about it when he mentioned you were coming. Pretty much the opposite, in fact."

"That's good to hear," Alice says with a smile, albeit a wan one. "Nico and I are closer now, but it's still a bit tenuous of a relationship. Makes this harder, because I do want to help. Thank God he has his trust to pay for him to stay in this home, which is wonderful for him, but he still relied on Margaret in so many ways ..." She drifts off here for just a moment but then shakes her head and does a half shrug.

We're back by the mailboxes, but Alice doesn't seem like she's in a big hurry, so I risk continuing our conversation just a little longer.

"I'm so sorry, that's such a shame for both of you. Nico is lucky to have you. My, umm, well I guess I understood from my mom that Margaret had been ill or something. I didn't realize this was a surprise."

She moves her head slightly up and down in sorrowful agreement but doesn't reveal anything about how Margaret actually died. All she says is "Life is always so much more complicated than you think."

Alice peers up the staircase, but before starting to climb she adds, "Oh well. I'd better go up now, but I'm glad we met. It was nice of you to come see Nico. He doesn't get a lot of visitors. You know, you're welcome to come to the memorial service. It's Friday at seven p.m. at Yeates Funeral Home on Rockville Pike."

I thank her and tell her I can find it, and with that we part ways.

Back on my bike, my adrenaline is in full surge and I'm on a high, thinking I've accomplished something big, although I'm not sure why. Now that I've met Nico and Alice, I'm starting to feel like I really am invested in this Margaret Crawford person, almost as if she really was an old family friend or something. My problem now is that she wasn't, and there's no one I know who can tell me more about her. In a flight of imaginary absurdity, I suddenly want to call up my mom and ask her to tell me more about Margaret Crawford and what she was like way back then. Poor Mom. She's an engineer by training and is now a program manager for a big defense corporation. She might consider Montessori school administrator a bit of a demotion. I picture her there anyway, greeting the parents and knowing all the kids' names. She'd have been good at it; my mom has the patience of Job.

The fantasy is getting me nowhere, and I decide it might help to talk through the day's events, lay it all out and maybe a next step will present itself. I want someone who gets it, who won't think I'm completely crazy, and who might have a suggestion or two to add. I'm just over a mile from Austin Hill hospital and head in that direction.

CHAPTER
EIGHT

When I get close, I stop to text Karen to see whether she has a few minutes to chat, and she calls me right back.

"Hi!" she says. "This is unusual! You're near the hospital? You're okay, right?"

I assure her I'm fine and blurt out, "I just met Nico and Alice Munney and wanted to tell you about it."

"What!" she exclaims. "Oh my God! I have to hear this. It's taco Tuesday; meet me in the cafeteria and let's have lunch. My treat!"

"You got it," I reply, grinning even though she can't see me. "Be there in ten."

The hospital is big, with long, winding hallways, and it takes me more than ten minutes to reach the cafeteria after I hang up the phone and find a place to lock my bike. Karen is standing at the entrance with a gray-haired bearded man, and when she sees me, she waves me over.

"This is Dr. Ben," she says. "He was here when I got here, and when I told him you were coming over fresh from speaking with Nico and Alice Munney, he wanted to meet you. Dr. Ben, this is Lily Piper."

We somewhat awkwardly bump fists (the COVID handshake!) and then head over to the taco line, where we do the small-talk thing as we wait.

Dr. Ben is the guy who wouldn't let Margaret's death get brushed aside, so I'm interested to meet him in the flesh. He looks fairly ordinary—when I say gray-haired, really it's just the sides of his head and his beard that are gray. The top of his head is completely bald. He is hefty but not fat and probably close to six feet tall. His attire is business casual, with brown oxford shoes, a button-down shirt, and slacks, but no tie or jacket. He has an air about him that is pleasingly amiable, even sort of jolly, if that's a word you can use to describe someone other than Santa Claus. I like him instinctively and see why Karen felt she could trust him. He asks whether I had trouble parking and seems impressed when I explain that I came by bike. He tells me he hasn't been on a bike since he was a kid, which he feels is probably a shame, since he'd heard there are a lot of great bike paths in the area. I tell him that's true, and that it's never too late to start. Karen starts telling us about her kids doing charity rides for MS, and pretty soon we're at the front of the line, paying for our tacos and scanning the place for a table. It's busy, but we find one tucked away at the end of a row of windows.

"How on earth," Karen starts in, "did you meet Nico? I mean, this can't be coincidence, right? *And* Margaret's sister? How did you find them? What did they say?"

The presence of Dr. Ben makes me a little shy, but I came here with the intention of telling Karen the whole story, and since I have no idea how to sensibly explain the meeting any other way, I go ahead and tell them the truth. They both kind of gawk at me. I don't take it as judgmental; they're not appalled. It's more simple astonishment that I would conceive of such an action.

Dr. Ben breaks the silence first with "If you don't mind my asking, what in the world possessed you to do such a thing?"

Karen nods vehemently, her demeanor silently dittoing "Same question." I start feeling embarrassed, not so much about having confessed to masquerading as a family friend and drawing my unwitting mother into the ruse (although maybe a little of that), but more about the truth of my own motives. I'm not ready yet to open up about the fact that I spent the last few years in an abyss of depression, that after isolating myself for the whole of that time

I'm a little lonely and want to extend the camaraderie of the night before by extending the interest in Margaret. I'm embarrassed that the mystery of Margaret and how she died is, of all things, one of the first things that has piqued my interest enough on a nonworkday to get me out of the house before noon. That's the real me, the real answer, but just at the moment it feels too revealing. So instead I tell them about my reflexive thought the night before about my beloved former babysitter Tessa, the forcefulness of feeling that I wouldn't want how she died ever to be in question, and that I would want the perpetrator to pay. I don't come right out and tell them I've decided to look into Margaret's murder myself, but I do confess that after viewing Margaret's houses last night online, I felt like checking out Nico's place today. Seeing where and how people live makes them come alive for me. Once I actually found Nico's facility, though, things just took on a life of their own.

Dr. Ben looks at Karen and then at me. "Well," he says, "Wow. You know, I think I'm impressed. I'm other things too, but honestly mostly impressed at your gumption. And I empathize with your instinctive sense for the need for justice. I feel the same way, although not for any of my old babysitters." Here he smiles, dare I say, impishly? "The little I remember about any of them isn't particularly endearing."

I'm really starting to warm to Dr. Ben, feeling all aglow inside from his "impressed" compliment, and my absurd interest in Margaret and her family feels validated. Karen was right: he comes across as a kindly, bookish superhero. Older guy, but oh so cool.

"You two should know, though, that this is now a police investigation." He is speaking very quietly, so we have to lean in a little to hear him. Cue the conspiratorial huddle-up. I'm loving this. "That means that they're also out there looking into Margaret and her family, among others, so be sure to stay out of their way. Don't confuse things for them. If they find some stranger has suddenly shown up with questions, lying about her connection, well … they might want to take a closer look at *you*." He speaks this last sentence with an eye to me, and while it is said lightly, it takes me a little aback.

I'm glad and relieved to have confirmation that the police are investigating, but yikes, I don't want to be someone they think needs questioning. My heart races as I silently exhort myself to watch where I step, but Dr. Ben has roused Karen's curiosity, and she asks him more about it.

"Like, what are they looking at? What have you heard? Do they have a suspect?" she asks.

Dr. Ben's elbows are leaning on the table, and he cups his hands to his mouth, looking at each of us and then around the room by moving only his eyes. Then he shakes his head side to side slightly and sort of sighs.

Still talking very quietly, he says, "Look, you two, anything I tell you, make sure you keep it to yourselves, as we don't need the whole hospital rumor-mongering—not that they aren't already. I've worked with Dan Ridley, the main investigator, in the past, so we're friends, and he's told me a little about the case so far. They're still only checking into whether there really is foul play here, so no suspects yet. But if there *is* foul play, there might be a financial motive." He looks at Karen. "People here see this whole thing as 'my fault' for calling Margaret's death not natural. That's ridiculous. I call it like I see it, and truly I don't want her—or anyone—to have been murdered. But I also want to know if I'm really right in my suspicions, or way off base." Now he looks at both of us and adds, "Dan gets this, which is why he's telling me things. Let's make sure he doesn't get into any trouble for that."

Karen nods, and I do too. With that, Dr. Ben collects a few pieces of trash from the table onto his tray and stands up.

"That's all I know, folks, and now I gotta go. Nice meeting you, Lily. You watch yourself out there."

I nod again, this time with a smile, and Karen gives him a wave. We look at each other across the table.

"That," she says, "was amazing! Seriously, he told us a lot! I'm glad you decided to come."

I agree on both counts, but Karen also has to get back to work, so we don't linger for much longer. She half-jokingly tells me to come back next taco Tuesday, and I half-jokingly say I'll be there. Who knows? Maybe I will.

I make my way home at a leisurely pace, taking in the sight of fall colors beginning to appear. Tessa and Frank are both at work, the kids still in school, and I have the place to myself, so I decide to get in the hot tub. I love the hot tub, but usually I only go in when Tessa is there, or sometimes late at night, when I'm wide awake and at my loneliest. Then I take comfort looking up at the stars while the heat and bubbles feel soothing and safe. This afternoon is different. I don't feel lonely; I just want to be outside while relaxing after all the biking. I lie back and muse about the morning's discoveries.

Although our conversation was brief, I gleaned some key pieces of information from Alice. She mentioned a trust that pays for Nico to live at Sherwood, and she used an unusual word to describe his occasional interpretation of events: "paranoia." Add to that Dr. Ben's mention of a possible financial motive. Are these all related? Could Nico's childlike mind misunderstand the use of the trust, maybe thinking he should get to use the money for whatever he wants, and get angry at Margaret if she won't let him?

I wonder whether I can find out more about this trust. Who controls it? How much money does it entail? I lie back a little deeper and feel the sun hitting the top of my head just right. I close my eyes and start to drift off.

"Lily!" shouts a bathing-suit-clad Julie as she runs across the deck and leaps in. She's not supposed to do that, but I'm not the hot tub police, and it's nice to be so unabashedly liked. She paddles up to hug me and then starts leaping up and down in the water as she tells me, "We're having a Halloween party! It's gonna be so awesome! Christopher and I are going to be Minions!"

Frank and Tessa throw some amazing pool parties, although I don't usually go; I help Tessa set up and snag a few snacks, but then I take off before guests arrive. I just haven't wanted to be around company. Halloween seems late in the season for a pool, but as Julie leaps and twirls and jabbers away about their plans, it does sound pretty awesome. I have a fleeting thought that maybe I'll actually attend this one. People. Food. Chitchat. It's not so bad. Then comes a second fleeting thought—that Margaret's funeral will have people, food, and chitchat. If I go, will the official police find that suspicious? Surely not. Alice invited me, so I feel like I have every right to attend. A few hours ago, I was looking for people who knew Margaret. What better place to find them?

43

CHAPTER
NINE

The next day is a long one for me, as I'm subbing in for Will in the evening as well as leading my own day classes, so I don't get much chance to do any more digging right away. Redd and Miller come in in the afternoon, but I don't mention my trip to Nico's yet. It feels as though Karen should be the one to initiate info sharing on our case, for one thing, and I'm also kind of in the zone, focused on the sensation of my own body as we go through the movements during each class. I'm feeling good and remembering how I got here.

Moving into the pool house was a saving grace; it gave me time and space, but it wasn't a cure in and of itself. I was still stiff, sore, overweight, and inextricably melancholy. One of the worst characteristics of a state of depression is the simultaneous desire to sleep all the time while enduring continuous insomnia. Sleep is an escape; when you're asleep, you don't have to think about what to do or worry about what you're not doing, but you never seem to wake up refreshed. You wake up to the fact that it is time to confront the day, and that is not appealing. You are also dead tired. But late at night, you can't sleep. You're wide awake, anxious and frustrated. I wanted to help myself, to make a change. I'd make vows to myself about exactly what I would do to turn over that new leaf, but I had no stamina to follow through. Apathy and lethargy were my constancies. Movement was painful, sitting was painful, and my brain was foggy and unfocused. I desperately wanted the old me back—the one who had ambition and never enough time in the day to do everything—but I couldn't rouse myself enough to make a move. To fight for the right to pursue happiness is one thing, but how do you fight for the drive to want to pursue it? I did find that it helped a little to look forward to something, even something small. One of those things turned out to be watching Tessa glide across the water early in the morning.

At first I'd take my coffee and sit in my comfy chair by the window and just watch—no sound, no TV, just a live person in her own world going back and forth against the backdrop of whatever the day brought. Sometimes there were beautiful pink and orange streaks, sometimes the sky just went from dark gray to blue, sometimes the pool was covered in mist, and sometimes it had little ripples from the wind. It was the same but different every day. It was so appealing that eventually I started joining Tessa in the hot tub postswim. We didn't speak much, but she seemed glad that I came out. Toward the end of June, the water had warmed up, and I started going into the main pool. Tessa swam her laps, and I just did whatever: a little swimming, a little floating, some dolphin dives. I didn't have the drive to do a workout or anything, but moving around in the water felt good, and it didn't make my back or my joints hurt. It made the hot tub afterward feel twice as nice, too, so I kept at it. I started sleeping better at night. It was all so subtle that I don't remember feeling any better, particularly, but I must have, because at some point over that summer I started to take my bike out occasionally. I'd decide on some simple destination, like Starbucks, and ride there, get a cup of coffee, and sit outside playing games on my phone until it got too hot. Then I'd ride back. It was nothing extraordinary, but it got me up and out to the shopping center. When they put up an advertisement for a part-time barista, I felt I could handle it. And frankly, I needed some income. I took the job, and on a whim one day I walked over to the Eye of Horus yoga studio, which is in the same shopping center, just to check it out. I signed up for the first set of sessions and never stopped.

Seeing me now, it might surprise people to hear that when I first started yoga, I would come to class and fall asleep. Seriously, as soon as we completed the initial warmups and standing poses and started work on the floor, I'd end up just lying down and dozing off. At the end of the class, I'd wake up feeling refreshed. Eventually one day the instructor tapped me on the arm and asked me if I'd like to try to finish the poses with the rest of the class. He sat down with me later that day, saying that he thought that rest was the thing I needed most when I first came in, so he always let me be. But he felt that I was ready for more now and would benefit from working through the poses. I was touched by the attention he paid to me and the thought he put into my well-being. So I did start making an effort to do the exercises. I began by only doing a few moves, but staying awake and then finishing with the class. After a while, I could keep up with the class for the entire hour.

I got stronger and really started to enjoy it. The Horatic approach suited me perfectly. Its symbology helped me visualize my own healing process, and the movements made me feel looser and freer in my own body. The more I did, the more I wanted to learn, so I went through instructor training and got certified. In the back of my mind, I kept thinking one day I would return to college, start over exactly where I'd left off, and continue as if nothing had happened. Instead, when my original instructor left the studio to pursue other goals, I applied for his spot. From out of nowhere, I suddenly found myself with a career that felt like a calling—one that I loved.

Haisley breaks into my reveries when she appears at 8:00 p.m., our last class of the day. She gives me a surprised smile when she sees me.

"I didn't expect you to be here!" she says, and I tell her Will couldn't make it this evening.

"That's just as well, because I've been wondering about Karen and her murdered woman. Have you talked to her? Did she tell you anything more?"

I can't give her much of an answer, as I need to start the class, but when Haisley stays after to help clean up and we're alone in the kitchen, she repeats her question. I'll feel bad if I tell Haisley all the latest now, since I didn't say anything to Redd and Miller, but I also don't want to say nothing and admit later that I lied. I decide to leave out the details of how I got to my current status and cut straight to the chase.

"Apparently her son Nico has a trust that pays for him to live at Sherwood, and they think there might be a financial motive for the murder. I wonder if that means the trust, but I don't know how those work."

"Oh! Interesting. Nico has a trust? Small world. I mean, it's not the same, but I have a trust myself," Haisley surprises me by saying.

"You do? Wow! How do you know it's not the same?"

"Because, to be more specific, I had one but it's closed out now. My grandparents set one up for their grandchildren to go to college. The money had to be disbursed by the time the youngest reached the age of twenty-five, which is yours truly and I'm twenty-six. So it was time limited. Nico's trust sounds like one that continues indefinitely."

I can hardly believe my luck that I have a living, breathing example of a trust fund recipient right here in front of me. I lean against the counter, and Haisley does the same as we continue talking.

"Can I ask … how does it work?"

"In our case, my uncle was the executor, I guess because he was the oldest. My cousins and I would write to him when we needed some of the money, and he'd send it to us, and at the end of each year he'd divvy out money to the others to keep it all equitable. I was lucky because my parents paid for me to go to college, but the trust makes it possible for me to go to grad school. Last year, a few months before my twenty-fifth birthday, he sent us each a final lump sum to zero it out and closed the account."

"So now you are rich!" I say clapping my hands in pretend glee, and we both laugh.

"I wish, but no," says Haisley, shaking her head, still smiling. "Our trust wasn't that big. It won't even cover all my tuition; it just helps a lot. But assuming Nico's continues indefinitely, then it's probably more like an annuity."

"Umm ... I don't really know how those work either."

Haisley laughs again at that. "I just mean he probably gets the interest so the principal remains intact. To throw off enough interest for a monthly income that pays for a place like Sherwood, it would have to be quite a bit."

We're still leaning against the counter, but Haisley turns her head to look meaningfully at me and gives an exaggerated shrug. I look back and give an exaggerated nod.

"Aah, now I see. And where there's money, there's motive."

"Could be!"

"You said your uncle was the executor for your trust. Do you think Nico could have been his own executor? Or, more likely, Margaret? If it was Margaret, I wonder how Nico will access his funds now."

"That's a good question. I'd have guessed Margaret was the executor, but maybe not. Maybe the dad? Either way, it could be set as an automatic payment. That way, even if Margaret is the executor, it won't matter that she's dead, at least not right away."

We finish up, collect our things, and walk companionably out the door. Haisley has been a font of knowledge. I tell her thanks for the info, and she grins.

"You bet! Back atcha!"

At home, I check for news articles about the murder but am disappointed to find that none of the local sites or TV stations have picked it up. Have the police given up? Did they decide it wasn't homicide after all? That can't be! Dr. Ben is taking flack for his finding; he wouldn't stick his neck out if he wasn't sure. I have to find a way to track this thing, to make sure the person who did it doesn't get away scot-free. Margaret was a person, a mother and a sister. Just like Tessa. She is important.

It's not official news, but I do come across Margaret's obituary. The writeup has a nice flow, concise but still conveying affection. This must be Alice's work, and my admiration for her increases. Margaret Crawford, I learn, was in fact Dr. Margaret Crawford, a scientist with triple degrees in botany, genomics, and bioengineering. She hailed from Pennsylvania, moved here to work at the National Institutes of Health in the 1990s, and then left the government at some point to pursue private practice and start a family. The ex-husband doesn't get a mention—the divorce must have been bitter—nor does any boyfriend or partner, with the article stating only that she is survived by her son Nico and her sister Alice Munney & (Gordon).

I read through several times, noting that Margaret's parents are deceased, that she herself was sixty-five years old when she died, and that she retired at sixty. Maybe I'm reading too much into this, but I have a feeling Margaret was a bit of a party girl; the one hobby described is her avid interest in craft beer, and the fact that she took pride in having tasted every brew ever on tap at some place called Everything Beer. If you pay attention, there's value in the details. I've now learned that Nico has no brothers or sisters and that Alice is married to someone named Gordon. Since no other siblings are named, there probably aren't any. All in all, a small family circle. Is there anyone else? I hope to find out more at the memorial service.

TEN

When Friday morning dawns, I pretend to myself that it's just another day, but I know it isn't. I'm starting to feel nervous about showing up at a stranger's funeral—a stranger who was murdered, no less. I swim a few laps with Tessa in the pool but don't mention it to her. Why don't I? Is it because deep down I know I'm getting involved in something maybe I shouldn't? I shy away from dwelling on that possibility too much and concentrate instead on my plan. I wear nicer clothes than usual today, all dark colors but not black—nothing that might beg questions. After work, I don't go home, but over to the grocery store for a sandwich and potato salad. I've decided to keep my ears and eyes open but my mouth shut as much as possible, not make any waves, be as unobtrusive as possible. From the grocery store, I wander over to Starbucks for a cup of coffee, and I order an Uber from there. My driver drops me outside Yeates Funeral Home right at 7:00 p.m.

I enter into a foyer, where a short line of people has formed to sign the guest book. It's a small space, and there's no comfortable way around them, so I wait for my turn. I'm thinking I'll just scribble something illegible and leave it at that. When I get to the book, though, I realize the next space is at the bottom of the page and see an opportunity. I sign my name slowly and take the time to provide full address and phone number—this is to cover the fact that I'm reading all the names before mine. Before I begin, I flip quickly to the first page and give it a skim. There's Alice Munney with an address in Boston, and quite a few names with addresses at Sherwood Independent Living. On my page, I take my time, skipping over addresses on Margaret's same street to home in on anything remotely incongruous. I see some indecipherable scribbles (how rude!), a few first names only, and some names with no address. What are they hiding? I memorize these as best I can and determine to note them down in my phone as soon as I get inside.

There is a medium-sized crowd, with an unusual abundance of people with various types of handicap. A few people are wearing masks, and I decide to dig mine out of my purse and put it on, hoping I'll be a little less recognizable that way. As we all mill around, I hear snatches of conversation but nothing nefarious—just Margaret's neighbors and former colleagues greeting each other with the usual platitudes. There is no viewing, but there is a table with many pictures of Margaret taken throughout her life. She was cute as a child, vibrant as a student, and serious as a young professional. In pictures with Nico, she is smiling when the photo is staged but more somber in the candid shots. The most recent photos show she hadn't aged well. Most people don't, but even so, I feel sorry for Margaret for having deteriorated to such an extent. The more I look, the more real she seems, the more complicated her life, and the more tragic her passing. The pictures don't reveal any other clues that I can see, and I'm glad enough to hurry through and sit down just as the service starts.

Alice Munney stands at the front, looking conservatively fabulous in a black turtleneck over a black-and-white plaid skirt and boots. She thanks everyone for coming and starts talking about her sister. She is an engaging speaker, and I learn quite a lot. Margaret, she informs us, was no wallflower; she was fun and adventurous and was usually the instigator when they were kids and got into trouble. She was good at school and studied science, eventually getting her doctorate and a research position at the National Institutes of Health, here in Bethesda. She loved her job working on the famed Human Genome Project, where she met the man she would later marry.

They tried for a long time without success to have a child, but just when Margaret thought it might never happen, their beloved Nico came along. A lot of people smile and turn to look at Nico when she mentions this. Nico looks around, raises his hand, and calls out "That's me!" which garners some laughter. Alice doesn't say anything else about the marriage, but she does tell a few cute stories about Margaret and Nico. She closes by saying, "Margaret wasn't perfect, and she wasn't in what you'd call her heyday. Those of you who knew her knew that she was plagued by health issues. But ... she still had dreams. Inside she was full of life, and she left this earth much too soon. None of us were ready for this, and I miss her all the more because I expected her to be around for so much longer." She starts to break down a little then but still manages to invite anyone else who would like to share memories to come up to the front.

Several people take up the offer. Her best friend tells us about their escapades on a brewery tour in Virginia, and that Margaret couldn't wait to go on another one in Germany next summer; one of her old colleagues from work recounts how her keen sense of humor made staff meetings tolerable. Nico remains seated, wearing a suit and tie along with his bicycle helmet and cane. The man next to him, though, eventually stands up and comes forward. He's maybe a little older than I am and not very tall, but his body is thick and teddy bearish, and his reddish-blond hair is already starting to thin at the front. This turns out to be Geoff Turner, Nico's house captain, who explains that Nico asked him to say a few words and read a poem on his behalf. This Geoff does, and he then says a few words himself. He tells us that he'd started to get into trouble in his teens and at the age of twenty-two found himself barely avoiding prison, sentenced to eight hundred hours of community service, which he served at a facility for disabled adults. He discovered he liked it, and eventually found and applied for his current job at Sherwood Independent Living. Nico was practically the first person he met there, along with Margaret, who was a constant, supportive visitor. Geoff especially appreciated that Dr. Crawford invited him over to her home one Thanksgiving, when he had no other plans, and how cheery and pleasurable the holiday was. He isn't as good a speaker as the others, but his obvious emotion leaves a lot of us—yes, even me!—a bit choked up.

The whole thing lasts only about an hour, and I head for the door. Another line has formed to say a few words to Alice and Nico, but I don't join it. I doubt they'll notice, and I don't want to risk getting into a chat with anyone about how I "know" the family—what if I end up next to someone who really is from Nico's Montessori? I Uber home, pour myself a mug of tea, and eat about a million miniature cookies as I consider the evening. In particular, I think about Geoff. His clunky speech touched me, but I remember that originally he went up to speak on behalf of Nico. In fact, Geoff was beside Nico pretty much the entire time and seemed to know exactly how to help him navigate the affair. Helpful, yes. But also clearly someone with an enormous amount of influence over Nico, someone with the ability to manipulate him. Someone with a criminal past no less, no matter how reformed he purports to be now.

How much money is in Nico's trust? Who controls it now? Can Geoff get his hands on it through Nico? I hope the police are looking into these questions. Can ordinary citizens find these things out?

I'm going to try.

CHAPTER
ELEVEN

I don't want to get too far ahead of my partners in crime—crime investigation, that is—so I call Karen at work on Monday and tell her I went to Margaret's memorial service. She wants to hear all about it, and we agree to meet later at the Iguana. Redd and Haisley are at my midmorning class, so I let them know our plans. They are welcome to come if they want. When I walk across the parking lot at the end of the day, I find that they're all there, sitting at the same table we sat at before. Even Miller is there—someone must have texted—and they're excited at my arrival.

"Lady, you are crazy!" says Miller. "I like your style."

"Crazy like a fox," says Redd, shaking his head. "Our Lily has hidden depths. What were you thinking, girl?"

"I told them," says Karen, with a "what could I do" kind of shrug. "They've been hyper ever since."

"You're our hero, so we ordered you a glass of wine," Haisley says with a grin, which explains why the waitress has already placed a glass down in front of me.

I had been expecting only Karen to come, but I'm glad that they're all here, and I feel sort of flattered to be the center of attention. I settle in, putting chips and salsa and jalapeño poppers on a little plate, and begin. Karen knows everything up to the funeral service, but for the benefit of the others I go through the whole bit about being curious about Margaret, checking out her houses on the realtor sites, which made me curious to see where Nico lives, my bike ride over, and my spontaneous decision to offer condolences ostensibly from my mom. I already told the same story to Karen and Dr. Ben and Tessa and Frank, and it all seems very normal to me by now. Not so to my audience, who go from gaping at me to eyeing each other as if to say, "Are you hearing this?" and then back to me, askance. Karen takes over for a while, recounting our lunch with Dr. Ben, and then I finish up with what I learned at the service.

Redd looks at me with raised eyebrows. "You do want to be careful, Lily. Dr. Ben is right; you don't want to get mixed up in something the police are trying to investigate."

Miller looks at him and exclaims, "Police? That's what you're worried about? What about the *guy*?" She turns to me. "What if this maniac notices you poking your nose in and decides to come after *you*!"

Miller has a way of speaking that always sounds emphatic, and its effect is often a little comical. In the safe normalcy of the Iguana, her response to Redd makes us laugh. However, while proclaiming the perpetrator a homicidal maniac seems a little overboard, Miller has a point. Margaret and her family seem real to me, but her manner of death does not. I need to remember that it is.

"Anyway," chimes in Haisley, "how do you know it's a guy? Maybe it's a girl."

I smile, thinking she's jokingly making sure we're all approaching this politically correctly, but Karen nods her head.

"That's true," she says. "I've been wondering about Alice Munney, just because of the money angle. Alice is the executor of Margaret's estate, so she probably also takes over executorship of Nico's trust. I think trustees can do almost anything. Remember the whole business with Britney Spears? I mean, it's not the same, but probably similar. If she gets control of it, she could do pretty much whatever she wants with the money, especially since Nico doesn't seem like he has the capacity to realize what's happening or do anything about it."

Redd looks thoughtful. "Could be. Or, what if it doesn't go to Alice—what if Nico just takes it over? In fact, even if he just *thought* it would go from Margaret to him and was wrong, it could give him a motive."

"I don't know about Nico." I look over at Redd and take a sip of wine, pondering. "He can't even walk without a cane and can have an epileptic fit at any moment. Also, it's hard to explain exactly what it is, but he's definitely mentally ... compromised. I just don't see him planning something like this. Even if he was just overcome by emotion, I'm thinking he would sort of fall apart. He wouldn't know what to do next."

"Yeah, I get that." Redd nods. "But I was thinking maybe he could be in cahoots with Geoff. Or Geoff on his own: maybe he figured he could manipulate Nico out of his money—if Nico had the money. He already fessed up to having a shady past, he knew where Margaret lived, and he knew about the trust. He might think this was a way to boost his income."

"That's exactly what I was thinking about last night!" I exclaim. "Geoff seemed pretty sincere about how much he appreciated Margaret and seemed sad about her loss, but you do never know. It could be a ruse, or he could have liked Margaret but found the money too tempting. And he definitely has a lot of influence on Nico. Rightly or wrongly, he might have thought he could get his hands on the funds if Margaret was out of the way."

"Oh yeah," agrees Miller. "Once a criminal, always a criminal. But what I want to know is, Where is the ex-husband in all this? Isn't it always the ex? He should definitely be a suspect."

Now Haisley looks a little doubtful. "I guess they should look into him, but haven't they been divorced for a long time? And isn't he in Italy? He wasn't at the service, was he?"

"I don't actually know," I say. "Maybe. I wouldn't have recognized him even if he was there. But at any rate, he wasn't one of the ones who stood up and said something."

Karen has me considering Alice, too. I don't want it to be Alice, but that's not a good reason to rule her out. She might have a motive, and she definitely had access. She was angry when Margaret's body got autopsied; could it be she really was afraid of what they might find? Something to think about later.

Our discussion turns jokey and lighthearted as we continue on through another round of half-price appetizers and drinks, widening and widening our list of suspects, topping each other's suggestions with ever more outrageous possibilities. Maybe the butler did it. Maybe it's Freddie. Or Jason. Or bigfoot. When we settle the bill, our waitress says, "Thanks guys. See you next time," and it dawns on me she is the same waitress we had before. She recognized us. *Hey, that's pretty good!* I surreptitiously check her name tag ("Star") so that I will know it next time. I mean, there will be a next time, won't there? I'm really starting to enjoy this. I want there to be a next time.

It's getting dark, and Karen gives me a lift home, putting my bike in the back of her big SUV. It's the first time she's visited me here, and I can see she is in awe. The pool is lit up and beautiful, nestled in the privacy of the trees.

"Oh my God. Oh, wow! Lily, this is amazing!"

It's a nice reaction, so on the spur of the moment I invite her to the Halloween party, telling her to bring her whole family. Tessa won't mind; in fact, she'll be delighted that I have a friend. Karen immediately says yes.

"They will love this!"

After she leaves, I decide to calm down from the excitement of the evening with a mug of spiced apple chamomile tea. Chamomile is the king of relaxing teas, and the spiced apple gives it an illusion of sweetness—which I intensify with a tablespoon of honey. I'm sitting in my comfy chair with my mug, contemplating upping the sweetness a bit more with a box of miniature cookies, when I hear a knock on the door. No one ever visits, so I assume it must be Tessa and open it without thinking or checking.

Whoops.

It's not Tessa, but a man standing there. I'm disconcerted, and a little frightened. He asks me if I'm Lily Piper, and reflexively I nod. As my adrenaline rockets, my mind races and I realize I've seen him before. *But where? Not someone from my past; I've seen him recently. Not a yoga client, and not anyone who's just stopped by to check out the studio. The Iguana? No, it's dark in there, and I didn't pay the least bit of attention to the people around us.*

Waaait a minute. The funeral service. He was there. Jesus, it's him. It's really happened. Miller's guy, as in the guy *guy—the homicidal maniac.*

I stand there and break into a cold sweat. *Was he suspicious when he saw me there? Did he stalk me and find my address? Is he here to stop me from asking questions? To silence me?* I wonder whether Frank and Tessa will hear me if I scream. I think so, but I don't scream. I don't want to seem hysterical, but that is a dumb reason not to scream for help when confronted by a homicidal maniac.

The man holds up his wallet to show me a badge and identification card.

"Montgomery County Police," he says, "I'm Detective Dan Ridley. I'd like to ask you some questions."

Oh boy. The police, in the form of the very detective Dr. Ben told us about. You'd think I would be relieved, but in fact, the second I realized I was too concerned about appearances to scream, I also realized that I didn't really think this stranger at my door was a homicidal maniac, or even a run-of-the-mill murderer, coming after me. Why would he? I was just one of dozens of other attendees at Margaret's service. So in the space of less than two seconds, I had gone from blithe, to bat-shit terrified, to wary but no longer afraid. When Detective Ridley said he was the police, my freak-o-meter shot right back up to one hundred. It's not like on TV, when the actors play it super cool and lie with charming abandon. I freeze up in the face of authority. I am a law-abiding citizen who has lived her entire life in law-abiding suburbia. My mouth is so dry I literally can't speak, so I just nod again and step back to let him in.

I sit ramrod straight in my comfy chair and gulp my tea. Ridley takes a seat opposite on the sofa. He's about the same age as Dr. Ben, but tall and thin with a full head of salt-and-pepper hair. He's wearing nice-looking standard business attire: a dark jacket with a crewneck sweater, contrasting slacks, and leather chukka boots. He is a little brusque in his mannerisms, which to me comes across as dauntingly authoritative but polite. He reaches into his pockets to extract a pair of glasses, which he dons seemingly unconsciously, along with a pen and a notebook. He opens the notebook and starts in.

"I understand you're friends with Nico DiSilvio. Or rather, your mother knew his mother, Margaret Crawford? I'd like to get her contact information, as we'd like to talk to her too."

At least that explains one thing: Nico D. I'd wondered about that from time to time. This, of course, is the merest of passing thoughts as I contemplate how to handle what is happening right here, right now. More to fill the silence and give myself some time, I blurt out, "Dr. Ben said you might want to talk to me."

I hadn't thought about what effect such a statement might have on the detective, and his reaction flusters me even more. His eyebrows shoot up, his eyes widen in bewilderment, and even his mouth sort of opens as he stares back at me.

"Dr. Ben? The medical examiner? You're acquaintances?" He manages to deliver this coolly, as if he had that one also already prepared in his notebook, but his initial reaction had already let the cat out of the bag. His wheels are spinning, and that's not a good thing.

Let's not kid ourselves, I know this is not something I can handle. So I blabber instead. I tell Ridley the truth, starting with Karen's quandary during tea circle at the studio and all the way through to the funeral. Once I start, I can't stop. At first my voice is kind of high and squeaky, but the more I blab the calmer I get, and by the time I stop for breath and down the last drops of my now cold tea, I'm back to my normal self—so much so that I enjoy a tinge of gratification at Ridley's rapt attention. When he knocked on my door, he was probably expecting a five-minute recap of my talk with Alice outside Nico's apartment that day, maybe some impressions of the service, and, of course, what he really wanted: my mom's contact info. Routine, in and out, on to the next. Instead he got a tirade of craziness and lost the possibility that my mom would have anything to contribute whatsoever. He hasn't touched his notebook. He looks at me with eyebrows raised high.

"Well," he says. Now he puffs his cheeks a little and shakes his head as he lets the air out. "This is a new one." Another head shake, but this time he smiles a little. Just a little, but still.

"Let me try to summarize here: you have no connection to Margaret Crawford whatsoever, but you heard about her suspicious death and got so curious about it you sought out her son, faked a story to meet him, and even went to her memorial service ... because ... I'm sort of lost here. Did you think you would find out what happened to her? Solve her murder? What exactly was it you were you thinking?"

Now I realize my heart rate is back to normal, but my emotional state is not. I'm wiped out, and he has caught me: there isn't a good answer to this question, other than maybe more truth. I revert to full blabber mode, this time telling him things I didn't even tell Karen or Dr. Ben. I tell him about my long, lonely recovery from the accident, the depression that set in, and how my vivacious personality turned solitary and restrained. I tell him how the murkiness of Margaret's death sparked a passion and interest I had been yearning to feel again, and how the burgeoning friendship of the group from that day in the tea circle when Karen told us about the accidental autopsy was filling a relationship void. I truly had not thought about solving the mystery as much as just wanting to keep an eye on it and maybe investigate it to whatever extent I could, to have a reason for conspiratorial huddle-ups and happy hour meetings at the Iguana. Putting everything into words like this, out loud, made me see how pathetic it must appear to someone else, but it was still something

60

of a relief to get it out in the open. Ridley took it all in, and he was actually sympathetic.

"I see. I'm sorry for what you've been going through. For what it's worth, it sounds to me like you're well on your way to full recovery. But regardless, I really recommend that you find a more, let's say, conventional outlet? I don't know what is really behind the Crawford autopsy findings, but there's something there. Your friends are right; it feels normal, and for you even fun right now, but things can turn dangerous and get out of control very quickly. That's why the police are involved, and that's why I'm here talking to you now—to find out what happened to Margaret. How about you let us do our job without interference, and you keep yourself nice and safe. Sound good?"

"Oh yeah," I grin sheepishly at him. "Of course."

"Good." He looks at me as if he's going through an internal debate. Instead of getting up to leave, he continues. "Look, since you have been around the family, let me ask you this: did you by any chance meet or see Nico's father, Lou? Or did you glean any idea where he might be?"

Now it's my turn to shake my head.

"No. Nico and Alice both mentioned that his father went to live in Italy, I think when he and Margaret first got divorced." I cast my mind back to the service because the name "Lou" rang a bell. "There was a woman at the funeral who was talking to a couple. On my way out, I heard her say something about Lou considering coming but not thinking Margaret or her sister would have wanted him there. I didn't think much about it, because at the time I didn't know who Lou was."

"Can you describe her or the couple? Or do you know who either of them were?"

"No idea who they were. The couple seemed older—maybe seventies? The woman had her back to me, so I don't really know what she looked like. That's it."

"Might be a start if we can run them down. Good memory," he says as I glow a little.

"Do you think he did it?" I ask, emboldened.

At this Ridley puts back his head and laughs quietly before shaking his head at me with a smile.

"We're quite a ways away from that, Ms. Piper. For now we'd just like to talk to him. We're pretty sure he's back in the States temporarily, but we don't know where he's staying. I went to the service in part to see if he would be there, but he never showed. The comment you overhead suggests he's here in the area if he was close enough to have considered attending. Most definitely something we'd like to check."

His comment makes me glow again, and I'm starting to warm to him, but Ridley is done with his questions. He gets up from the sofa, all business again, and tucks his glasses and notebook quickly back into his pockets.

"I'll be on my way, but this is my card. Please do let me know if you think of anything else that might be pertinent. Just don't go looking for stuff."

He delivers his last sentence with a meaningful stare. We've ended, I think, on fairly good terms, but he is not someone who will be trifled with. He's warned me off, and I'd better take heed.

As soon as he's gone, I breathe deeply to calm myself down and assess. Upon reflection, the evening has ended rather successfully. Not only do I know for sure now that the police are investigating Margaret's death, but I also know the detective in charge. What's more, I now know Margaret's ex-husband's name is Lou DiSilvio and that he might be right here in the DC area. I decide to celebrate with another cup of tea and several handfuls of miniature cookies.

The big question now is, Where do I go from here? Do I leave it alone, secure in the knowledge that Margaret is in professional hands and that I might get in their way by hanging around? My head says that is the sensible thing to do, but my heart rejects it. I don't want to stop. Having a mission feels good; happy hour at the

Iguana feels good; helping people feels good. I love that warm glow that comes from feeling valuable. My presence at the funeral service helped a little, didn't it?

What should I do? What will I do?

CHAPTER

TWELVE

I'm dying to talk to someone about the Ridley visit and my own ensuing dilemma, but for once, not Tessa; she would worry too much. So when I don't see any of the others from our little quintet at the studio, I text Karen to see whether we can meet for lunch again, and she replies with a "sure—same time same place!" and a thumbs-up. My last morning session ends at 11:50, and I take an Uber over to the hospital. There's no Karen when I get to the cafeteria, so I text her and wait at the entrance.

"As I live and breathe, if it isn't Ms. Lily Piper," says a now familiar voice. I turn to see Dr. Ben approaching with a smile. We do our fist bump thing, and I tell him I'm waiting for Karen.

"She might be a while," he replies. "There's an administrative all-hands meeting going on, and they always run late. Let's go on in. You can let her know we'll be waiting as close as we can get to the table we had last time."

I check my phone, and there's still nothing from Karen, so I text her about Dr. Ben and where to find us, and follow him in to the lunch line. After loading our plates, we walk along the bank of windows until we find a table. It's not the same one, but Karen can't miss us. Up till now Dr. Ben and I haven't talked much, but he keeps smiling at me with that impish gleam in his eye.

"I have a feeling you already know Detective Ridley came by," I say once we're seated.

"Oh yes. He called me first thing this morning. Told me you two had quite a little tête-à-tête!" He's still smiling at me, but not unlike Dan Ridley, he is also shaking his head. "He's never had anything quite like that happen before, and it really threw him. Worried him too, a bit—it's so easy to get caught up in something you think is innocuous only to find out too late you've gone too far."

"He said pretty much the same thing to me last night. I just don't want Margaret to get swept under the carpet, so if the police are definitely investigating, then I'm happy. I mean, you were right, right? They're sure now it was homicide?"

"As far as I'm aware, the police share my opinion that Margaret's death was a homicide. But an investigation really is just that: trying to determine what happened and who or what played a role. So … Dan and his team are looking into it. It's impossible to say right now what they'll find, or whether they'll be able to gather the evidence that would be needed in a court of law."

Dr. Ben is looking at me with an expression somewhere between kind and quizzical. He senses my determined need for closure, but he's not sure why I'm so wrapped up in this. I can't explain myself any more than I already have, so I don't really try. Instead I tell him what's exasperating me most right now.

"I'd like to follow the case, but it hasn't even made the local news, so there's no information laid out for the public. I don't want a murderer lurking around, and I want Margaret to have some kind of final say. And you know what else? It really bugs me that whoever did this would have gotten away with it if it hadn't been for a totally random mistake!"

"That's certainly true." Dr. Ben nods his head and blows air through his nose—not quite a snort, but enough to indicate his own sense of wonder. "It's actually a bit of a fluke she even came to Austin Hill. Nico and his house captain, Geoff, found her in bed Tuesday lunchtime, the day after she died. Nico was there for a visit, and I guess Geoff drove him over. Geoff called 911, but neither one of them had the wherewithal to decide where her body should be sent, which is how she ended up in our morgue in the first place. Random, as you say, in a very real sense."

"Nico and Geoff, huh? Are either of them suspects—or maybe both of them? I mean, you know, first ones to find the body," I ask him.

Dr. Ben smiles over at me. "I imagine they are persons of interest, but that is Dan Ridley's purview, not mine. You surprise me though. You really think Nico could do this?"

"It would surprise me for sure, especially if he was by himself. But Geoff admitted he's had problems with the law in the past, and he obviously has a lot of influence on Nico. Maybe if Geoff thought Nico could get more money out of this, he could have done the heavy lifting...?" I start to repeat some of the theories from the Iguana but sort of drift off, as I really can't picture how this could happen, and I really *really* can't picture Nico acting as he has been if he'd actually witnessed his mother being murdered. Is it possible that's just how his mind works? Maybe he grieves and thinks about the now differently than the rest of us. It's way beyond my meager understanding of the human psyche, so I shrug a little back at Dr. Ben and say, "It definitely seems unlikely, but stranger things have happened."

"I know what you mean, and you do never know. I'm sure Dan won't disregard them out of hand."

Dr. Ben has apparently decided he's told me all he's willing to say. Or maybe that's all he knows. In any case, he changes the subject.

"Tell me, when you're not playing amateur sleuth, what do you do for a living?"

I tell him I'm a yoga instructor.

"Have you ever heard of Horatic yoga?" I ask. He shakes his head. "It's really a blend of yoga and martial arts, especially tai chi, and a few other things mixed in. Its founder researched practices from all over the world, trying to determine the ideal way to tap into and strengthen the totality of what makes us human."

"The totality of what makes us human ... sounds audacious. What was driving him?"

Dr. Ben seems interested, and this is one of my favorite subjects, so I tell him more about the history and philosophy behind Eye of Horus yoga: how it was introduced in the 1970s by an Egyptian American who was also, in fact, an Egyptologist with an interest in traditional healing; how he himself suffered terribly from a wide range of ailments throughout his life; and how his search for relief led him to define a philosophy of wellness based on some of the tenets central to ancient Egyptian beliefs, and to develop a method of physical rehabilitation and exercise to be its foundation.

"I'll be darned! I've never heard of it before," says Dr. Ben. "Why Eye of Horus though? Why not use the sphynx or the pyramid or some other icon of Egypt that's more familiar to Americans?"

"Because of the symbolism specific to the eye. Ancient Egyptians associated it with healing both of the body and of the spirit."

I explain how, according to mythology, the eye was wrenched out and pulled to pieces by Horus's evil uncle, but it was magically restored and made whole again. Because of that, it was associated with health and the power to cure, and became the symbol for ancient physicians.

"It still is today," I add. "The *R* with the cross at the bottom in the emblem for medical prescriptions originates as a depiction of the eye of Horus."

"Of course!" Dr. Ben tosses back his head and laughs. "I did know that but hadn't put the pieces together. Now I get it. Ingenious."

"There's even more to it," I continue, excited because Dr. Ben now seems even more interested. I pull up a picture of the eye on my phone, and point to it as I explain that it is made up of six parts. Each one symbolizes one of the five senses—vision, hearing, smell, taste, and touch—with the last piece symbolizing thought. Together they represent the human body. At the same time, each part of the eye of Horus also equates to a unit of volume, and these units were used to depict measured amounts of things like flour and grain—or, if you were a physician, medicinal herbs.

I explain that one of the tenets of Horatic yoga is the belief that we are made of many parts that work together as a system, but all together we are also something more. Now I find and point to a picture showing the fractional amounts each part of the eye depicts, which are ½, ¼, ⅛, 1/16, 1/32, and 1/64, and continue, "If you add all those fractions together, you get sixty-three sixty-fourths, so one sixty-fourth is missing from the whole. Some Egyptologists think that this last fraction symbolized the divine, a part of each of us that is not of this world. It could be described as the soul, or the spirit, or the light within, but however you put it, this last piece acknowledges that life is more than the sum of its parts, and that to be a whole person, truly healthy, we must be sound not only in our cells and bones but also in our spirits."

Dr. Ben has moved my phone closer, enlarging the images and studying them. There aren't a lot of people who have the patience for this type of thing, and I am surprised at how engrossed he seems. The phone hasn't dinged, so I know Karen hasn't responded to any of my texts yet, and I lift my head to check and see whether she is here somewhere, looking for us. Nope, no Karen.

"It's fascinating, really, as a way to conceptualize life, but how does it work in practice?" asks Dr. Ben, giving me back my phone.

"The basics aren't very different from other types of mind-body exercise traditions. The idea is that you need a healthy, functioning physical body first in order to reach clarity and freedom of mind, and mastery over your emotions."

I tell him about the power of the poses. While a lot of people recognize that you can rehabilitate injuries or alleviate things like back pain through stretching and performing certain movements, and yoga is a popular way to reduce stress, I describe how you can also do poses to improve thyroid function, asthma, liver function, digestion—very specific physical ailments like that. Doing certain poses also releases concomitant emotions. Once you feel that and are conscious of the impact of your movements, I explain, you are much more self-aware in every sense.

I remember when I first started at Eye of Horus how much this way of looking at things resonated with me. I find myself telling Dr. Ben how I didn't think the postaccident Lily was really me: I looked different, I felt different, I thought differently. While I knew so much of this had to do with changes in my brain as a result of that trauma, it made me wonder who really is "me"—the physical person in the mirror, or the one whose mental state comes through in the pages of my journal? Is the real Lily the me I remembered and wanted back? Or is she the one I became as I healed? I had to believe there was something more, something beyond all that—some spirit of Lily that could encompass them all—and that that Lily also must be part of the equation. The final ¹⁄₆₄ felt like the perfect way to explain it.

We've finished eating, but Dr. Ben doesn't seem to be in a hurry to leave. On the contrary, he seems to be enjoying our conversation as much as I am.

"You know, Lily, you and I are in a remarkably similar business. As a medical examiner, I often find myself contemplating exactly that, the question of what really makes up what you call that final sixty-fourth."

Now it's my turn to gawk a little. What is he talking about? What do forensics have to do with movement and self-actualization? I ask him what he means.

"Here's a question we like to put to new students: what's the difference between a dead body and a live one?"

It's such a bizarre and obvious question that I'm flummoxed by it. What is he getting at? I give Dr. Ben a smile and a big shrug, guessing, "One's a person and the other is a body?"

"Very nice!" Dr. Ben smiles broadly. "That's an excellent answer! In fact, I think I'll use that the next time it comes up at our medical examiner conventions! As you see, though, the reason it's a hard question is because on the one hand it's so obvious, and on the other it's not obvious at all. There is no real difference; all the elements are there in each, all identical except for the fact that in one the parts are moving and in the other they are still. It's not much different from a car that's turned on or one that's turned off"—here he sees my expression and winks—"aah, but so very different, isn't it? We are so much more than our body parts, but it can be hard to show exactly how. I will keep your Eye of Horus in mind from now on."

The conversation has gone in a captivating direction, but it ends abruptly as Karen comes hurrying up.

"Lily! I'm so sorry! We had this all-hands, and I had no idea it ran on so long! I left my phone at my desk. I feel so bad—I didn't even answer your texts but came right down. Hi, Dr. Ben. Oh gosh. I'm glad you found each other and managed to get some lunch before you have to go back. Sorry sorry sorry."

She collapses into a chair and lowers her head into her hands, peeping up at us like a sad puppy as she repeats her sorries. Dr. Ben and I pooh-pooh this and tell her not to worry, as we had a nice chat. It's true too. I'm delighted with how it worked out, as my mind is going a million miles a minute thanks to our little exchange. Dr. Ben says he does need to be going, though, and gives us a wave as he takes his tray to the trash. I get a cup of coffee and stay with Karen as she eats her lunch, and catch her up on the Detective Ridley visit, but we don't have time to talk about it much, as she, too, has to get back to work.

We're leaving the cafeteria together when Karen says, "Oh, by the way, about the Halloween party ..." I'm thinking she's going to tell me she can't come, but that's not it at all.

"I kinda sorta, well, I was so enthralled by your house and pool and everything that I told Miller about it. So now she's dying to see it, and I'm not sure how this happened, but, I mean, you know Miller. She's such a bully. I think I may have invited her to come. And bring her kids."

This is hilarious! So very Miller. But in fact, I'm thrilled, and I know Tessa will be too. There is plenty of space, and now I'll have two people to talk to. I tell Karen not to worry, that this is great, and we're both laughing as we part ways.

It's funny how answers sometimes come to us in ways that we don't expect. I had intended to talk to Karen about what I should do next, if anything. Do I keep nosing around the Margaret mystery on the down-low to appease my curiosity and, frankly, prolong the "fun"; or do I do the safe, sensible thing and just let it go? The conversation with Dr. Ben had the effect of pushing "whether or not" to the background while inviting some enticing points of enquiry to the fore. Talking about the elements of a body made me think of DNA. That reminded me that at the funeral Alice said Margaret met her husband working on the Human Genome Project.

I don't feel as if I'm investigating Margaret's murder; I feel as if I'm checking a few historical facts triggered by an unrelated conversation, so it's as though it doesn't count as taking action when I do a little googling on the Uber ride back to the studio. I read that this project was a venture to identify the entire genetic sequence for *Homo sapiens*. The NIH website notes something about it being the genetic blueprint for building a human being—talk about audacious!

Back at Tessa's after work, I am contemplating my discovery again as I swim laps up and down the pool. I'm swimming at a good clip, which is necessary to keep warm, but it's also a way for my body to keep pace with my thoughts. How interesting that the description of Lou DiSilvio's early work so neatly fits the very conversation I had with Dr. Ben—what is the total makeup of a human? Is it just the parts, or are we something more? I wonder about Lou himself: did he, as they accumulated and mapped each tiny DNA component, also wonder about that extra transcendental something? Did he find a gene for the human soul, or did he get frustrated because he could not? Okay, this last thought is maybe too far a flight of fancy. But I do wonder whether he considered these things, or whether instead he believed that once the genome was complete, he had all the pieces. Does he see people as just a set of building blocks, like a car with an on and off switch? Could he kill someone? It's a spurious question, of course, not at all fair. I know nothing about this Lou. I know virtually nothing about Margaret; I have to remind myself that I've never met her.

It's the period of the gloaming, darkening but not truly dark yet, and while the patio and pool lights have come on, I have the sensation of the forest closing in, and being all alone and far away in a secluded sylvan lake. Despite the unseasonably mild October weather, the water has chilled considerably since the summer. When I first noticed Tessa swimming in March, I couldn't imagine how she could stand it, but now I'm finding I love swimming in cold water. It's definitely a shock at first, but if I stay in and swim, I start to feel a kind of thrum inside my core. Eventually it spreads, so that a fiery warmth runs all through my body. As long as I keep moving, I feel invincible. When I do get out of the pool, that warmth always stays with me for a few minutes, and along with it comes a subtle sense of tranquility and joy. I think this must be akin to a runner's high, and the feeling remains even after the chill begins to set in and it's time to head for a nice, hot shower.

When I finish my laps this evening, I wrap myself in a towel and stand on the deck, enjoying the crisp bite of autumn that has taken over now that the sun is gone. Frank sees me from the kitchen window, and opens the French doors to call out, "Hey, Lily—lookin' strong! We're having pizza delivered. You're welcome to join us— should be here in about fifteen minutes."

Pizza around the island of their big, comfortable kitchen sounds wonderful. I thank him and tell him I'll be right in. The bright cacophony of the Corbins' dinner, with the kids talking over each other, getting up and down for who knows what reason; the clattering of cups and plates; and the delicious aroma of pizza, proves a stark but not unwelcome contrast to the quietude of the pool. It brings me back to the here and now, and there's something about the noisy boisterousness of this big family that appeals to my only-child self. It's fun to be in the middle of it all. Tessa is the calm, quiet center. She is beautiful, blue-eyed, tall and willowy, with blonde hair that falls below her shoulders. But Tessa is no ethereal model; she loves to take on tough physical challenges and works hard to keep fit; running, swimming, and biking (real biking, no motor for her!) are her mainstays, but she does it all. Frank is nerdier, with black square-framed glasses that match his hair, and he loves to goof around. He's in good shape too, but his attitude toward fitness is more playful, his activities haphazard compared to Tessa's clockwork workouts. They complement each other well, and they're a popular couple in Mattaponi.

After dinner Frank and the kids go to play some kind of board game, so Tessa and I stay in the kitchen to clear up. There isn't much—we stack the plates in the dishwasher, and she stuffs the pizza boxes in the outside garbage can. When she comes back in, she picks up the bottle of wine Frank opened at dinner and peers through it against the light; just over a quarter of the bottle is left.

"We may as well kill it. Want to?"

"Sure!" I smile, pushing my glass across the island to her. There's probably half a glass in there for each of us. Just right. We go into the living area and make ourselves comfortable. We talk about swimming first, and then she asks me about my day, so I tell her about having lunch in Karen's cafeteria again.

"Aah! The mystery of Margaret Crawford. Did you hear any more about that from Karen?"

"Funny how it worked out. I ran into the medical examiner, who recognized me, so we ate our lunch together while we waited for Karen. He happened to mention that it was Nico who found Margaret."

"I see. Does that make Nico the primary suspect? You said before he's disabled. Could he even have done it?"

"I've been thinking about that. He seems frail; he's very skinny, and he can't really hold his balance for long without the cane, not to mention the epilepsy. And then, his mind is very … 'childlike,' I guess, is the word. He's not someone you can talk to about complex topics. But even little kids have wild tantrums, and maybe Nico is stronger than one might think, at least in his arms—the balance issue wouldn't affect that, right?"

"Good point—maybe not."

"Nico's aunt Alice mentioned a couple of times that he had some paranoia. What if he got paranoid about his trust money—say, he thought Margaret was stealing it—and he was trying to either get her to admit it or was threatening her or something by pushing her under the faucet? Just the weight of his body could have held her down."

"I suppose that's not impossible," says Tessa as she sips her wine, "but the ME said she was found in bed, right? So how did he get her there? And come to think of it, how did he get back home?"

I correct myself, telling her that it was actually Nico and Geoff together who found Margaret. "Maybe Geoff saw it unfold and took advantage of an opportunity, like if he thought this was a way to get access to Nico's trust fund. Nico's not sophisticated enough to commit a crime and then cover it up, but Geoff probably could. He might even be able to convince Nico that Margaret had fallen on her own after all, or that Margaret really was still alive when he tucked her into bed."

I sip my wine too, contemplating. Let's say it was an accident, the result of a paranoid tantrum. Could Nico have had an epileptic fit brought on by the shock? Maybe he's acting so normally because he doesn't remember anything. Geoff could so easily take Nico home and never let on that anything untoward had happened.

My conundrum rears its head with a vengeance: keep digging, or leave it alone? I don't voice it to Tessa, because I know she'd tell me to leave it to the police, and I know she'd be right. What should I do when the answer I want is not the right answer?

For the moment, I stall. Back home in my comfy chair, I play games on my phone and do no more searching. Determined to get a good night's sleep, I manage to steer clear of the mini cookies, but it doesn't help. I sleep fitfully, dreaming disturbing dreams that I can't remember when I wake up.

CHAPTER
THIRTEEN

I n the mail, I receive a nice thank-you note from Alice Munney; it's probably the same note she sent to everyone who attended Margaret's service, but I thought it showed some class. On my phone I receive a strange text:

> Hello. Testing 123. Tonight on tv is a repeat of the
> live version of phantom

I do a number lookup and realize it's from Nico. He must have found my phone number in the guest book that I signed, although I can't imagine why he would take the trouble to add me to his contacts. I don't have a clue what he's talking about, so he probably texted me by accident, but the conflagration of the two messages propels me into thinking all the more about Margaret and what happened to her. I check WTOP and other local news sites for information on her case, but there's nothing. I really wish I knew who was responsible. Was it one of these people who I've actually met? I want to know more but am not sure how. I'm stuck.

On Thursday, the four "regulars" and I are all together sipping tea after class with only one other client, an older lady, also in the circle.

She inhales deeply and asks, "What is that smell? Licorice?"

I explain that this is a chai tea with ginger, cinnamon, and cardamom. She's probably smelling and tasting the cardamom, which, I explain, has a hint of fennel that sometimes tastes like licorice. It also tastes of cloves and citrus and acts almost like a sweetener. Cardamom is an unsung powerhouse, thought to help with inflammation, improved oxygen intake, and maintaining lower blood sugar. It's beneficial in other ways, too, but doesn't get the press of spices like turmeric and ginger. When the circle breaks up, Miller helps me collect the cups and bring them to the kitchen to wash, and she rolls her eyes at me.

"You and all your teas! I thought she'd never leave."

"Oh, Miller. I only wanted to show her some encouragement. She's an old lady and maybe needs some friends."

"Old? Are you kidding? That's hard living for you. She's forty-six. She's been in recovery for a while now, but for decades she was a heavy user."

I'm dumbstruck. Only forty-six? Not only is she younger than my mother; she's younger than Miller. I can't believe it. She looks, frankly, terrible. I immediately make a promise to myself: *I will never use drugs. I will never again touch alcohol.*

Karen, Haisley, and Redd have gathered their things and put on their jackets, but instead of leaving they gravitate over to us in the kitchen. Redd says they heard we had another meeting with Dr. Ben and want to know if he told us anything of interest. Karen starts to tell them about my visit from Ridley, and I start piping up about Lou. There's a general uproar of exclamations and questions, and Will pops his head in.

"Hey guys, sounds like you're having fun, but we've got people already arriving for the next class. Any chance you could take this somewhere else?"

"Oh, sorry, Will. Of course," I say with a huge grin at the others, my eyebrows raised in a question.

"Ig-ua-na," sings Miller.

"Don't ask me twice; I'm in," says Redd.

"We're getting jalapeño poppers," says Haisley.

As we set off across the parking lot, I revise my promise: maybe an occasional drink will still be all right.

A waitress in her early twenties with dark skin, multiple ear piercings, and frizzy midlength black hair, whom I now recognize as Star, smiles and waves at us as we enter, calling out "Hi, guys!" on her way to the kitchen. We begin seating ourselves around the same table we did before. Is this now our table? Sweet! We've only been here, what, maybe three times? But it feels comfortable and familiar. Does this mean ... are we Iguana regulars now? That is so cool.

We give our orders and sit back, relaxed.

"This is more like it," says Redd. "Now let's hear all the juicy details—but one at a time, please!"

So we go through everything—the visit from Ridley, the conversation with Dr. Ben, my google results. They fall over laughing at my thinking at first that Miller had been right and Ridley was the maniac knocking politely at my door to do me in.

"Our little group here is just starting to get fun; we'd miss you!" says Haisley.

"Fun?" says Karen. "You're having fun? What a bunch of ghouls!" she smiles. "But I have to say I'm glad to have people I can talk to about this and blow off a little steam. Sure would feel bad if it cost us Lily's life."

"Yeah, I feel like the party would kinda end with a thud just as we're getting known around here," says Redd, circling his finger around "our" table.

"You know what," declares Miller, "we need to figure out what to call our group. You know, so when we need, like, an emergency get-together announcement we can just say, 'Calling all whatevers, drop what you're doing and report to the Iguana immediately!'" We whatevers whoop and clap at that and turn our focus to the various possibilities.

Karen starts off the bidding with "How about Lily-pads? No! Wait, I know: Lillipops!"

"Cute!" says Redd. "Or maybe we need something a little more formidable. Lily-Hammers?"

"I like Tiger Lilies," chimes in Miller, and I know she's remembering that sleeping tiger is my favorite pose to end class.

"What about Pandas?" says Haisley. There is a brief silence as we look at her in confusion, and then Redd cracks up, snorting beer through his nose.

"Well," Haisley shrugs and smiles a little shyly. "Kinda like kung fu pandas. Did you guys see that movie? It's awesome!"

"Oh brother," groans Miller. "No Pandas. What do you think, oh wise one Lily?"

She's calling me that because I'm the one who stands at the front of the class, the one who always leads them to the next step. At the moment, though, I'm totally stumped and can't think of anything. Fortunately, I get something of a reprieve from Star, who is back at our table to clear plates and ask whether we want anything else. We tell her we're trying to think of a name for ourselves, and she flicks a hand at us dismissively, saying, "Oh, that's easy; we already have one for you! We call you guys Five-Bucks-and-a-Beer 'cause the girls always order the five-dollar happy hour wine, and your token male here always gets a beer."

That gets us laughing. We love it! I still can't think of anything, so we decide to let things percolate for a bit before we make a final decision. As I make my way home, I realize I've done it again. I accepted a social invitation and enjoyed myself. I even allow myself a moment of smugness. Sure, I still go up and down, but I think, maybe, outgoing Lily is back ... at least a little? Maybe a little. I do love our Iguana gatherings.

When I get home, I notice right away there's something wrong. My trash can and recycling bin have been upended, and trash is spread all over my back patio. I look around, and all is quiet, but I suddenly feel alone and vulnerable. Tessa and Frank are probably at home, but I can't hear anything and can't see their lights from this vantage point. For a second, I actually contemplate calling Detective Ridley, but I decide that's not a good move just yet, and in any case, his card is inside. Should I go inside? I stand still again, listening, but all is silent. Am I being silly? We've had problems on and off with raccoons, and this has happened before. But not in a long time. Is it raccoons ... or ... something else? Miller's maniac rears his head in my imagination, but I push it back down. It's not helpful, and not rational. *Don't be dumb*, I tell myself.

I go around toward the main house, and now I do see lights on in the kitchen, so I knock on the French door.

"Hey, kiddo, come on in," Frank welcomes me. I tell him that I forgot my key and ask if he could let me into the guest house.

"Sure thing." He gets the spare out of a drawer and hands it to me, saying, "Here ya go."

"I think there might be raccoons ..." I tell him, not taking the key.

Frank laughs. "Well, you probably already scared them away, but let's go take a look." He grabs a flashlight and walks with me over to the patio. Whew.

"Oh, yeah, looks like it. Gotta be careful to make sure the bin enclosure is latched tight. They're gone now though. Here, let me help you clean this up."

Frank opens my door and turns on the light, and it's obvious no one is inside. I thank him and tell him not to worry and that I'll clean the mess up myself, but he helps me anyway. When we're all done, Frank returns to his kitchen and I enter mine, feeling safe and secure once again. I'm shaken, but not really scared. In my heart, I am pretty sure it's raccoons. We haven't had problems with them since Frank installed lattice enclosures around the bins, but the doors are too heavy for the hinges, and the latch doesn't quite align anymore, making it difficult to catch. Sometimes in frustration I just leave it, but up until now everything has remained undisturbed. It's freaky timing, of course—right when I've been warned that getting involved in a murder investigation can get dangerous.

I decide there's no need to call the police about probable raccoons, but I'm also not going to sit on a suspicion of mine that has been building over the past few days. *If* someone came here and went through my trash, either to scare me or to find out more about me, who would that be? The stamp on my letter from Aunt Alice shows it was mailed from Boston, so presumably she is now back home. Nico is, well, Nico. But Geoff ... Geoff found Margaret, Geoff has influence over Nico, Geoff has a past, Geoff is young and strong, and Geoff had access to the memorial service book with my name and address. I need to find out more about this guy.

I turn on my laptop and start searching, only to discover he's remarkably easy to find on Facebook and Instagram. Geoff Turner is a guy who likes to post; his entire life is on display here, and it's not at all what I expected. Because he'd been in trouble, I had assumed he grew up in a household with little money, but this couldn't be further from the truth. He grew up in Potomac, an area so wealthy Bethesda is quite the slum in comparison. He attended two different, very expensive, private schools; old posts show jokes from friends that imply he was kicked out of both of them. He has hundreds of "friends" on his pages, but judging by the photographs there are really just two main besties. Their primary common interest is music; there are tons and tons of pictures of them at concerts, along with comments and links about bands, band members, lyrics, and new releases. There's no girlfriend, and his status is single. The next most prolific subject of Geoff's postings is a group he calls "the League."

The League has six members: Nico and his roommate Erik; a girl in a wheelchair whose face is always twisted to look up rather than toward the camera; another girl with a shaved head, glasses, and combat boots; and two somewhat older men—say, thirties. One of the men has Down syndrome, and the other is permanently bent over and walks with two canes. They go on all kinds of outings together, and Geoff's postings show photo upon photo of the League members out somewhere, smiling happily. I have to scroll back in time many pages and years to figure out why "League." It turns out that's a curtailment of the full name. As I eventually discover, when the group really took off, they decided to name themselves the League of Extraordinary Buddies. When I see that, I can't help smiling. Now that's a name! I imagine sitting at our table in the Iguana and laying out League of Extraordinary Buddies as my suggestion for our own name. Then I imagine the look on Miller's face, and my smile gets bigger. Of course, I would never dare. Continuing my surfing, though, it is touching to see how much time Geoff devotes to these guys. Lots of superhero movies, some local college theatrical productions, bingo games, botanical gardens. Comments and links indicate that for about a year, Geoff has been looking for a slightly used Sprinter van that's in good condition, but affordability is an issue. He posts that the bigger van would be more comfortable for the League, and he could camp in it on weekends when he goes to concerts.

You can't tell the truth of a person by what he or she puts online. People don't post what they don't want other people to know; and they often do post pictures and videos that show them in a particular light—more beautiful and more talented than they are in real life. What comes through on Geoff's pages are years of patient commitment and lasting relationships. A good, kind guy. Someone who would want to help a buddy out in a pinch. Or is this picture even real? Am I any closer to knowing whether he is capable of murder?

I close the laptop and turn on some music, relaxing into the soft melodies. I'm bushed. Trolling through social media is tiring. When my depression was at its worst, I swore off it completely. That didn't turn out to be realistic over the long run, but I've managed to steer pretty clear of it for years now, and I do believe less is more in this regard. The amplitude of other people's lives gets overwhelming. But there was a lot that was on Geoff's pages that made me smile, a lot that seemed sweet and authentic. Whatever else I was expecting to find, that wasn't it. If nothing else, the activity has lulled me and I'm completely over my alarm at seeing the upturned trash. What reason would he have, truly, to come after me as opposed to anyone else at that service? The thought seems almost silly now.

What doesn't seem silly at all, though, is to imagine him as someone who would go to great lengths to help Nico, maybe even cover up a murder for him, especially if it was an accident. What if this is one of those instances where a good Samaritan does a bad thing, thinking it's the right thing? Would the exceptionally solicitous Geoff think he's helping Nico by concealing a devastating mistake? Now *that's* something worth pondering. I want to go back to Sherwood and see these two again. I want to look for more subtle hints about their characters. Is there some tell that I might note in Geoff's demeanor—some nervous tick that would reveal something is weighing heavily on him? Maybe!

Now what excuse can I use for a visit?

───── C H A P T E R ─────
FOURTEEN

The next day, I have one morning session, but after that I'm free. I'm not sure yet what to do about visiting Sherwood again, so I decide to go back to the "source" and ride my bike to the hospital to see Karen. Maybe she's learned something new. This time I go up to her office because it's a little early for lunch. The door is open, and when she sees me, she waves me in, but I can see she is distressed about something.

"Are you okay? Is this a bad time?" I ask, a little confused because just twenty minutes ago, when I'd texted, she was enthusiastic about a visit.

"Yes, yes! It's fine; it's good. I'm glad you came. But have a seat and give me one sec; our chief administrator called a minute ago, and I have to check something."

I settle into the chair opposite her desk, and she starts tapping on her keyboard as she tells me, "It's just kind of sad. A woman named Irene Li gave birth here four days ago. Well, to be accurate, not even: she was at home early in the morning, and the baby came out all of a sudden, terribly premature. The woman called 911, and they brought her and the baby here. Poor thing, born at twenty-three weeks and weighs less than two pounds. Mom was doing fine—she stayed two nights and was released—but of course the baby is still here. She'll be in the NICU for months. But guess what? The mother just died. They don't know why yet. I need to find out who is responsible for the baby now."

83

She's looking at her screen, and I stay seated and quiet. Poor woman. Poor little baby.

"I'm pulling up her intake and insurance forms," Karen continues. "Irene Li, age thirty-nine." Karen reads something on her screen, and her expression changes from sorrow to ... puzzlement? I wonder what's up.

"This is her address," Karen says to me and reads it out. She looks at me. I look back. It's as if we both know something is weird here but don't know what it is. I think it hits us both at the same time.

"Wait, no way," I burst out first. "That's Margaret Crawford's old address. The house she sold when she downsized to the townhouse."

"That's what I thought too, but that would be bizarre. Are you sure?"

I open the Zillow app on my phone, as I had reviewed these properties several times since that evening with Tessa and Frank. I check history, and there's no mistake; it's the same address.

"That is a strange, strange coincidence," Karen says, looking spooked.

"They don't know how she died?"

"No, but I'm sure there'll be an autopsy, probably here. They're going to want to know if there was something we should have caught before we released her, among other things." She checks her watch. "You know what? Let's go see Dr. Ben. We can swing by his office and go to the cafeteria after."

Before we go, though, Karen has to makes a few calls. The first one is to a person named Tom Peary, but he doesn't pick up, so she leaves a message. She's standing at her desk, and looks over at me as she speaks slowly and clearly into the phone: she is calling from Austin Hill Hospital, it's about Irene Li, and she would like Mr. Peary to get back to her as soon as possible. She gives her name and number both at the start and at the end of the message. It's very professional, and I'm impressed. Then she calls back the chief administrator to say there is a complication and she'll need a little more time. I listen as Karen explains that there is no father recorded on the birth certificate, and no spouse for Irene. There is an emergency contact, a Tom Peary, who is listed only as "friend," and she just left him a message. With that, Karen locks her screen and we're on our way.

We put on masks to go down the hall, since they are required everywhere except in administrative offices and dining facilities. As we go down the elevator, Karen calls Dr. Ben to let him know we're coming, but there's no answer. She shrugs and says he might not be there, but he might just be on another line or something. When we get out of the elevator, it's a bit of a hike to get to his office, but eventually Karen stops, and we both remove our masks as she knocks on the door.

"Come in."

She opens the door, and in we go. All four of us gape at each other for a millisecond, because sitting across from Dr. Ben is Detective Dan Ridley.

"Well, well," says Dr. Ben. He introduces Karen to Ridley and adds, "Lily Piper, I believe, you've already met."

"Uh, hi," says Karen. She swivels her eyes at me for a second, only now realizing what it is we've walked into, and then looks back at them. "I'm sorry to interrupt, but it's actually good that you're both here. Are you talking about Margaret Crawford by any chance?"

Neither says a word for a second, and then Dan Ridley replies, "As a matter of fact, we're discussing a different case. Why do you ask?"

"Oh, sorry, none of my business, of course. But something just came up regarding Margaret, and we thought it was strange. We were going to run it by Dr. Ben."

"We?" asks Ridley. "Does Ms. Piper work in this hospital too?"

"Oh, uh, no. We're just friends. Lily stopped by, we were going to have lunch, but it's still a little early, so we were sitting in my office. When she came in, I'd just gotten this call from the chief administrator."

I can see Ridley is taken aback at seeing me here, still involved in this, so I give him a nice, innocent smile. Hey, I'm just visiting a friend. It's not illegal.

"Okay. What was strange about it?" Dr. Ben asks this time, moving things along.

"It wasn't really the call that was strange," Karen says, and she goes on to tell him about Irene Li, the baby, and her unexpected death. "I was checking her intake forms, trying to find out who is the baby's father, and noticed her address. It's Margaret Crawford's old house—the one she just sold."

Dr. Ben and Ridley stare at us, then look at each other. They know all about our search for Margaret's properties online, so they know how we know the house was hers. But I imagine what's going on in their heads is similar to what went through mine and Karen's—*What are the odds? Could it possibly be coincidence?*—mixed with some bewilderment that the two of us are here giving them this information.

"There'll be an autopsy," Dr. Ben says to Detective Ridley. "They're going to want to know why this baby's mother died."

"Oh yeah," Ridley kind of sighs back to him, "we're going to want to know how she died too." He's waggling his head side to side a little, thinking. "Could be just a fluke. People buy and sell houses all the time. But I'll let my team know. We'll take a look to see if there's any connection between Margaret and this Irene Li."

Ridley turns his head back to us and asks Karen, "Did you find the father? I'd like to speak with him."

Karen explains about the birth certificate not listing one, just this Tom Peary, "friend," point of contact.

"I see. When he calls you back, please let him know we'd like a word. In the meantime, I'll take down his information."

Karen is ready for this, and she's already written his name and number on a yellow sticky note, which she hands to Ridley. He thanks her and turns back to Dr. Ben.

"As a point of reference, how unusual is this—for a woman to die right after having a baby like this?"

"It's rare, certainly, but it does happen. Sometimes there's no apparent cause and no early symptoms that would signify a problem. Stroke, heart attack, amniotic fluid embolism—these can all fatally occur postpartum even if the mother feels fine right after childbirth and shows no indication of risk."

"Good to know," says Ridley grimly. "Okay, regardless, we'll want to see what the autopsy reveals as soon as possible."

Again he turns from Dr. Ben and back to us, saying, "Thank you for the tip, ladies. Just keep in mind that we're the ones doing the investigation here, okay?"

He was looking at me rather than Karen as he finished speaking, but we both reply, "Yes, of course."

We head back to the elevators, and I'm planning to leave since Karen is clearly busy, but as we're walking, she gets a call on her cell phone. She stops and looks at me as she answers it. I don't hear the other side, but Karen responds, "Oh, hello Mr. Peary, thank you for calling back so soon. Can you hold on for a minute? I'm in the hallway heading to my office."

She looks around and darts into an empty break room, gesturing at me frantically for a pen and paper. I go into the room with her and gesture back that I'll type notes on my phone. She puts her phone on a table and goes on speaker to continue the conversation.

"Are you still there? Good, thank you. I'm from Austin Hill Hospital and called because Irene Li listed you as her emergency point of contact when she checked in a few days ago."

"Yeah, I got your message. Is she all right? I mean, she checked out already; I drove her home. Is the baby okay?"

"The baby is in intensive care. But I'm very sorry to inform you Ms. Li passed away."

"Wait, what? What do you mean 'passed away'? You mean she died? How can that be? I thought … I thought she was fine. I took her home and made sure she was okay before I left myself. Are you sure? What happened?"

This is a hard conversation to have, and Karen's face is a vision of stress and dismay, but she's holding herself together better than I would and is able to speak to him calmly.

"Yes, and I'm so sorry to have to tell you in this way. Ms. Li did leave the hospital in apparent good heath after delivering her baby, but something must have happened. She was found dead in her living room this morning." Karen looks over at me as she says this, placing both hands up to her face and covering her nose and mouth for a second, shaking her head as if to say, "This is horrible; I don't know how to have this conversation with this poor stranger." I feel for her, and with no way to render her any actual assistance I unconsciously mimic her same face-covering action, shaking my own head in empathy.

There is stunned silence at the other end of the phone, and Karen continues, a little rushed now, filling the pause with an answer to a question he may or may not have asked now but might wonder about later. Or maybe she's just giving him time to collect himself.

"Her neighbor noticed that her back sliding door was slightly open and was worried she'd left it by mistake. He couldn't get a response from knocking or phoning, so he went in just to make sure everything was okay—no animals had gotten in or anything—and found her. He called 911, but it was too late."

"Oh. Oh my God. Irene. I can't believe it. Thanks for letting me know, I guess. Do I … need to do anything?" His speech is slow as he takes this all in.

"We're trying to locate her next of kin, and also the baby's father, as none is listed on the birth certificate … is that you, by any chance? Or do you know who we should call?"

"Oh, ah, okay, yeah, uh, no … I'm … the baby's not mine." He's quiet again, but this time Karen waits, not wanting to distract him from his train of thought. "Irene and I got together through happEver—it's an online dating company. We just met in person for the first time about two months ago. I knew she was pregnant, of course; she was totally up front about that and so happy and excited to be having a baby, but she never mentioned the father to me. I just figured, I don't know, he was out of the picture and she wanted it that way." He is quiet again for a few seconds, then adds, "Jesus … sorry, I'm kind of in shock here. I couldn't believe it when she called and said she'd delivered the baby; it's so early. And now this. Man. Anyway, you need next of kin. I know she has a brother, but I don't know how to contact him. You might see if some of her colleagues at work know more. She was a program administrator for advanced analytics at the National Endowment for Scientific Development. She's been there for a long time, so some of the people there must know her pretty well."

"Okay, thank you. You have my deepest condolences." Karen pauses before adding, "There is just one more thing: Detective Ridley from the Montgomery County Police would like you to contact him. Do you have something to write down his number?"

"The *police*! Why? What do they think happened?"

"I don't know precisely, but among other things, they also need to find the father and next of kin."

Silence.

"Huh." More silence, then "Whatever. What's the number?"

Karen reads it off Ridley's card, and with that they hang up. She lets out a long breath and looks at me.

"Well. What do you think?"

"I don't know what to think. He didn't sound evil or anything. He sounded like what he said: shocked by the news. So pretty normal. But everyone sounds normal to me. What will happen to the baby?"

"I guess it depends. I'll have to try and find that brother. Poor little thing. Her name is Victoria, by the way. I saw it when I checked the birth certificate."

We continue along the hall to the elevators, Karen to return to her office and I to my bike. What a strange morning this turned out to be. I keep going over it again and again: is this a coincidence or something else? All thoughts of Geoff and Nico are, for the moment, relegated to the back burner as I absorb this new development.

Back home I'm surprised to see Tessa in the pool, swimming laps, and I decide to stop for a few moments. I sit cross-legged on the edge, watching her go back and forth. I still find it soothing to watch her swim; she has such a smooth, effortless stroke. She looks as if she's going really slowly, but that's just an illusion. Even going all-out, I can't keep up with her. She's looking down, of course, executing perfect flip turns when she reaches the end of the lane, but at one point she stops to clear her goggles and notices me sitting there. She smiles and glides over, resting her elbows on the edge next to me.

"Don't stop," I tell her. "I'm just watching in awe. You don't usually swim in the middle of the afternoon. What's the water temp, by the way?"

"That's all right, I'm about done. I'm playing hooky. After taking the twins to dental appointments this morning, I didn't really feel like going back to work. Figured it'd be nice to just get in and move a little. Today's reading is sixty-seven degrees, so it's definitely dropping. You still going to be okay?"

I give her a big smile and two thumbs up. She's not talking about my murder case; her question has to do with an event that we're both excited about—an upcoming winter cold-water swim challenge, which Tessa does every year. It's a series of four open water swims, one in each of the months spanned by the winter season. They aren't races, the idea is just to see if you can get into the water, no wetsuits allowed, and swim to a designated buoy and back—about four hundred meters in all. I felt proud and thrilled when she asked whether I wanted to join her for the first one in December this year. I knew she wouldn't have asked if she didn't think I could do it, and that alone showed me how far I'd come. Thinking about it is a little scary—it's a long way to swim, and open water isn't like the pool; you can't see the bottom—you can't see much of anything. Add to that the cold; water in the fifties is vastly different from the air. It can feel as if your skin is burning and takes your breath away. But we're doing it together. Tessa says she'll swim next to me the whole way, and if I freeze up or just get stuck, she'll be right there. It'll be so fun. We're going to drive up early to collect our T-shirts and event swag bags. A lot of other swimmers will be there too, of course. There are whole clubs that organize and do these things. It's daunting, but that's part of the excitement, and it makes me feel as though I've arrived. I'm not a heavy, pathetic lump anymore. I'm not watching from the sidelines. I'm an athlete, a swimmer.

Tessa smiles back and hops out of the water. "Want a cup of coffee?"

I join her in the kitchen, where Frank has just brewed a fresh pot. It drives Tessa crazy that when he works at home, he often uses the kitchen as his office, spreading out across their island. He and I chat for a few minutes while Tessa showers off, and she comes back into the kitchen just as we're sneaking the last of their Oreos. She gives us a look of mock severity but doesn't say anything.

"Lily says the woman who bought Margaret Crawford's house just died," says Frank, barely coherent as he finishes chewing and swallows his cookie.

"What? Seriously? Was it … she wasn't murdered, was she?" Tessa asks me.

"They're not sure yet what happened to her. She'd just delivered a baby but had been well enough to go home. The police are going to see if there's any link between Margaret and this other woman, Irene Li."

It's a relief to talk about this morning's revelation, and I recap the rest of it as we drink our coffee. Frank asks some of the same questions as Ridley and Dr. Ben, focused as we had been on the strangeness of the coincidence, while Tessa asks a number of questions about the baby. It's so sad and so shocking for this poor tiny thing, barely alive herself, to suddenly become an orphan. We talk about Tom Peary a little too—poor guy, gets himself a nice online hookup and then suddenly all this. Eventually, though, our coffees are finished and Frank has to get back to work. I gather the empty mugs, put them in the sink, and head back home.

Trying to distract myself, I do some general chores: check the refrigerator and pantry to see what to do for meals and start making a list for the next grocery run, make the bed and tidy up a little. I never did have lunch with Karen, so I heat up some soup while flipping through catalogues that have come in the mail. I look around for my phone to play my games for a while and realize I've left it in Tessa's kitchen, so I decide to kill two birds with one stone. I gather up a load of laundry and go into their mudroom and put the laundry into the washing machine. Then I continue down the hall to the kitchen, where Frank is still at the island.

"Tessa walked down to the bus stop to pick up the kids," he says, not looking up.

"That's okay—just came back to get my phone."

Now he does look up. "I've been thinking about that house," he says with what I recognize as his all-innocence-but-secretly-mischievous expression. "Figured it wouldn't hurt to make a phone call. Wanna stick around for it?"

Oooh, interesting. We both know we have no business prying, but Frank can see that I'm champing at the bit to find out more, and he seems to have an idea how we can do that. I nod back, all innocence myself, and slide onto one of the counter stools as he tells me what's got him thinking.

"I rechecked the records on the property and noticed a few things. One is that the house sold significantly under market value compared to its comps. Another is that it was sold through a dual agency." He can see from my expression that that means nothing to me. "Dual agency in Maryland is when the agents for both the buyer and seller work for the same firm," he explains. "You don't usually do that unless there's a special circumstance. Seller's agent was a Sara

Blankenship. Who knows? Maybe she can tell us something. It's worth asking." He puts his phone on speaker and dials.

"Richardson Layman Realty, Sara Blankenship."

Frank introduces himself and says he's calling about an online inquiry he received, and he gives the address of Margaret/Irene's house. "I don't see it listed, but this person seemed to think it was going to go on the market soon. Since you were the agent for the previous sale, I thought you might know if that's true."

She's quiet for a second and seems cautious in her answer. "No, it isn't listed, but as a matter of fact, your inquirer could be right. There's a possibility it will go back on the market. Are you his realtor? Or are you looking to list it yourself?"

"No, nothing like that—it's out of my area; I only work Mattaponi—but I was online, and one of our chat requests opened up, so I took it. I don't even know the guy's name. All I know right now is that he's user Reggie2525. But he seemed pretty interested, so if you are the listing agent, I'd be happy to refer him to you."

Sara Blankenship warms to Frank at this promise and becomes a little chattier. "This area is amazing. Seriously, already? What is this? Some kind of ambulance chaser or something? Oh well, never mind, thanks for calling. What makes you say he's really interested? Maybe he's just shooting in the dark."

Ambulance chaser, I think. *Interesting choice of phrase.*

"Could be, but he did some research already. He noticed the house went pretty cheaply last time and wondered if there was something wrong with it. Maybe he's looking for a great deal on a hot location, or maybe he's being cautious and doesn't want to buy a money pit."

"Huh. Well, there isn't anything wrong with the house. It could definitely have gone for a lot more. My original client was the seller, who contracted with me to list it but then took it off the market almost immediately. Said it was a misunderstanding—she did want to sell it, but specifically to a friend of hers. So that's what we did. The buyer and seller set the price between the two of them. We got another Richardson Layman agent for the buyer, and I was the broker. If it had stayed on the market, the seller could easily have gotten another $400K, but this is what she wanted to do. I just can't *believe* how fast news gets around. I only got off the phone with the police, like, an hour or so ago, which is how I know it might go up for sale again. The previous buyer just died. And now here you are calling."

"The police? Whoa, wait a minute, was this, like, a murder? Was it inside the house? Reggie2525 sure didn't mention anything like that."

Frank is looking over at me meaningfully as I sit, quiet as a mouse. Well, well, well. So Margaret and Irene did know each other; they must have been good friends for a sale like that. How would their paths have even crossed? I'm listening intently, thinking that if the police called Sara, then Ridley is already onto all of this. I'm relieved that I now get to be in the know without feeling like I need to pass the information on to him and reopen the scab that is Lily, constantly in the middle of an inquiry where she has no business. I'm quite impressed with Frank; it's like he does this all the time or something. *Keep going!* I urge him silently. *What else can this Sara Blankenship tell us? Did the police tell her this was a homicide case?* But he's in his element and needs no encouragement from me.

"Am I right in assuming you'll be the listing agent? Hey, good luck to you; people get awfully shy about what they think might be a haunted house."

"The police wouldn't say whether or not there was an actual crime. God, I hope not; people definitely shy away when that's the case, but they were also calling to ask about that last sale, and they wondered if I knew anything about next of kin. To be honest, I was looking at my files from the sale when you called, because I do remember a relative being in the mix. I'm really sorry she died, but yeah, I'd like to get the listing."

"Makes sense ... I guess if the owner is dead, it's part of the estate now. It'll probably still have to get through probate or whatever, but that can go fast. Or was there a spouse?"

It sounds like Frank is just thinking aloud, and in fact I suspect that's exactly what he's doing—he's thinking like a realtor himself, mulling over the implications of a house suddenly vacated following an unexpected death.

"No—no spouse. The buyer was a single woman who apparently wanted a house with a yard in a good school district. She didn't have any kids but was planning to, I think. She was Chinese descent, you know? I couldn't tell how old she was. Had a good salary—some government job, I remember. Even so, by herself she could never have afforded a house in that neighborhood, so she was lucky her friend was willing to sell so low." I hear her tapping keys in the background. "Oh yeah. That's right. She had a brother in Canada who wired a sum for the earnest money. That was it; the buyer needed to sell her condo to come up with the rest of the down payment. He might be next of kin ... I'm going try him anyway. Hey, look, I gotta go. If that Reggie guy or anyone else contacts you about this property, you pass them on to me, all right?"

"You bet! Thanks for the info. Hope you get that listing!"

Frank hangs up and turns back to me. "Well, kiddo, something to chew on, isn't it? What are the chances of two friends, who at one point each owned the same house, dying under suspicious circumstances within such a short time frame? If I were the police, I'd sure be looking into it."

"Yeah, wow. Curiouser and curiouser. Thanks for the call; my eyes were popping!"

He gives me a wink and a smile, and I take my phone with me this time as I head back down the hall to change over the laundry. What's really going on here? Margaret was found in bed but had drowned. Irene was found in her living room—but could she have been drowned as well? My head is whirling. The Margaret–Irene connection opens up possibilities well beyond Nico's trust. Was there another financial motive? Why was the sale for so much below the market value of the house?

I check the local news again, but there's still nothing there. I know Ridley's team is checking into links between Margaret and Irene, but what have they found? Are their deaths related? They must be! But what does that mean? Are they close to solving this case? I wish I knew more. I think back again to my "raccoons" and wonder whether I should call Ridley after all. I tell myself I want to be reassured that this isn't a murderer angry at me for butting in, but I know that, really, I'm just looking for an in to ask how they're doing. I'm batting the idea back and forth in my head when my phone dings. It's another text from Nico.

CHAPTER
FIFTEEN

The text I receive is long and convoluted, riddled with typos. It appears to be about a pair of sneakers—the pros and cons of different brands, which to buy. I read it several times, trying to make sense of it. Obviously it has once again come to me in error. Should I text him back and tell him? Just ignore it? Then another text comes in, and this is no mistake—it has my name on it. He's sent a YouTube link to something called *QUEEN – Who Wants to Live Forever – BSO Los Immortales (substitulos español)*, and he's written the following:

> Good morning Lily. Please enjoy. On my calendar
> I see a special day is coming soon and you get to
> see it first. That's if you're in Australia

What the hell? I think about this. Is something up with Nico? Are these bizarre messages his way of calling for help? I had mentally discarded my suspicions about Geoff in light of Irene Li's death, but why look a gift horse in the mouth? Staring me in the face is a perfect reason to visit them again—not to mention the fact that I do, sincerely, want to get to the bottom of these texts.

The next chance I get, I ride over to Sherwood Independent Living, contemplating the way best to approach this. Instead of going straight to Nico's, I decide to check with Geoff first. This is easy to do, because there is a first-floor door with a placard that helpfully announces "House Captain, Geoff Turner." I press the bell, and a few seconds after someone calls, "I'm coming," Geoff, in short sleeves, cargo shorts, and bare feet, opens the door.

I go through my now familiar rigmarole about how I know Nico, and Geoff nods with a big smile. "Oh, sure," he says. "I know who you are. Come on in."

For a second, I waver, not sure I should go into his apartment alone. But I don't see how I can avoid it, since, after all, I'm the one who initiated this meeting. Up close, however, I notice how small Geoff is—I mean, that teddy bear physique makes him at first seem bigger than he is, but he's not very tall. Now I see that his hands and feet are no larger than my own, and his knees and calves look slight indeed. I'm pretty strong now, and I probably weigh as much as he does. No way he could overpower me. So in I go. I tell him I'm sorry to bother him but wanted to check on Nico; I explain about the odd text messages, and Geoff starts to laugh.

"Oh, man, sorry about that! Nico just does that. It's like once you're in his phone, you're fair game." I'm showing him my phone with the texts, and he starts nodding.

"Yeah, I see what happened. The second one about the shoes really was for me. He likes to do a ton of research before buying anything at all. But since he sent you that first note, your number was right above mine, and he probably accidently hit it. No wonder you were confused."

He moves on to the next text and says, "Uh huh, Nico loves to be cagey. Is there a holiday coming soon? Halloween, right? That's probably the special day, and Australia's time zone is ahead of us. I guess Australia celebrates Halloween—who even knows. Nico doesn't get out much, so he spends a lot of time watching TV and YouTube. If something catches his interest, he texts it to someone. He doesn't really think about what other people might be doing at any point in time or whether they're interested in exactly the same things he is."

"Oh, okay," I say. I think about that for a second, finally deciding it's a little odd but not particularly worrying. I'm also not picking up any vibe at all from Geoff other than chill amiability. "And Nico's all right? This is normal, you're really sure? I mean ... should I answer?"

"Yeah, yeah, he's good. You don't have to do anything, but he'd love it if you reply. Don't need a big message, just say, like, 'Hello.' He just wants a little interaction."

"Just 'Hello'? Like this?" I type "Hello" into the box and show it to Geoff. He nods, and I shrug and press send. Almost immediately, Nico 'likes' it. I show that to Geoff too. He gives me a thumbs-up.

"You made his day! And don't worry; he won't blow up your inbox or anything. He seems to pick contacts totally at random. You might not get another one for weeks or months. But if it bothers you, I can talk to him, tell him to leave you alone."

"Nah, don't worry about it. I don't want to hurt his feelings."

"Oh good, 'cause I think he likes you. He was disappointed you didn't stay longer at Dr. C.'s service."

Oh, yikes. I was noticed—both for coming and for disappearing. And what does that mean, he likes me? Like, he *like*-likes me? Thinking of Nico is making me regress back to childhood verbiage. But it's sweet, and oddly flattering. It also explains why he plucked my number out of that guest book and put it in his phone. I feel a little bad now for not going over to him at the funeral.

Geoff must see something in my face—I'm terrible at hiding my emotions and probably look a little guilty—because he says, "I don't suppose you'd like to go on up and just say hey to him now, would you? He won't keep you, I promise. It'll be like five minutes. He'll be super happy you showed up, say a few words, and then he'll be like, 'Thank you for coming. Goodbye.' That's what he does. But it'd *really* make his day!"

I couldn't have scripted it any better, but I play it cool and say to Geoff, "Sure, I'm already here; I may as well." I'm thinking this has been something of a waste of time, but I may as well finish what I started. I climb the stairs to Nico's, and as it turns out, Geoff was absolutely right; it played out exactly as he described. But it was an exceptionally interesting five minutes.

"Hi, Lily," Nico says as he answers his door, bicycle helmeted as always but sans cane. "It's nice to see you. Come in."

I have to say, he is very polite. I say something along the lines of I got his texts, was in the area, decided to drop by. All is smooth sailing up to that point, but then we falter and head into awkward silence. Grasping at straws, I bring up the only thing we have in common—his aunt Alice—and mention I got a nice note from her in the mail.

"Oh, yes, Aunt Alice has been really nice. She came all the way from Boston right away and took care of everything, which was especially special since she was just here earlier in the week."

Just here? Whoa now, this is news.

"She was? Gosh. You mean she was here right before your mom ... uh ... passed away?"

"Yes. She took me out for breakfast that Saturday."

Margaret died on Monday. I wonder whether Ridley knows this.

"That's amazing. Did you tell the police?"

"No. They didn't ask any questions about that."

"I see," I tell him, thinking how to play this. Ridley really does need to know, but I don't want it to come from me. I feel like we have such a nice thing going now, and I don't want to ruin it.

"You know, Nico, I bet they'd be impressed you remembered that and decided all on your own it was important to tell them. The police left a card with you, didn't they? Probably Detective Dan Ridley?"

"Oh yes, that was him, and his card is over there on the bulletin board with all the other ones people give me. See? That's my dentist, and all my doctors. My stuff is on the left; Erik's is on the right. I keep all the numbers on my phone, too, just in case I want to text." He waves his phone at me, and I allow myself a gleeful internal chuckle. Ridley is in for a treat; I hope he likes Queen.

"Well, maybe you should call and tell him. He'll probably be really happy to hear from you."

Nico has stopped waving his phone and is now staring at it. I think he's just checking to make sure the number is there, but then I hear Ridley's voice mail on speaker. I freeze in panic, but it's too late to do anything. I had wanted to do more "coaching," but it turns out not to matter. Right on cue, Nico leaves a message. And it's perfection.

"Hello Detective Ridley, this is Nico. I thought you should know that my aunt Alice took me to breakfast the Saturday before my mom died. Goodbye." Nico presses End Call with a flourish and looks up at me. "There, all done."

It happens so fast I can't quite believe it. Nico, you are a jewel.

"That was *perfect*," I tell him with all my heart. "He'll probably be so impressed you did that that he'll be back to talk to you again. You know, it's fine with me if you don't want to mention I was here. That way you can take all the credit. You totally deserve it."

"Thank you. I don't mind if I do. I guess you'd better go now."

And just like that, I've been shuffled off. I float down the steps. Ridley will get some good information, and I'm probably home free. I feel elated, even triumphant. I climb back onto my bike and ride home singing "Don't Stop Me Now."

Even when you're in the midst of something big, life carries on. One might say life gets in the way, but it's more like all the mundane things you still have to do add to the general action and sweep you along. I'm dying to talk with Karen and the others, but there's no time for another Iguana meetup. All of us have stuff we need to do, so we fall into a kind of game-of-telephone system: when we see each other individually or in partial groupings, we pass along what we hear to the next person. In between, we're texting or chatting online. It's chaotic, which only keeps the interest and excitement going. It's a fun new dimension to our group.

Late in the evening, I see Karen online and open up a chat.

> (Me) Hey Karen! You there? I found out Margaret and Irene knew each other. Also, Irene's brother is in Canada—had you heard?

> (Karen) OMG you're amazing! How did you find out? I did find the brother. His name is Andrew Li—lives in Vancouver. Parents are also still alive, but in China. Did you talk to Tom Peary or something? You playin' with fire, girl!

> (Me) What? Why? No Tom. Is the brother going to care for the baby? Did you talk to him? Did he say anything else?

> (Karen) Isn't that how you knew? Dr. Ben told me Ridley told him Tom Peary was the one who recommended a realtor for Margaret to sell her house. And yes I did—brother was pretty shocked. Don't think they communicated all that frequently

> (Me) Tom Peary knew Margaret? Hey—this is a lot to type. Can we call instead?

A second later, my phone rings.

"How do you know they knew each other?" starts Karen.

I explain about Frank's phone call, swearing her to secrecy. "So what's this about Tom Peary?"

"Yeah—interesting, isn't it? It's true he and Irene met online, but it's not a new thing. He's still claiming they only just met in person, but they've been in contact for almost two years. I guess Irene told him she had a friend willing to sell her house to her but they didn't know how to do it, so they wanted a realtor. He knew one and gave her a name, which presumably Irene passed along to Margaret. I don't know though ... baby Victoria was born at twenty-three weeks. So that means Irene got pregnant while she was in contact with Tom."

"That's weird all right. Tom's not the father, but he's okay with her having someone else's baby?"

"Exactly. He's gotta be lying about something. I mean, he didn't seem jealous or anything when we talked to him on the phone, remember?"

"No, he seemed fine with the baby, even told us he was the one who brought Irene home from the hospital. Maybe he knows there was no guy. Like, maybe he figured she went to a sperm bank or something but didn't want to tell anyone."

"Funny you mention a sperm bank; her brother mentioned that too *but* told me basically the opposite. He described Irene as a hyper type-A personality, very exacting regarding herself and everyone else. She never mentioned having a boyfriend or a partner of any kind to him, but she did want a child. He said she *didn't* want to go to a sperm bank. She thought the people who run those things can be sleazeballs who just use their own sperm, and she didn't trust that hundreds of siblings wouldn't one day come out of the woodwork."

Karen tells me that according to Andrew Li, Irene was considering adoption but was worried she wouldn't get approved. He thought maybe she had been, though, because all of a sudden she wanted to trade her condo for a house with a yard and was having difficulty finding something. Margaret was a godsend—willing to sell at an affordable price.

"Oh, wow. There is definitely a disconnect here. Maybe Peary really is the father but didn't want to be?"

"I've been wondering that too. The police want to do a DNA test to check. After all, Tom Peary was the last person to see her alive. He says he made sure she was okay before he left her, but who really knows?"

"But why kill Margaret? Wait ... do they think the deaths are linked?"

"I don't know what the police think. It's still weird that they died so close together, both maybe murdered. But you're right; if it was Tom, why Margaret? I can't figure that one either."

"So what does happen to the baby? If it's Tom's, does he take care of it? But what if he really did kill Irene?"

"I know, poor little Victoria. If Tom's really the father, then she's his responsibility unless they can prove he murdered Irene and put him in jail. If that happens—or if Tom's not the father and they don't find one—the brother might be the ticket. He told me he lives in a small apartment and already has a thirteen-year-old son, but said he'd talk to his wife. If no father can be found, they might be willing to take the baby."

The whole thing seems screwy. We talk over the possible implications of the Peary connection following a slew of different assumptions, but we don't feel as though we're any nearer to a story that makes sense. It's getting late, so we reswear each other to secrecy—me not to disclose Dr. Ben as Karen's informant, Karen not to rat out Frank—before hanging up.

I'm considering all these new possibilities when I realize that I forgot to tell Karen about Nico and Alice Munney's earlier visit. Oh well, it'll have to wait. *Wait for what?* I ask myself. *The police have this well in hand, I've done my one good deed for Margaret, I can drop all this, keep myself safe, and move on with my life.* As soon as the thought enters my head, my whole being rejects it. I'm not ready to let this go. I love the energy it's giving me, the sense of being part of something important, and the fun of our little group. And the more we discover, the more desperate I am to know: what's going on here? Why did someone want to kill Margaret and Irene?

I need a new plan, and the next day when I see Redd at one class and Miller at another, we chew over the possibilities that these new pieces of information offer.

"What if it's the house," Redd considers. "Maybe someone left some kind of buried treasure in there and is trying to get access to it. You hear about this stuff happening."

"But Margaret didn't live there anymore."

"Yeah, but what if this person thought Margaret knew where it was? Shoot, maybe she put it there. So someone was trying to get it out of her—like waterboarding, you know? That's how she drowned! Maybe he even got what he wanted out of her and so then went over to the house to get the money but ran into Irene."

"Interesting. Do you think it would be someone they know? Tom Peary? Or the ex-husband, Lou?"

"Could be. Could be that guy Geoff too. You know, it could even be Alice Munney. Maybe that weekend she saw Nico she also went to Margaret to force her to tell her where the treasure was. Yeah, yeah, this could be it," Redd is thinking hard. "So Alice has to fly back to Boston for work or something, but as soon as she has a reason to come back here, she goes to the house to get the treasure. Maybe she thought Irene would be out at work that day or something. She wouldn't necessarily know Irene had been pregnant."

This strikes me as a pretty good theory—one I hadn't considered. Alice might even have had a key from when Margaret lived there, and could let herself in. *Hmm.*

"Why did Margaret sell so low to Irene? Do you think that's relevant?"

"Good point. Maybe. What if Margaret knows there's a treasure but doesn't know where it is; she's got health problems, but Irene promises to look for the treasure and give it to her if she sells her the house!" He's excited at first that the theory appears to be holding, but then he kind of laughs and shakes his head. "I don't know, Lily. We could sit here and suppose all day. We don't even know if there really was a buried treasure."

Miller's mind is working furiously, her theories all over the place. "Lou might still have a key from when he lived there. You know what? I bet Lou and Alice had an affair! They're in it together to get the money!"

"What? Where is that coming from? And what does that have to do with Irene? You don't think Tom Peary's suspicious?"

"Oh yeah! You're right. I think he's probably the baby's father. Wait a minute … have they found Lou yet? What if Tom killed Margaret *and* Irene *and* Lou? Seriously, listen: Maybe Lou and Irene were having an affair and Tom found out! Lou is the baby's father!"

"Wow, Miller! Make a few leaps, why don't you. Even if they were having an affair, why kill Margaret?"

"Oh yeah. I dunno. Lemme think about this some more."

Despite the will-nilly nature of these theories, they've given me ideas on where to concentrate. I think Redd could be onto something. Was there a big sum of money somewhere in Margaret's old house? Did Tom Peary know about it? Did Alice? Or Geoff? Or Lou? Also, Miller had a good question: where is Lou? Is he in Italy, or is he now in the DC area? And could she be right and he's either a victim or a target also?

Regarding the house, Nico might be a source of information. He may or may not know about a buried treasure, but maybe he's seen something and just doesn't know what it is. Maybe I'll go check in on him soon, just to say hi. If I ask the right questions, he might tell me about it.

Over the next few days, I don't see Haisley or Karen at the studio, but everyone's texting.

> (Karen): I like Nico having a raging tantrum and Geoff covering, but why kill Irene?

> (Me): Did the police ever find Lou? I'm wondering if he's involved

> (Miller): Or dead

> (Karen): Nope! Lou is alive! AND he's in Arlington! He normally works in Italy at a university but he's here now on sabbatical. Police are trying to see if he profits from Margaret's death or has any link to Irene

(Miller): Hah! I knew it. It's always the ex

(Redd): I think it's the house. Maybe Tom makes money murdering homeowners and getting kickbacks on their house sales?

(Miller): Alice is in on this, she has to be. Maybe she and Tom had an affair. She killed Alice for the money and then found out about Tom and Irene and killed her too

(Redd): Alice is dead?

(Miller): Sorry—I meant Margaret

(Redd): ok

(Me): Maybe Alice killed Margaret but Tom killed Irene. Two completely separate crimes

(Karen): Why does everyone think Alice is guilty?

Oops. I told all the others but forgot to go back and tell Karen about my second Nico visit.

(Haisley): It might be Sara Blankenship

There is no immediate response to this. Then, a little later, there comes a reply:

(Miller): ???

(Haisley): She wants to list Irene's house, right? Well, RL are the listing agents for Margaret's townhouse. Maybe she's the connection

She includes a link to the listing.

(Miller): Hey why is this group suddenly named Pandalilies? How do I change it? We're not pandas

Karen sends a laughing/crying emoji.

(Miller): Pandas are fat and slow and stupid

Haisley sends an animated gif of a horrified panda saying "What?"

(Karen): How about we name ourselves the Idjats?

Ha ha, I think, *very clever*. The Eye of Horus is called the udjat eye, rendered with various spellings.

(Me): No! We are NOT idiots!

Karen sends a shit-eating-grin face, and more emojis from the others follow.

(Me): No name decision unless it's unanimous! I like pandas, but don't think they're right for us

(Redd): Yeah. We're not fat

These interactions continue through the week. New information, new theories, confusion, silliness. I have noticed that this is what we do. We are deeply interested in one particular subject—the mystery of Margaret and Irene—but almost anything will throw us off onto a tangent. I don't mind at all; in fact, I relish this. I think maybe this is how it happens. What I mean is, when you grow up like I did, making friends occurs so naturally, so spontaneously, that you don't even think about it, you just take it for granted. It was easy; they were just there. But after the accident, and years of eschewing contact of any kind, I found myself no longer a student but a fully-fledged grown-up, with a job and an independent life. That's when it hit me that I had no clue by what process one actually connects with others and becomes friends. So I watch this thing, whatever it is, with these tea circle regulars, and let it run wherever it will. One thing brought us together, but what happens when that's over? Maybe somewhere in all these tangents another thing will bond us, and another, and so on and so on. Maybe that's all you need.

To me, the big news was about Lou being in Arlington—on sabbatical, Karen had said—so he could have been here during the time both women died. What might that mean? I want to organize my thoughts and get all the different theories straight, so after work I go down to the canal towpath for a walk while it's still light. This is a marvel of a local attraction for walkers, bikers, runners, and the like. It's completely level, hard-packed dirt and gravel, and extends for almost two hundred miles. I love that on the path I am surrounded by nature, with no need to worry about traffic or even crossing a street, and I can't get lost; it's the perfect place for moving meditation, or just thinking. It's right after work for most people, and a lot of them have the same idea, so while I stroll, I idly check out the different body types and apparel that pass by. Because the weather has been all over the place, I see everything from joggers in shorts and tank tops to walkers wearing jackets and knit hats. I watch a couple of runners as they come toward me, a man and a woman. The woman, in particular, holds my attention because there is something just a little "hitchy" in her gait. I'm trying to guess whether it's maybe something in her feet or legs that bothers her or whether she's tight up top and it's affecting her stride. I'm leaning toward a neck or shoulder problem when they slow to a walk and the man says, "So it *is* you! Hi there, Lily. I've been wondering if I might see you here one of these days, although I was expecting a bike. Ben tells me you're an avid cyclist."

I can't believe it. It's Ridley, and I didn't recognize him—probably because of the out-of-context thing, along with the fact that he's drenched in sweat and wearing running shorts and a baseball cap.

"Oh, hi, Detective Ridley!" I reply. "Sorry I didn't say anything; I was lost in thought. No bike today, just a walk. Looks like you two are runners."

"Trying to be." He smiles. Then he turns to the woman and introduces us.

"This is Lily Piper—you know, the one whose application to the police academy is pending. Lily, this is my wife, Toni. Also Detective Ridley, incidentally."

They both look like people who take fitness seriously. Dan Ridley has that deerlike thinness you see in dedicated runners. His wife is about his same age, give or take, and has some muscle. At a guess, I'd say she's more into something like CrossFit than pure endurance. I envy the sculpted arms hanging casually from her sleeveless shirt, and the way that shirt clings easily to her waist without highlighting any bulge. She's smiling kindly at me, though, and I forgive her her perfect body.

"Nice to meet you," I tell her, flashing my own smile.

"Pleasure is all mine! Pay no attention to his teasing. It's just that you've made a big impression on Dan. He tells me you're quite a bulldog, digging hard into one of his cases. Keeps him on his toes!"

I'm supremely flattered to find that he's talked about me outside of work, but I'm shy about this too. I hope I'm not blushing when I reply, "Well, just a little armchair digging maybe. I'm curious, that's all."

"Oh, you're an *armchair* investigator, huh? Then I guess we'll have to punt your application over to state," says Ridley, at which Toni punches him in the arm.

Still smiling, she explains, "That's just a little interforce rivalry you're hearing. He's county, I'm state— 'cause I'm better."

I grin back at both of them, "Oh, boy! Your dinner table conversation must be fun!"

They laugh at that but don't contradict me.

Ridley says, "We're parked in the lot by the next mile marker. Care to walk with us?"

I'm surprised and pleased at the invitation, and I agree immediately. It means turning around and going back toward home for me, but I was about to do that anyway. One must take advantage of opportunities whenever and wherever they arise.

"Tell me, Lily, what have you been looking into lately from that armchair of yours?" Ridley asks.

I tell him about checking out Geoff's social media presence, and all the pictures and comments about the League. I confess my surprise at his background—that I'd made the assumption he'd grown up struggling.

"Geoff, huh? Some reason you're concentrating on him?"

"I just wondered about him. For good or ill, Geoff has a lot of influence on Nico."

"Ah," Ridley acknowledges. He grins over at his wife and adds, "See? Got my own internet sleuth!"

"Internet's good!" Toni smiles at me again. "You just have to take what you find out there with a grain of salt. Things can get twisted around."

"I know," I assure her. "I've been looking for articles in the local news but haven't seen any reporting. I just want to know what really happened."

"You and me both, Lily," says Ridley. "And I appreciate how your mind works; the address thing was quite a leap. But I always worry when a private citizen gets involved. Bad things can happen."

"Do you have a suspect? Someone in particular I need to look out for?" I ask.

At that Ridley looks at his wife and sighs; she looks back at him and laughs. "I see what you mean!" she says.

"Look, Lily, let me just say this. The case is still open, presumed homicide, and we haven't yet apprehended the perpetrator. So stick close to the armchair. You don't want to find yourself accidentally caught up with the wrong person."

I agree immediately and back off the subject, switching instead to their running. They tell me they're training for the Philadelphia Marathon. Today they did what Toni calls a ten-mile fartlek run.

"We do some miles easy and some fast. I'm beat, so walking this last bit feels good."

"That's awesome," I say sincerely. "Good luck! You guys are amazing! Have you been doing other things, too, though? I ask because it looks like your neck, or maybe your shoulder, is sore." This last I direct to Toni, whose turn it is now to stare at me in surprise.

"My shoulder," she says. "I don't know what I did or when, but it's been bothering me for weeks now. How on earth did you know?"

I grin and explain that when I first saw them jogging, I noticed that her stride wasn't completely smooth.

"Try this," I say, twisting my arms in front of me and pushing with my palms, which is the upper-body portion of eagle pose.

Toni tries the pose and exclaims, wincing, "Oooh … aaaah … that hurts so good!" Then she circles her head and shakes her arms. "Left shoulder's definitely tight."

"Sometimes runners don't realize they're clenching their shoulders, or it can happen if you do a lot of work on the computer. One can tighten up more than the other. Doing that can stretch them out a little."

"Nice!" Toni says, and I see Ridley give his slight smile.

"Pretty good," he says.

We've made it to the mile marker, and they head up to the parking lot while I continue along until I reach my own turnoff. Of course, he didn't give me any information. But now I know where to find him if I do feel like I want to "accidentally" bump into him again. More importantly, I feel as if we know each other as people now. If there's another raccoon incident, I can call him as a person just wanting a policeman's take, not necessarily as someone reporting an actual incident. I find this comforting, like a safety net. And of course, his little aside about appreciating how my mind works has me swooning on the inside. Ironically, despite their warnings, this interlude with the Ridleys has inspired me. I want to find something else they haven't thought about. So they're on to Geoff and Tom Peary and Lou and Aunt Alice. What about Aunt Alice's husband, Gordon? Only Alice signed the book, so he wasn't at the funeral. Why not? If there's money somewhere, Gordon would likely be as aware of it as Alice. As soon as I get home, I google Gordon Munney.

CHAPTER

SIXTEEN

O n Thursday, the four of us "Whatevers" finally end up together again in class, and everyone wants to share theories and maybe clear up some of the confusion over the facts that we've been bandying around so haphazardly. Karen volunteers to help me clean up, and we're Swiffering the floor when Redd comes over with his arms up and open in question mode.

"Well?" he says. Karen and I don't have time even to ask "Well what?" before Miller appears and claps her hands.

"Okay, gang, it's go time! Iguana in five. Haisley's meeting us there."

Redd grins. "Thank you! That was my question." Karen and I grin back, zip through the rest of the cleanup, and grab our jackets and bags. We're all out the door in less than five.

Star spots us almost the minute we walk in the door. She's carrying a big tray of drinks, but she smiles broadly and cocks her head toward the back, where Haisley has snagged us our table. She's also got a big smile on her face as we come through and settle ourselves on benches and chairs. No one even looks at the happy hour menu; we already know what's on it and what we want.

"So what do we think, guys?" I start off. "Is it the house? Or is it the people who are all in this together somehow?"

"Seems like that's the thing to figure out first," agrees Redd. "How 'bout we bat them both around a bit and see where we land? I'm thinking house. Here we have two women who die unexpectedly under very similar circumstances, one who just moved out of the house and one who just moved into it. Seems to me the strongest connection is the house."

"You mean like ghosts?" squeaks Haisley, wide-eyed. "Or some evil presence like Amityville or something? I don't know about that. Even if that's what it is, I think you have to be in the house itself, you know? I think it's like they can't get you if you're somewhere else. So it wouldn't explain Margaret."

"Seriously?" Miller looks over at her with knitted brows and a don't-be-dumb expression.

Redd smiles gently at Haisley but shakes his head, saying, "No, I wasn't thinking ghosts." He explains his theory about treasure being buried in the walls. "Maybe not literally the walls, but you know what I mean. There's a big stash hidden somewhere on the property."

"That's a possibility," muses Karen, who is hearing this for the first time. "If that's the motive, then Alice and Lou are the most likely to know about it and want to get their hands on it. Possibly Tom Peary knew too, if Irene told him."

"Or the house might just be an offshoot of Margaret and Irene knowing each other," I say, adding in my two cents. "Tom Peary is trying hard to convince everyone he's not Victoria's father, but he sure is the most likely one. What if Irene told Margaret the baby was Tom's, and Tom killed them both to keep that quiet because he didn't want a baby? Or Tom could have met someone else and wanted to break up with Irene but now felt trapped."

"Yeah—it's always a love triangle type thing with murder," says Miller. "Here we have an ex, and a boyfriend, and ... I don't know. Cherchez la femme! Well, that or money."

"Oh, hey! Speaking of love and money ... I've been googling Gordon Munney, Alice's husband," I tell them. "He owns a chain of brewpubs. It doesn't have a real website, just a Facebook page, but a lot of people have posted questions like, 'What happened to the one on such-and-such street.' I'm thinking he used to have a bunch of locations around Boston, but now there's only one or two left. Margaret was into craft beer … maybe she was supporting the brewpubs but stopped, so he had to start closing down."

"Yes! And what if she stopped because she and Gordon had an affair that went bad! What if Alice found out and got angry," adds Haisley.

Silence follows this, and then Miller asks, "How old was Margaret?"

"Hey! Older people fall in love, you know," says Redd, his tone of voice making us laugh.

I tell them about Margaret's recent pictures at the funeral and admit that if he'd been Margaret's husband having an affair with Alice, I would have believed it in an instant, but the other way around seems unlikely. The brewery support, however, does seem Margaret-like.

"I'll bite," says Redd, "So what else would make her stop?"

"I've been thinking about that." I reach for the nearest apps and put some on my plate, then take a bite before continuing. "She sold her house for less than it was worth. What if she and Gordon were finagling the books and Irene found out and was blackmailing her? That would explain the sale and also explain why Margaret stopped supporting the brewery—she was low on funds or just figured the game was up." No one else seems to notice, but I raise imaginary arms in a celebratory touchdown signal. I've been dying to use the phrase "the game is up."

"Ooooh yeah …" Miller is nodding emphatically. "Blackmail. Definitely. So Alice or Gordon kills Margaret, and Irene tries to blackmail whichever of them did *that*, and that's who kills Irene! It explains everything!" Miller raises her glass to us and takes a sip.

"It's actually a good hypothesis," says Karen, "but I can't get Tom Peary out of my head; there's just something off about where he fits in with the baby."

Redd laughs and shakes his head. He takes a sip of beer and plops a handful of nachos onto his plate, saying "It's as if the more we find out, the more possibilities there are, and we're just chasing our tails. Sure is fun to think about though!"

We toast to that and break out of our serious mode into something more on the happy hour relaxation spectrum.

Miller takes over. "It's so true, it is fun to think about! We've all really bonded over this. What are the chances? Just look at us, so diverse! We got a guy who's black; me, Vietnamese; and we span, like, four decades in age. Who would have thought?"

Miller, Miller—straightforward almost to the point of inappropriateness, as always. I'm at a loss for words after her outburst, but Haisley jumps right in.

"Don't forget me! I'm Hispanic."

We look at her in surprise. She has dark auburn hair and spectacular green eyes. Looks don't mean everything, but I'm sure that if any of us had been asked to guess her ethnic roots, no one would have said Hispanic.

Miller of course is direct, and skeptical. "Your name is Haisley Gilchrist, and you're Hispanic?"

Haisley grins and nods her head. "I use my middle name; my full name is Ana Haisley Gilchrist. My dad is Scottish, maybe with a little English and Irish strewn in, but my mom is Colombian. Her mother's name was Ana."

"Do you even speak Spanish?" Miller again.

This time Haisley shrugs a bit sheepishly. "Umm ... a little. I took it in high school. But even my mom isn't perfect at it; she came here with her parents when she was only five years old."

Now Redd breaks in before Miller has another chance, saying, "Ana is a nice, international name. Easy for everyone to pronounce. You don't want to be called Ana?"

"It sounds kinda dumb, but when I started middle school, I noticed that all the cool girls had cool, unusual names. So I just started off telling everyone I go by Haisley, and that's been it ever since. Now I'm so used to it I don't think I could change back."

"And were you one of the cool girls?" asks Redd.

"You betcha!" A beat passes. "Well, actually, maybe not one of *the* cool girls, but I had my buds. It all worked out."

"It is a pretty unusual name," acknowledges Miller. "I don't know any other Haisleys."

"It's my dad's mother's maiden name. Her first name was Eilidh, by the way, spelled E-I-L-I-D-H, and fortunately my parents didn't saddle me with that one—I would be doomed forever to misspelling and mispronunciation. But speaking of unusual names, *Miller*, what's your story? Lots of Millers over in Vietnam?" Haisley shoots this comment with another grin. The drinks and bar food are having an effect, and we're in a teasing mood.

"Ha ha ha!" replies Miller, tapping her nose and pointing back at Haisley. "You got me! Nope, no Millers. My real name is Uyen, but, you know, same problem as your Eilidh: no one here can spell it or pronounce it. It's pretty normal for us when we immigrate to pick an easy, American-sounding name to use. I was fifteen when I came here, and I didn't know any, so I asked my friend what the most common American name was. She told me "Miller," so that's what I picked—I had no idea it was a last name, not a first name! Took me years to figure it out!"

We all break up laughing at this, not least because of the sight of Miller herself, who is almost in hysterics at her own mistake.

"Woohoo!" cheers Redd. "Guess what—I'm a last-name-firster too! John Redd was our preacher, and he passed away just before I was born, so I was named in his honor. Tell you what, though, I learned my lesson: it's a bear going through life with a last name for a first name and a first name for a last. Everyone always gets it backwards. My kids all have normal first names." Redd's full name is Redd Thomas. I can see the problem.

My turn now. "I don't have a last name for a first name," I tell them, "but I was also named for someone who died shortly before I was born. Not a person though. Lily was our family dog. My parents still have a big picture of her on their living room wall."

"Ooooh," coos Haisley, "that's sweet!" Redd and Karen laugh, nodding in agreement.

"Oh brother," says Miller. "But maybe you're lucky. Did they have any other pets?"

"Sure did! A cat named Pookey and one of Lily's puppies, named Pepper. Fortunately, they both remained alive and well all through my birth and toddlerhood."

"Whew!" Redd pretends to wipe his brow. "You did luck out. Pookey Pepper Piper is a mouthful!" We toast to that and then turn to look at Karen.

"I got nothin'," she says, shaking her head.

"Come on, girl! Think!" says Redd with exaggerated desperation. "Tell us your middle name is Ms. Simpson, for the ghost in your attic!"

Karen does that Karen thing where she puts her head in her hands and shakes it side to side, peeping up at us with her eyes. "I blame my parents. My middle name is Marie. I have no idea why they picked either one."

Redd throws up his hands while Haisley and I also affect dejection. Once again, we're off on a tangent, but I'm enjoying it. We're learning a lot about each other, and it really does feel as though we're a gang of friends now, hanging out at our regular table, no matter what picture we may present to the rest of the world. Miller's right—it doesn't make sense, but we fit. I haven't truly fit anywhere in so long. I just sit back and watch it happen, basking in the warmth of it all.

Later, though, tucked up in bed, I realize how foolish my postulations really were. Lots of things make perfect sense when you're sitting in a bar, drinking and hamming it up with your friends. In reality, I had been so hell-bent on making an extraordinary leap, to impress Detective Ridley with my brilliance, that I hadn't considered all the things that make my premise specious. I have absolutely no evidence whatsoever about any relationship—financial, romantic, or otherwise—between Gordon Munney and Margaret. Does wine make you telepathic? I don't think so, but my phone dings, and there's a text from Haisley.

(Haisley) Did you see the menu?

(Me) Umm ... huh?

(Haisley) He's not broke, he's retiring

Haisley sends a link followed by a shrugging emoji, a laughing/crying emoji, and a smiley. The link is to the menu of Gordon's brewpub, but it's not a normal online menu, it's a pdf of what is likely the four-page paper foldout that sits on all the tables. I enlarge it on my phone and take a look. The first three pages are exactly what you'd expect to see on a menu, with what's on tap, appetizers, entrées, and the like, but the last page—the back—has a pen-and-ink drawing of a shop front, followed by a few paragraphs telling the story of the pub. Haisley is right; it's in the last paragraph:

> It's been a great ride, but when it's time, it's time. The year of our 40th anniversary, we sold our expansion locations to the big boys. Alice and I want to enjoy our golden years, living out our lives in a manner to which we've only dreamed of becoming accustomed! It's not quite last call, though, so don't worry, fans. I can't bear to let go of the flagship. We'll keep this one going for as long as we can.

At the very bottom is the handwritten signature "Cheers! Gordo." So much for my theory. Who would think of looking at the menu? I text Haisley my thanks, ruefully telling myself I need to be more careful about jumping to conclusions. I don't form another plan immediately, but Miller, it turns out, has been doing some research of her own. It isn't long before she has some interesting things to share.

CHAPTER

SEVENTEEN

The Halloween party is late afternoon the Saturday before Halloween. I help Tessa and the kids put up decorations around the pool, while Frank puts out extra lights, folding tables, and chairs. They have Halloween candies in dishes here and there, and over by a big picnic table are coolers full of wine, beer, and sodas. They're also going to provide grilled hot dogs, but the party is mainly potluck. The rest of the picnic table will be filled by all the plates of food, desserts, drinks, and candy brought over by the guests. The place looks fantastic when we finish up and go inside to change into costumes.

I've been thinking about my costume for days now, figuring out how to dress up without spending any money. I own a pair of leggings that are white at the top and black down around the calves, so I put those on. Then I add a black turtleneck shirt underneath a white scoop neck shirt with the sleeves folded up a little. I don the black sneaker booties that I like to use for walking in the winter, and I look in the mirror. Pretty good, I think, and it's not just the costume. It's taken a long, long time, but in the three plus years since I've been living here, I've lost weight. I'm still what a kind person might call stocky, and still too thick around the middle for my liking, but I'm solid and fit now. I can look in a mirror like this and not be horrified at my reflection.

I walk over to the main house and go into the kitchen, where Frank sees me and says, "All riiiight! Storm trooper!"

I throw my hands in the air and do a one-second victory dance to celebrate him getting it on the first guess.

"Wait a sec," he says, and he runs off somewhere. When he comes back, he's carrying a white trucker hat with a black front and bill. There's a logo on it, but it's dark gray on black and barely noticeable. I put the hat on and look back at him.

"There ya go." He smiles. "That's it."

Tessa comes in dressed in a fabulous Moana outfit, although she has prudently swapped Moana's authentic top for a long-sleeved Hawaiian shirt tied at the waist. It's warm for Halloween, but not that warm. She looks me up and down and guesses, "Skeleton?"

Darn.

"Nope. Storm trooper."

"Of course!" she says, and now Tessa races off, only to return a few seconds later with a huge squirt gun that she hands over to me. It's lime green but has a black shoulder strap, so I sling it over my back, put my fists on my hips and stand with my legs slightly apart, glaring at her. Tessa smiles broadly.

"Love it!" she says. The kids love it too, and I love theirs: Christopher and Julie, now aged nine, are dressed as Minions, in yellow shirts, blue overalls, and yellow knit hats with mason jar lids stuck on to look like goggles. Charlie is a seven-year-old Spider-Man. Last week Tessa showed me a picture of him in the school Halloween parade, surrounded by the other eight kids in his class dressed as Spider-Man. Brielle, at five, is adorably conflicted; she's wearing a white doctor's coat and plastic stethoscope paired with a glittery blue skirt and glittery pink sneakers. Tessa reads my mind and confirms she put this together herself.

They're too excited to stay in the kitchen for long, and in any case, guests start arriving and soon people are milling around, oohing and aahing at everything. It turns out October is a wonderful time for a pool party, even if no one is swimming. Frank has put their two full-size ocean kayaks and three kid-size kayaks into the pool, and kids are zipping around in these. As the evening proceeds and more people arrive, princesses, avengers, dragons, cowboys, and vampires pile into the vessels. It's as if Disney has shipwrecked and all the characters are now squeezing into too few lifeboats. They don't seem to mind, as the increasing challenge of staying afloat and steering makes it all the merrier. Tessa has wisely hired a lifeguard to keep an eye out so parents can enjoy the party on dry land.

Into this scene walk Karen and her husband with their two kids, carrying some kind of dish that looks like eyeballs, and Miller—whose husband couldn't come—with her four kids, and brownies iced in purple and orange. Their eyes get huge as they take it all in. *Oh my God!* I see them mouth over and over. I introduce them to Tessa, and she tells them how happy she is they could come. She points to the food table, saying "Help yourselves to anything!" as she turns to greet more newcomers.

The kids break away almost immediately, and Karen's husband goes over to the grill to meet Frank, so I take Karen and Miller on the tour. I show them my guest house, and then we go around the pool, past the trickling waterfall toward the old diving well, which has been reconfigured with a wooden dock jutting into it, and along the other side, where I point to a hidden slide that spills out from an island grotto in the middle of the pool. Back on the near side, we head toward the picnic table and check out the signs affixed to the brick back wall of the main house. The original pool rules are there, exactly as they were when the public pool was open. They're pretty much what you'd expect today, with "no running" and "no gum" near the top, but rule six, "no hairpins," gets a giggle. Next to the pool rules is another original: a big metal square, a bit faded now, but dark blue with a red growling bear head encircled by red lettering that reads "MATTAPONI BEARS SWIM TEAM"; underneath in smaller italics is written "*Go Bears!*" Lastly, right above this is a gem of an antique store find that Tessa couldn't resist purchasing: it's a dark green sign with big white letters: "BATHING SUITS FOR RENT." They especially love that one.

"Oh man!" says Miller, "That is so funny. That's a real sign? People really used to rent bathing suits?"

"That is awesome!" Karen agrees, laughing at it. She looks around and adds, "This whole thing is awesome. I've never seen a house with a pool like this!"

We help ourselves to plates of food and drinks, and make our way to one of the little tables to sit down. I unsling my squirt gun and lay it on the ground. Miller does the same with the stuffed toy walrus she had slung over *her* shoulder, as she has come dressed as an Eskimo.

"I thought it would be colder!" she says, in answer to our unasked question about why she chose this costume. "I wanted to wear a coat."

"Uh huh," says Karen, examining the walrus. "This is a manatee."

"Oh, shut up."

We eat and chat about the pool, about their kids, and about yoga. But pretty soon we can't help ourselves: we're back on the topic of Margaret Crawford and Irene Li. Miller surprises us by saying she has an update for us. I'm seeing that Miller loves our little group and "our" mystery almost as much as I do. She can't leave it alone either. She tells us that wills in Maryland are public information once a person is deceased, and are available online. So she looked up Margaret Crawford's will.

"It came with a letter of instruction that was also online, but altogether it was pretty short and simple. Nico gets everything. And yeah, her sister Alice Munney is named the trustee for him, but the letter gave the name of a law firm that is already managing the money, and its fees are covered by the trust. I don't really know, but I kinda got the idea that this firm manages the day-to-day things and disburses the money to Nico, so Alice would only get involved if they had to make a big change. If that's true, I don't see how she could take over and start using all the money herself."

We think about that for a minute.

"But you say if there was a big change, she'd be the one to make the decision?" Karen asks. "What if Alice just decides to change law firms. She could fire the current one, saying she's going to use a firm in, say, Boston or wherever she is. Then she could just not hire another one, couldn't she?"

"Yeah, maybe," concedes Miller, looking deflated. "She probably could. But then what? She still has to pay Nico's expenses; she's not gonna leave him homeless, is she?"

"You're right, and it makes Alice less likely a culprit in my eyes," I say. "I've been thinking we haven't really considered the ex-husband very much, but we should since he was here so fortuitously. He just happens to be on sabbatical a few miles away when she died, when normally he's in Europe? That's some coincidence. Or you know what, this just occurred to me: maybe Margaret had a boyfriend. That opens up possibilities that we haven't even considered."

"Oh yeah, that's good," says Miller. "Maybe there was a boyfriend and he did it. Or maybe Nico didn't like the boyfriend. Remember: you told us he gave Alice the cold shoulder because he thought she had something to do with his dad leaving. And he and Geoff found the body? Nico could have visited, he's angry, maybe he hurts her by accident."

We talk about this a little, and I tell them my theories about Geoff and Nico. Miller jumps on this last idea immediately, proclaiming them the new number-one suspects, but Karen is more circumspect. We eat and drink quietly for a few minutes.

"What about Irene? Did she have a will?" I ask.

"Nope. At least not one recorded in Maryland, so I'm assuming no will," Miller shakes her head.

There's another brief pause, and then Karen leans in and drops her voice a little. "Actually ... I don't think it's Nico's trust. I'm not supposed to know this, but the police think Lou DiSilvio was involved in some kind of con. Lily's right; we shouldn't just skim over Margaret's ex."

My eyes open wide, and so do Miller's. "What do you mean? What kind of con? How did you find out?"

"Remember how Margaret's tag got mixed up with that other body's? Our chief administrator put me in charge of a process improvement project to ensure that never happens again. It's been high priority, and I've been working with different departments for the past couple of weeks. Anyway, we've got something everyone seems to think is good, and I needed to go over it with Dr. Ben, to have him sign off on it."

Karen goes on to explain that she took the paperwork down to his office in the basement and knocked on the door. She heard his voice but couldn't quite make it out, so she opened the door and peeked in, only to realize he was on the phone.

"He was talking on the phone and pulling out drawers, looking through his desk for something, so he didn't realize I was there. I could see he was busy, so of course I left; but just as I was closing the door, I heard him say 'DiSilvio.'"

Karen couldn't help herself. She shut the door quietly and stood outside, listening.

"I could only hear Dr. Ben's side of the call, and even that I couldn't hear very well, but I think he was talking to Detective Ridley."

She was able to glean that Lou owns a company here in the States and he's been in Arlington since September, catching up and doing work related to that.

"So he *was* here for both deaths," I jump in, wondering to myself whether he has an alibi for either one.

Karen nods, and what's more, she tells us, the police have been digging into his company files, finances, email—everything, under suspicion that it has defrauded the government out of millions of dollars of research grant money.

"Oh man! So it's *money*! And Lou is a scumbag! I knew it!" exclaims Miller. "His company's stealing from the government? Maybe Margaret was going to turn him in!"

"This is huge!" I agree. "Maybe it *is* why Margaret was killed. Did Dr. Ben say anything about Irene?"

"He sort of did. I heard him ask if they found any connection between Lou and Irene …"

"And?" Miller and I both prompt.

"Well, I don't know what the guy on the other end of the phone said! But Dr. Ben kind of sighed. You know, like an 'oh, well' kind of sigh? I think the answer was probably no."

Miller and I deflate.

"Maybe just not yet!" Karen chimes back in. "They're still investigating, right? Maybe they just haven't found anything *yet*." We all perk up at that possibility.

"Hey, speaking of Irene, did you ever find the baby's father?" asks Miller.

"Tom Peary is balking. He didn't want to give a DNA sample, so we're stuck until either they find a way to compel him or he changes his mind. No one else has come forward, and none of her work colleagues have any idea. I talked to two women supposedly close to Irene, and neither of them even knew about Tom, never mind anyone else. Irene held her cards pretty close."

"Why doesn't he want to give a DNA sample?" I ask.

"I don't know, and he doesn't have to give a reason. But if you ask me, it's suspicious," says Karen. Miller snorts in agreement while I nod my head, thinking furiously. It's as if the pieces are starting to come together, but not quite.

All three of us are quiet again, tasting all the desserts on our plates. Then the kids start to come running over, telling their moms numerous exciting things, and we get up to free the table. Karen goes to find her husband, and I see them in conversation with another couple. Miller gets embroiled in a cornhole game. I move around collecting trash but also find myself meeting and chatting with other guests. It seems like it gets dark all too quickly, and people start to say their goodbyes. Karen and Miller both hug me, exclaiming over and over how much fun they had. Miller's youngest positively beams up at me and begs me to have her back in the summer so she can go swimming. I tell her of course she has to come back! I'll hold her to it. Miller laughs and says they don't swim much; they might have to rent some bathing suits.

CHAPTER

EIGHTEEN

I push Margaret out of my head for most of the rest of the evening, helping Frank and Tessa with cleanup and storing away all the goodies people have left. But much later, half sitting and half lying on my comfy chair, I feel exhausted but my mind won't stop running. Lou has been here all along. He owns a company and was running a scam. Did Margaret know? Maybe. I'd considered blackmail before, and now I wonder about it again, only this time with Margaret the offender. That could have gotten her killed. But if so, then where on earth does Irene fit?

I surprise myself by waking early the next morning. Looking through the window, I see Tessa swimming laps. Since I've been mostly swimming after work lately, it's been a while since I went in with her, and I miss starting the day in this way. Instead of turning on the coffee pot, I feel myself smiling as I change into a bathing suit, grab a towel, and walk out to the deck. The air has a hint of late fall smokiness, and a light fog hovers above the pool. The water temperature has continued to drop, and I go down the ladder very slowly, acclimating for at least a minute between each rung. Once I'm in there's one last bit that needs to get wet. I take a deep breath, put my feet on the wall, and push off, immersing my head under the water. It is cold cold cold, but now that I'm all the way in and swimming, the excitement kicks in. I concentrate on finding that thrum, and it doesn't take long before I feel wonderful. I'm no longer cold; I'm energized, and my strokes are rhythmic. I could go forever. When we do get out, the sun feels stronger and brighter. Is it really, or is that just an illusion? We wrap ourselves in our towels, enjoying the "runner's high" sensation. When Tessa heads toward the hot tub, I follow.

"Aaaaah," she says with her eyes closed. She peers over at me, heavy lidded, for just a second and then settles back again. "I'm glad you invited some friends to the party. Looked like you were enjoying it—were you?"

"I was! I'm so glad I went, and I'm really glad they came." I explain to her how I invited Karen, really, but then Miller bullied an invite out of her, which starts Tessa laughing.

"They both seem great. I hope I can meet the rest of your crew sometime," she smiles and is quiet for a few minutes before continuing. "Your swimming is looking fantastic, by the way. But I have something I need to tell you." She turns her head toward me again, and now her eyes are fully open. "I won't be able to do the December challenge. We just found out that's the day of Julie's hip-hop recital."

I try not to show any reaction as I take this in. Julie started hip-hop dance lessons this year, and she's been bebopping all over the house for months. This will be her first recital. Of course, Tessa must go. But I'm sort of in shock. I can't possibly do the cold water challenge by myself; I'm terrified. Somehow I manage to play it cool for Tessa.

"Oh! Hey, don't worry about it. I mean, maybe I should go to her recital too—we can do one of these swims another time."

"Oh noooo! No, Lily, please, please, please don't let this derail you! You're registered; you've been training! I'll feel so bad if you don't go! We'll take the minivan with the kids, and you can take the car. I don't want it to be my fault that you miss out."

Tessa is my best friend; she's done more for me than I can ever repay. The least I can do is not be the cause for her to feel bad. She deserves a medal, not a guilt complex.

"Well, then, sure, if Julie won't be upset. I'll pick up both our T-shirts. Seriously, it's fine! I'll send you a picture when I'm all done," I say with an easy flap of my hand, calm and confident.

"Good for you," Tessa sighs with relief. "Julie won't mind at all—of course we're going to video the whole thing. You two can sit together and watch it over and over and over. As many times as you want. Can stand. And many more."

"Wonderful, deal!"

We're both smiling as we lean back in the bubbling cauldron. I'm sincerely happy to see that Tessa is happy. But dear God, what have I gotten myself into? I don't think I can do it. I've never swum anywhere but in a pool. There are no sides to grab onto in open water, and while the swim is in a lake, not the ocean, my imagination still runs wild wondering what creatures might be lurking beneath the surface. But I can't give up now; I have to do it—for Tessa.

There's a string of texts waiting when I get back to the guest house. It's my own fault, really; Frank sent me a link showing there's an open house for Irene's property this afternoon. I immediately forwarded it to the others, and Miller texted that she is going to go. Redd texted back, "Okay, let us know if you find out anything." Karen wants to go but can't. I want to go too, but I'm working; I'm taking over the second day of a weekend retreat. I send a reply exhorting Miller to pay close attention and report back, and I get a thumbs-up from her. There's nothing more to do, and the retreat takes over my full attention.

Eye of Horus puts on two-day symposiums about every other month. They attract practitioners from all the area studios, so they rent a large conference room in a hotel that is as convenient for everyone as they can find. The area instructors take turns as leaders and support staff. We do a lot of various activities, including our regular classes as well as some team-building games and some self-discovery exercises. We also provide a lot more detail about the development of Horatic yoga, and the purpose of the poses and flows. Today I lead a session that includes tai chi moves focusing on kidney health, as well as breathing exercises, traditional yoga asanas, and other stretches to open up the root chakra. I'm just following the outline that the retreat's lead instructor has put together, but as we all work through these moves together, I'm struck by how apposite this is for me. These are movements that help clear out emotions like fear and frustration and help build confidence, ambition, and mental strength. At the end of the day, I'm physically tired, but I do feel strangely bolder. Doing the cold water challenge on my own doesn't seem quite as daunting as it did this morning. And I'm more eager than ever to dive back into the mystery of whatever happened to Margaret and Irene.

Since I haven't checked my phone all day, it's no surprise to see another spate of texts. Looks like there was an attempt to get together at the Iguana, but almost everyone was busy. I really want to know about the open house, though, so I call Miller.

"Oh, hey, where were you?" she says. "You never answered our texts."

I explain about the retreat, and she says, "Oh, okay. Well, I'm going to Karen's after dinner—she said to come about seven. Why don't you come too?"

This habit of hers of inviting people over to other people's shindigs is hysterical. I reply right away that I'll be there, and I don't even tell Karen. When she sees me show up unannounced, she'll totally get it. In the meantime, there's about an hour and a half to kill. The hotel is near the DC line, and there are lots of shops and restaurants on both sides of the street. It's still light out, and the place is crowded with people walking along the sidewalks or in their cars, looking for parking. It feels good to be part of the pulse of the city, and I choose a direction on a whim. Before long I find a little Chinese restaurant, one of those places whose business is almost all carryout, but it has four or five somewhat shabby-looking tables where you can sit down. I go inside and order lo mein, and I play games on my phone until I look at my watch and am surprised by how quickly the time passed. My Uber pulls up to Karen's just as Miller arrives in her car, so we walk down the path together and ring the bell.

Karen takes one look at us and cracks up, sweeping her hand wide to invite us in.

"What's so funny?" asks Miller, noticing that I'm grinning like a maniac too.

"Nothing, nothing," Karen replies innocently as she leads us through to the kitchen. I see why she's been busy: the house still bears the remnants of a birthday party, with balloons floating along the ceiling and stray wrapping paper under the couch. The kitchen is cluttered with plates and serving utensils awaiting cleaning, but it is bright and cozy, and has one of those built-in niches with bench seating around three sides of a table. On the table sits more than half of a big sheet cake decorated in psychedelic tie-dye.

"Please tell me you guys would like some milk and cake," says Karen. "I don't know how we're going to get rid of this."

Miller and I are delighted; we most definitely would like some! Karen gives us big slices and big glasses of milk, and we sit at the table munching as Miller recounts the highlights of her trip to Irene's.

"My husband told me I'm crazy, but he still wanted to come too. I told him, 'Great, it'll be fun; just make sure you nod at everything I say and don't ask any questions.' So we went together, which was probably good; there were some other couples already there, and we fit right in. I think they got a lot of traffic today, so it'll probably sell fast."

"Was it Sara Blankenship?" I interrupt.

"She wasn't there, at any rate. It was some other guy from Richardson Layman. I forget his name, but who knows, maybe he works for her or something. Anyway, we walked through all the rooms, checking out the space. It was pretty nice—you know, older house but mostly updated. It was kind of bare though. I don't know if that's because she hadn't lived there all that long, or maybe she just likes a minimalist style. It just felt a little stark to me."

"Maybe a lot of stuff was already moved out? Maybe it was bad staging?" I ask, interrupting again.

"Maybe, but … *not*! Ms. Lily, you're going to have to just let me tell this story and get all the information out before you start asking questions."

Karen turns to me and says very sternly, "Ms. Lily!"

I shrug contritely, contain my urge to giggle, and mime zipping up my lips and throwing away the key. Miller stares at me for a second, ensuring full compliance before resuming her story.

"When we first went in, there was a woman in the living room, like, walking up and down the carpet and staring at it. It's a really pretty carpet—Persian or something. Anyway, we go all over the house, which is clean and neat but not much changed from when we first looked at it on Zillow; she hadn't torn walls down or anything, the kitchen was about the same. It was fully furnished, all that same kind of austere style. Mixed in there, though, you could see she was getting ready for a baby. She had a crib and a rocking chair all set up in her room, and the bedrooms upstairs were painted for a baby—really, really cute. There were some cubbies with diapers and little onesies and things folded and ready to go—all brand-new, I could just tell, nothing secondhand. Oh, and she'd had the basement finished. It wasn't fancy, just that vinyl tile on the floors, and the walls were painted. She'd put a couch and a TV and a little rug down there. She also had other baby stuff stored to one side, like one of those car seats that converts from back to front as the kid gets older, and a really nice stroller. Some other things still in their boxes. Just like in the bedroom—everything new, nothing preowned or hand-me-down. Everything was so neat it felt almost sterile. They didn't need to stage anything; they probably didn't even need to vacuum! My house is bedlam. That was true even before the kids; now it's just more so." Here Miller gives us a grin and a shrug, while Karen nods empathetically, and I help myself to another slice of cake.

"From the basement, we went out the sliding doors, which are definitely sticky and hard to move, to take a look at the yard. There's no fence or anything, just a concrete patio, then grass and a few trees. You can't really tell where one yard starts and the other one ends. People were walking their dogs along the greenway behind the houses—maybe that's how the neighbor noticed the door was open. It would be easy to see from there. When we're all done and head back up to the living room, the woman is still there. Now she's talking to the realtor guy about that carpet. I pretend like I'm waiting to maybe talk to the guy myself or something so I can listen in a little. And guess what."

Are we allowed to talk now? I'm afraid to say anything, so Karen asks, "What?"

"She's one of the women Irene used to work with. Turns out she had this big Persian carpet and nowhere in her house to put it, so when Irene bought this house, her friend says she can put the carpet in the living room. But it's, like, ten thousand dollars or something. Expensive anyway. Now the woman wants the carpet back, even if she has to hold on to it till maybe one of her kids buys a house where it can go. She just doesn't want to lose it to some new home buyer when really it was meant to be like a long loan and not a gift."

"Did she get to keep it?" I ask. Oops. I couldn't help it; it just popped out.

"Lily." Miller rolls her eyes at me. "I have no idea and I *do not care*. Didn't you hear me? This woman worked with Irene!"

I slap my hand over my mouth and shrink down, not daring to look at Karen. We're both on the brink of a giggle fit. Miller glowers at me a second before continuing.

"I'm all like, 'Oh, you worked with Irene? You're at NESD?' Like we must have so much in common or something. Then the woman asks if I know Irene, so I tell her, 'Kind of; I don't live far from here. My husband and I just want a bigger yard in the same neighborhood. Blah, blah, blah.' Ky—that's my husband—is looking at me like he doesn't know me, but he keeps quiet and plays along. He's the best husband in the world, even though he thinks I'm a total cuckoo bird. The woman was really nice; her name is Sharaya, and she starts

135

asking me if I heard what happened to Irene, and we're, like, totally bonding over the story. Sharaya said she was completely surprised when the police came in asking questions."

"They questioned Sharaya? About what?" Karen asks.

"That's what I asked, and she said not her, but some of her other coworkers. They seemed to think Irene was involved in some kind of fraud. I could see Sharaya didn't believe it. She was like, 'Fraud? Irene? No way.'"

I'm wondering if Sharaya got the rumors wrong; Lou is the one the police are supposedly investigating. But I don't dare interrupt again. The thought makes me want to giggle.

"Sharaya did say Irene could keep things to herself though. She never even said she was pregnant. She—Sharaya—said she was starting to suspect, but it wasn't super obvious yet. And guess what."

I can't talk because I'll definitely start giggling. Karen is on the verge but manages a straight-faced "What?"

"Sharaya says Irene was kind of a workaholic, never sick or anything. *But* she took four whole weeks off in the spring. Unheard of. And guess where she went."

We're not giggly anymore; we're agog. Karen says, "Where? Not … Italy?"

Miller taps her nose with one index finger and points at Karen with the other. "Yep. Italy."

Well, well, well. This is unexpected. I think through the timeline.

"The baby was born at just over twenty-three weeks, which means it was conceived in May sometime. May, as in this past spring. Did she get pregnant in Italy?" I wonder out loud.

"I don't know, but the timing sure fits. I mean, maybe she did some special fertilization treatment or something—in vitro, whatever—in Italy. She must have planned something, 'cause she knew she was going to get pregnant when she bought the house from Margaret. That's what the brother said, right? That she wanted a nice house in the right school district for kids?"

"Sure is," says Karen. "I think you're right; she went to Italy intending to get pregnant there."

I nod. "But why Italy for a treatment? Why not go somewhere here, or, if she wanted cheap, why not Mexico, or even Canada, where her brother lives? Are we all thinking the same thing? Lou was in Italy. That's a big coincidence, isn't it?"

"It is a big coincidence," Karen agrees. "I don't think the police have found any evidence that Lou and Irene knew each other, but this is pret-tee strange. Of all places, she goes to Italy, and bam, suddenly she's pregnant. You know what? They really ought to test Lou to see if he's the father. That'd be bizarre. Why would she and Margaret be such great friends, then? Why would Margaret sell her the house like that? You'd think Margaret would be mad about this or at least wouldn't want anything to do with Irene."

"Maybe Lou made her somehow, or paid her off."

"Maybe," adds Miller. "There are lots of maybes. And there's more: if Lou is here now, where does Tom Peary come in? I mean, why does Irene turn to this special friend to take her home from the hospital? If Lou is the baby's father, why doesn't she have Lou come?"

"She didn't put his name on the birth certificate. Maybe she never even told him she was pregnant? Maybe they broke up or something, and she no longer wanted him involved?" I'm tossing ideas out. I know we're onto something here but can't quite figure out the right sequence.

"Did they ever find out how Irene actually died?" Miller asks.

"Kinda, but not really. The chief administrator told me Dr. Ben is frustrated because he has suspicions that he can't prove. The autopsy results were apparently inconclusive. Well, sudden arrhythmic death syndrome. That just means her heart stopped, with no underlying cause identified. She's young, no known heart problems, so ordinarily the most likely explanation would be that it was a complication from childbirth."

"Huh. But Dr. Ben is suspicious? Why? I mean, is there something other than her connection to Margaret?" I ask.

Karen shrugs a little, saying, "I'm sure he checked for signs of drowning, like with Margaret, but he must not have found anything, because that would have been a big deal. What he told the chief administrator was that he noticed tiny hairline cracks in her ribs, which bothers him, because it opens the possibility that she sustained some kind of blow to the chest. Under the right circumstances, that could cause someone to go into cardiac arrest." Karen pauses to take a bite of cake and a swallow of milk.

"So she was murdered, right? Sounds like it to me," says Miller.

"It's not definitive. Did you know that pregnant women can sometimes crack their ribs from coughing? And I thought my morning sickness was bad."

"Mine was horrible!" chimes in Miller. "With my first one, I retched so hard I lost a tooth!" There's something about her delivery that makes us break out laughing at this, Miller most of all. "It's true!" she insists.

"So what does that mean for the police and their investigation?" I ask, back to business. I can't help it; I want to know.

"It means the autopsy doesn't show anything that indicates murder, and neither did the scene. So for now they can't call it homicide, but that doesn't mean it isn't weird. Technically Ridley is only investigating Margaret's death, not Irene's, and I bet that bothers Dr. Ben. He's suspicious of coincidences like this."

We keep talking and eat more cake and start to veer off on tangents, so I feel I can risk asking about irrelevant details.

"What was the realtor guy doing while you were with Sharaya?" I ask.

"Oh, you won't believe this! He saw us girls talking, so he went over to Ky to see what we wanted—you know, like why we had stayed behind—and Ky totally stalled him! He started asking about whether we'd be able to get a permit to build a garage, and just kept going! He's a total saint. They were really into it, and *I* finally had to drag *him* away. I bet that realtor is expecting a contract from us any minute now."

Miller can't help chortling at the memory. I love how much she enjoys laughing at herself; it's one of her most endearing traits. We take pity on Karen, finally, who is tired from the birthday party, as am I from the retreat, and Miller gives me a lift home. It feels like we got a key piece of the puzzle today, but I'm nervous about what to do next. Do the police know about Irene's trip to Italy? It feels as if we should give them a heads-up, but I'm not ready yet to let the cat out of the bag that we're still doing our own investigations.

Karen is online later that evening, so I open up a chat. She's been thinking along similar lines as I have been, and we both agree she's in the best position of all of us to glean more information about what the police are thinking. She's going to keep her eyes and ears on high alert and promises to let me know as soon as she hears something. She closes with a spy emoji and I respond with a winking smiley face. We get each other.

CHAPTER
NINETEEN

The next day is Monday, but it must be a teacher workday or something because the kids are off from school. It is gorgeous, cool and sunny. Frank and Tessa also took the day off and want to go kayaking, and I switch schedules with Will so he's doing the day classes and I'm free till five. Tessa and I round up the kids while Frank straps their two ocean kayaks to the top of the minivan, and we all pile in. It's a very short drive to the river, but they want to get as close as possible to where they can launch. Frank parks just off the canal towpath, and we work together to carry the kayaks down a skinny beaten path to a tiny beach of clay and stones. In a flip-flop from the Leprechaun 5K, they take the littles with them—Charlie sits cross-legged on the front of Frank's boat, while Brie goes with Tessa—and the twins stay with me. We're going to hike the Billy Goat Trail. It's not particularly long, but there is a lot of rock scrambling, which they absolutely love. Frank, Tessa, and the littles paddle off as we wave madly from the shore. I look around and notice that they're not the only ones with this idea; several dots of neon vessels are already visible on the water. It's a spectacular scene all around. The sky is bright blue, and the water, normally a kind of olive-gray color, has taken on an almost aqua hue. There's nothing but trees along either shore—oranges, yellows, browns, and maroons—all now dazzlingly near their peak.

I take off my shoes and socks, roll up my pant legs as far as possible, and wade in. I'm thinking about the cold water challenge, the fact that so far I've done all my training in the pool. I want to get a sense of what real open water feels like. At first I think it's not too bad, but after just a few seconds my feet are in agony. Ooooh, it's cold all right, much colder than the pool. I walk back up the bank and feel my stomach clench. *There's no way,* I think in desolation. I do a quick check on Christopher and Julie, who are using sticks to dig up pebbles and throw them in the water. They're fine. When my feet feel almost normal again, I wade back in, and this time it takes a little longer before it starts to hurt. I do this several times, and eventually I can stand there without feeling as though I need to get out right away. I walk up and put my shoes and socks back on. *Well,* I think to myself, *it is what it is, and it's better than it was.*

"Hey, guys, you ready?" I call over to the kids, and they both drop their sticks and come running.

The Billy Goat Trail turns out to be not only fun but also a great workout, and we're treated to beautiful views above the river all along the way. In places it can be surprisingly difficult to climb up and over the rocks, and I have to focus all my attention on (A) not falling myself and (B) making sure the kids don't get hurt or lost. Maybe I have the priority order wrong there, but Julie and Christopher are flying around like actual little billy goats, while I scrabble more cautiously over the terrain. After the accident, I couldn't climb the stairs to the townhouse, and even now I can be timid about testing my body's full capability. By the end of the trail, though, I'm giddy with confidence, jumping and running almost as much as the twins. I feel free, victorious.

Eventually we emerge back onto the almost disappointingly flat towpath, where we walk along until we came to a visitor center with—gosh! Looky here—an ice-cream shop! How very convenient! The kids get cones with some kind of brightly colored cotton candy flavor, and I opt for moose tracks. We make a pact not to tell their parents or the littles. As we start walking again, I give Tessa a call to see how they're doing, and we figure that by the time the twins and I make it back to the van and then follow the path down to the launch point, they should be just about there. Sure enough, we see them pulling up onto the little clay beach as we come around the last bend.

"Mommy, we got ice cream!" is the first thing both twins shout as they race the rest of the way down. Nice.

I give Tessa a big shrug and slightly abashed smile as I make my own way over to the boats.

"It was supposed to be our little secret."

"Excellent!" says Frank, smiling broadly. "Great decision!"

The littles start clamoring that they want some too, but Tessa shushes them, reminding them that *they* got to have "secret" chocolate bars out on the river. At that little confession, she gives me her own huge grin and oh-what-the-hell shrug back.

It's been a nice day, and by the time we get home I feel relaxed and a little sleepy. My mind wanders back to Margaret again, dwelling on the fact that Alice was here in town just two days before she died. Maybe my guard is down, or at any rate my usual inhibitions are at bay. It occurs to me that I have a relatively simple way to find out more about that visit. Maybe it won't work, but I don't see how it can hurt. I have an hour or so before I need to leave for the studio, so I pick up my phone and go totally old school: I dial directory assistance and ask for Geoff Turner's number.

"Hello?" I recognize his voice when they connect me.

"Hi Geoff. This is Lily Piper—you know, Margaret Crawford's friend's daughter?"

"Oh yeah, sure. Hey! How's it going? What's up?"

"Pretty good. I feel a little silly calling, but … after my last visit I haven't had any more texts from Nico. That's fine of course, but … I imagine life without Margaret must be hitting him for real now, and I just want to make sure I didn't do anything to upset him even more. Is he doing okay?"

"Ooh, that's real nice of you. Yeah, yeah, like I said before, he'll text out of the blue and then he'll move on to some other contact and you won't get anything for months. He's fine; you definitely didn't upset him. He was real happy you visited. But yeah, now that it's been a few weeks, I think he feels a little lost. We're all trying to be extra supportive to help him get through it. It's crazy the cops think she was murdered. What do you think about all that? You know they came back asking about Aunt Alice right after you were here the last time."

I'd had a different idea about how to bring up Aunt Alice, but Geoff's opening is too good to pass up, so I somewhat awkwardly jump on it. I wish I were a better liar.

"Uh, gosh. I mean, um, you never expect someone you know to be murdered. They came back about Aunt Alice? Did they, uh, say why?"

"She was here the weekend before Dr. C. died. Nico told them she took him to breakfast on Saturday. I didn't know until they came to ask me about it too, 'cause my buddy and I went up that Friday to New Jersey for a concert, and Nico never mentioned it. Man, that's bad."

His voice dropped significantly in volume for that last aside, conspiratorially.

Bingo. He knows something.

"What makes you say that?" I ask, also lowering my voice to match his.

"I was over for dinner with Nico in August. Dr. Crawford was upset that she and her sister were having a big argument. I didn't want to intrude on anything private, but Dr. C. brought it up, so I asked what about. She said Alice was suggesting maybe she was losing her marbles—those weren't her words, but something about cognizance. Alice was talking about coming down to check on her, and Dr. C. wanted her to mind her own business. She was real mad."

"Gosh, I wonder why Alice thought that."

"I think it was because Dr. C. sold her old house, although that doesn't seem so crazy to me. She was retired and having trouble with her heart and stuff, so why would she want to have to take care of a whole house by herself? But Aunt Alice knew Dr. C. was counting on the house to be her nest egg for big expenses later—like for assisted living or medical bills, you know? So she was real surprised about the sale. She was also surprised Dr. C. didn't say a word about it until she sent her her new address."

"Gosh, it is a little strange she waited so long to mention it. Maybe Alice was afraid Margaret was sicker than she was letting on ... or maybe Alice was afraid Margaret had been taken in by some scammer and had to sell the house fast to get money. That happens to older people a lot. Sometimes they even fall for the same thing more than once."

"Oh yeah! I didn't think about that. If Aunt Alice thought that, she'd come down to check all right."

I'm picturing Alice flying in from Boston and presumably confronting Margaret. Did the fighting continue, or did they make up?

"Did you say anything about all that to the police?"

"Yeah, actually, I did when they came to talk to me after the funeral. I didn't think it mattered really, since Aunt Alice lives so far away and at the time I didn't know she'd just been here. I hope I didn't get her in trouble."

"Oh, don't think that. If she's in trouble, she got herself in trouble. If not, no harm, no foul, right? Margaret can't speak for herself, so she needs you."

"I guess so. Yeah. Thanks."

"No worries. I'm glad Nico's surrounded by good friends. Thanks for letting me know he's all right."

We hang up, and I sit back, thinking hard. I take it as a good sign that Alice came down out of concern for her sister's well-being. But what was really going on with Margaret? And why wouldn't she tell Alice? Or did she?

I need to run this by the Whatevers. I start texting.

(Me): Was Alice still furious with Margaret? Or did she find something out from Margaret that made her go after Irene when she learned Margaret was murdered?

(Karen): Did Alice even know Irene? Maybe Alice was trying to warn Margaret about Lou. Didn't you say she didn't like the husband?

(Miller): Lou is in this somehow. The ex always is. I'm gonna see what I can find out about him

I send a thumbs-up emoji.

(Haisley): It could still be Tom Peary. He knew Margaret, too, right? He kills Margaret for not telling him about the baby's father, then kills Irene because he's mad at her

There's no immediate response. Then, a few minutes later, I receive the following:

(Redd): That's a theory

(Karen): They finally did get Peary to do a DNA test. I should find out soon if he's the father or not, since we really need to start billing someone for Victoria's care

(Me): Awesome! Let us know as soon as you do!

Karen sends a thumbs-up emoji.

We're on it. All of us. Checking in with the group always makes me feel better, but the fact is, there are few frustrations worse than being on the outside with a little knowledge and no way to look in and get your questions answered, no way to get the full picture. Racking my brains where else to look, a penny drops into place. I grab my phone and open the browser, certain I'll find something this time. Yes! Elation sweeps through me when I am rewarded with two brief but recent articles.

Searching for news about a local homicide, I hadn't found anything, but NESD is a government agency, so this time I went looking for government news items, and that's where I hit pay dirt. The articles were in *Federal News Digest*, the first one being just a blurb that Montgomery County Police were working with the Justice Department regarding a possible case of government fraud they had uncovered while investigating a suspicious death. The follow-up has quite a bit of detail, and I text out the link to all the Whatevers (we really do need a name for ourselves) and then read it through slowly myself.

According to the second article, the crime came to light as the police were looking into the death of Dr. Margaret Crawford, who, it stated, was retired from working as a scientific consultant for the Hartmann Chemical Company and several other small agricultural biotechnology corporations. They discovered that her business bank account—which had lain dormant since she retired—became active again about eighteen months ago, and over the course of that time she received sums of money from the National Endowment for Scientific Development ultimately equaling $800,000.

NESD—Irene's agency.

After the evening at Karen's, when Miller told us about meeting Irene's colleague at NESD, I had looked it up and learned that this is a federal organization that provides money to companies to research and develop cutting-edge innovations. As I understand it, they give grants for high-risk, potentially high-reward stuff that commercial businesses balk at because they're afraid it could turn out to be a big waste of money. Apparently it works; their website boasts that hundreds of companies and products owe their start to NESD seed money. At the memorial service, Alice had described her sister as adventurous, the one always getting them into trouble. It had seemed like a funny, sweet memory at the time, but now I wonder. Maybe Margaret hadn't changed all that much in sixty years.

I continue reading that evidence suggests Crawford and Irene

Li, a senior administrator, conspired together for Crawford to put in a fake proposal for a $1.3 million grant, which Li then approved on behalf of NESD. Of that, $800K was wired to Crawford's business account, while the balance went to a bank in Europe. The article notes that Irene Li is also recently deceased of natural causes but the Justice Department is continuing the investigation to identify any additional incidents and determine whether there were others involved.

I sit back, lost in thought. A lot of things do fall into place. Margaret is okay selling her nest egg house at a low price to Irene because she makes up the difference twice over with her share of the fraudulent grant money. Irene then doesn't need to come up with an amount of money that her tax records say she couldn't possibly have, but she still gets the house she wants and a nice sum of cash on the side. It also explains why Margaret was so angry with Alice for butting in—she wouldn't want Alice to find out about the fraud. Pretty ironic, Alice maybe afraid someone had swindled Margaret out of whatever small fortune she had, when it's basically the other way around. I can see it though. The feisty Alice who storms into the hospital demanding to know why Margaret's body was autopsied, threatening lawsuits, protecting her even in death, would absolutely be the type of person not to take silence for an answer, who would fly down to find the truth and set it right if she could.

So far so good, but there are still some things that don't fall into place at all. Why isn't Lou DiSilvio mentioned in the article? I interpret that as certainty he's not involved, but why wouldn't he be? Didn't Ridley find out about it by looking into his company's files? I'm also thinking about that European bank account. The article doesn't say whose it is, and maybe they don't know yet. Lou lives in Italy, and he would have a European bank account. Irene took a long trip to Italy when she got pregnant; she could have set one up then, or even already had it. And it sticks in my craw to see Irene's death described in black and white as due to natural causes. There's no way. I just *know* she met her death by the same person's hand as Margaret. Is there anything I can possibly do to keep the police investigating?

CHAPTER
TWENTY

I went to bed last night fired up, planning to take on the world, if need be, to get to the bottom of it all and make sure justice is served. The morning, though, brings weather that is finally turning truly fall-like, overcast and chilly. It's one of those days when all you really want to do is curl up under a blanket and do nothing, and my excitement from the day before dissipates. It's not just me—classes are emptier than usual—but I'm uncharacteristically spacy today. I've brewed what I consider my daytime comfort-food tea: it's black leaf Earl Grey blended with banana and coconut chips. Earl Grey doesn't have the bitterness you can get with other black teas but still has the caffeine. The banana and coconut chips are just for extra yum. I've been guzzling it all day to no avail. It's sort of a relief when five o'clock finally rolls around, but I don't really feel like biking home. I'm debating ordering an Uber when I get a call from Karen that jolts me wide awake.

"Hey, Lily, I'm glad I caught you. I know it's crazy, but can you come to the hospital? Dr. Ben and Ridley are sitting in the Nook, and Dr. Ben saw me and waved me over. I said I'd be right there and went to the cafeteria to get coffees. I could tell them I'm waiting for you because we're going to see a movie or something, so it would be normal if you came by and, you know, joined us."

I feel mischievous glee coming down the phone and want to do a high five and a happy dance myself.

"I'm coming! Be there as soon as I can!"

We hang up, and I order the Uber and lock my bike in the office. It's rush hour and bad traffic, but the lights are with us and it turns out to be a quick trip. Unbelievably, I'm fast-walking across the lobby in about ten minutes. The Nook is several sets of comfortable seating, meaning couches and cushioned chairs, on the first floor of the hospital near the entrance. It is considered one of the dining facilities because there is a kiosk that sells coffee, but at the moment it's closed and the whole place is empty except for Ridley, Dr. Ben, and Karen.

"You got here fast!" Karen greets me, handing me a cup of coffee, the twin to hers, which she brought down from the cafeteria.

I smile my thanks at her and nod my hellos to the guys as I take a seat. Dr. Ben and Ridley look at ease, as if they're both kicking back after a long day, shooting the breeze about nothing in particular. As for me, my spaciness is gone. If I can just finesse things right, I might be able to get some of my questions answered.

"Off to the movies, is it?" says Dr. Ben. "We're not going to make you ladies late, are we?"

"Oh no," Karen replies smoothly. "It doesn't start till seven. I was looking for you anyway to find out if Tom Peary's the guy we need to bill for baby Victoria's care. I heard you got the results from his DNA test?"

Before Dr. Ben can answer, Ridley's eyebrows shoot up. He looks at his phone, looks at Dr. Ben, and then lifts his phone to his ear, shaking it as if listening for a rattle. He looks at it again and says, "Oh? I don't seem to have an email from you."

Dr. Ben snorts a half-laugh, rolls his eyes at Ridley, and says, "No! There is no email! There was an anomaly in the results. We have to run the test again." Dr. Ben then says to Karen, "But I wouldn't hold my breath on Peary."

"You don't think it'll be a match?" says Ridley.

Dr. Ben shrugs. He tells us that Irene Li's brother Andrew had a lawyer send a letter to Tom Peary threatening to sue him for financial support for Victoria, operating on the assumption that

Peary is the father. That convinced Peary to agree to the test, so Dr. Ben suspects that Peary knows his DNA will prove he wasn't the father.

"Ah. You're probably right," says Ridley, almost to himself. He sighs a little and takes a sip of coffee "I'd still like to dot the *i* and get that report in the file."

"Won't be long," Dr. Ben promises.

"Still seems strange to me," says Karen. "I admit it's been a while since I was on the dating scene, but I can't imagine going out with some guy and him being totally fine with me suddenly becoming pregnant by some other dude."

Ridley laughs a little at that but shakes his head. "Not so strange, really."

He explains that Peary had a perfectly simple explanation for why he and Irene only met in person so recently even though they started communicating online a couple of years ago. When questioned, Peary said that when he and Irene first found each other's profiles and started corresponding, everything moved along nicely and he thought they had a lot of promise. But at the time, he was also corresponding with another woman from the dating site whom, at least on virtual paper, he also liked. Peary said that Irene sort of petered out; their communication just dwindled and stopped, and he never knew why. But he figured that's the way things sometimes go with online dating, and in any case, things were going well with this other woman, and they ended up going out for a few months. There were no real sparks between them, though, and they jointly called it quits. Nothing else was happening for poor Tom, and he found he kept thinking back to Irene. He contacted her again, and this time she was more interested. But she was also pregnant.

"I guess that's the way things sometimes go with online dating," Ridley finishes, and we all laugh.

Ridley is sitting with his long legs stretched out and his head sinking into the back of the comfy chair. Dr. Ben is equally relaxed; he looks a little tired, in fact, glad to finally have a chance to wind down. Neither of them seems to mind that Karen and I are sitting here. With nothing to lose, I decide to ask Ridley about the articles in the *Digest* and why Lou doesn't get mentioned at all.

"It said you discovered the fraud investigating Margaret's murder, that you went through his company files, and I remember you were looking for Lou when all this started. Why don't they think he's involved too?"

"Everyone did think so at first, Lily. And to be honest, I got a weird vibe from him. When I get that, it usually means someone is hiding something, but that doesn't necessarily mean it's something criminal. In any case, all the meat was in Margaret and Irene's files; Lou's company received some confirmation correspondence by mail, but that was probably just a fluke holdover from previous grants. There was nothing anywhere specific to Lou."

"But then ... why his company?"

"I didn't see the article, so maybe this wasn't in there, but Margaret and Lou started the company together while they were still married. Lou bought out Margaret's share as part of the divorce agreement, but as cofounder and partner all those years, Margaret knew all about the company. It was probably the simplest way for her to establish a front to put in a grant proposal; she'd even have the knowledge to cite its previous work to demonstrate past performance. NESD's paperwork shows that the contact information was Margaret's, and she's the one who provided the wiring instructions for the funds. Since Irene was doing all the administrative reviews, it passed easily."

"And no one noticed?" asks Dr. Ben.

"Nope. Not until we started asking questions."

Ridley seems comfortable elaborating, since he's no longer responsible for this part of the investigation. He describes how, as they pieced it together, it became clear that Irene, through her wealth of experience, knew exactly how to work the system. For one thing, she split the money across three fiscal years—that is, the periods when the money actually gets allocated in the budget, not when it gets disbursed. That meant it hit a much lower threshold for approval and oversight than it would have normally. Then she kept reassigning the technical overseer. She would assign it to one person, tell that person not to worry about it because it was about to be reassigned, and then every few months, that's what she'd do. Margaret sent in fake activity packets, but no one really looked at the details, thinking a new person would soon be responsible for it anyway. Eventually, Irene closed out the whole thing, designating it as having inconclusive results—no big deal; they expect that to happen to a large percentage of projects.

"Holy shit," says Dr. Ben. "Pretty daring. Obviously, I didn't know either woman, but I think I'm mostly shocked at Irene. Margaret may have had some rabble-rouser in her, but everything we've heard about Irene seems so straitlaced."

"I agree," says Ridley. "To me it smacks of either an act of desperation or maybe of taking advantage of an opportunity that fell so perfectly into her lap she couldn't say no. Maybe a little of both."

We fall quiet, absorbing this, and Ridley takes a glimpse at his phone. I have a feeling he's not checking for messages; he's checking the time. Any minute now, our gathering will break up and everyone will go home.

"So now you're done? Without finding out who did this?" My face must betray my desolation, because Ridley cocks his head at me for a moment and then smiles.

"We're never done until we're done," he says. "But while your enthusiasm is admirable, the NESD fraud is the Fed's problem now, and there's no evidence that says Irene Li's death wasn't natural. That leaves Margaret's unexplained drowning, and it's proving a tricky one."

I have to say something outrageous—something to keep him from giving up on what must surely be the reality that they were both murdered. I don't like coincidences any more than Dr. Ben. "What if Irene killed Margaret?"

I don't know myself where that comes from, but it certainly garners a reaction. All three of them put down their coffees and look at me. Then Ridley and Dr. Ben look at each other.

Dr. Ben gives another laughing snort, and his eyebrows shoot up in surprise, but I have to give Ridley a lot of credit: he doesn't dismiss this out of hand. He looks curiously over at me.

"What makes you say that?"

"We think maybe Lou is the father of Irene's baby. What if Irene told Margaret and they got into a fight or something? Maybe the shock of it all is what caused the baby to come out so soon."

Now Dr. Ben laughs out loud, throwing his head back and saying something like "Whoo-eee!" Karen, though, gasps and covers her mouth with her hands. Her eyes get even bigger.

"Well, that's coming a little out of the blue. We haven't found anything that shows Irene and Lou even knew each other," Ridley says, looking back and forth between me and Karen, disconcerted by her response. "Have you?"

Karen speaks up then and tells them about Miller's visit to the open house, running into Irene's coworker Sharaya, and the fact that Irene took a long vacation to Italy about the same time she got pregnant.

"We don't know what her plan was or what she did there or anything, but the timing is sure on the money, and, well, Italy of all places? Right where Lou happens to live? That just seems like too much," Karen finishes. Talk about a rapt audience! Dr. Ben and Ridley are both staring, metaphorically open-mouthed if not literally.

"I take it this is new information for you," Karen says.

"Sure is," Ridley concedes. "I can't believe it. We talked to Irene's manager and several of her coworkers, and nothing like this came up." He takes out his notebook, whips on his glasses, and begins flipping through, shaking his head. "She took her usual week off at spring break; that's it. Her manager said she always volunteers as a chaperone with the Girl Scouts."

"Maybe she didn't tell her manager," says Karen. "With virtual working, it wouldn't be all that hard to mush together being gone on vacation and 'working from home' for a few extra weeks. Irene could take calls on her cell, respond to emails, and attend her meetings via computer. Even if coworkers noticed, since she was so senior, they probably wouldn't question it. She returns to her normal routine, and pretty soon no one even remembers she was absent."

I don't know much about working in a big office, but Karen's suggestion seems possible to me. Neither Dr. Ben nor Ridley contradicts her; they must think it believable too.

"You know," Dr. Ben says, breaking the silence, "if Irene really did go to Italy, I agree with Karen and Lily that it would be worth it to check if Lou is the baby's father after all. It could certainly provide him a potential motive. Any chance of that happening?"

"Maybe. We can request a DNA sample for elimination purposes, and he might give one. He could also refuse, of course. But if we can find something specific that ties Lou and Irene, we could compel it," replies Ridley.

Dr. Ben smiles and nods at Karen and me, raising his coffee in salute. "Citizen sleuths!" he says.

"Citizen sleuths," repeats Ridley with his slight smile and his head shake. "The bane of all police forces, but they can be helpful sometimes too."

Karen and I look over at each other with our own smiles. *Yes, we can be!*

Soon after, we do break up to be on our way. Misty spit has turned into real rain, and Karen offers to give me a ride home. We jabber excitedly as we hurry to her car and clamber in, neither of us able to believe how the conversation turned out.

"You really think it was Irene? That came out of nowhere for me!"

"I don't know what I think," I reply. "I was desperate to find something that would keep Ridley focused on them both, and that just popped out."

"If we hadn't been sitting, we all would have fallen over when you said it." Karen laughs at the memory. "Interesting Ridley didn't just dismiss it. I wonder if deep down he really thinks their deaths are connected, but his team just can't uncover the evidence they need."

"I hope so. My worse fear is that we'll never know what happened to either Margaret or Irene. I'll wonder about it forever."

"Me too!"

We're quiet for a minute, and then I add, "Maybe Lou is the link."

"Maybe ... but if he and Irene were a couple, it sure is strange that the police couldn't find any correspondence or anything between them." Karen's right, and I have no response.

We've joined our fellow commuters, too many cars jammed into stop-and-go traffic. A lone biker is heading along the sidewalk, wearing waterproof reflective gear that I know from experience isn't enough to make his ride either pleasant or comfortable. I sit back luxuriantly in Karen's warm, dry vehicle and sympathize. Rockville Pike, with its six lanes of traffic and parade of shopping centers on either side, is not a place normally described as beautiful, but viewing it in the dark through the rain-streaked car window, all I really see are neon signs merging with vehicle lights, and it reminds me of Christmas. I feel an unexpected sense of peace and contentment come over me, which remains intact despite the inevitable distant sirens and occasional honks.

I know Karen needs to get home, her family probably waiting for her to have supper, so I tell her to let me out at the bottom of the driveway. The rain has stopped, and the automatic lights on top of the two large stone pillars that mark the entrance make it seem safe, but as soon as she drives away and I start to walk toward the house, it gets very dark. The further I go, the darker it gets, with nothing but woods all around and no stars. It feels spooky, so I quicken my pace and then freeze when I hear the sound of footsteps rustling through leaves. I'm almost too afraid to look, but my body instinctively whirls around to see what's behind me.

Nothing.

I start walking, and I hear it again. Is it a deer? A bear? A person? There aren't any bears this near to the city, and deer usually take off through the woods—you hear the rustling slowly taper off, not stop suddenly and wait. The incident with the strewn trash flashes into my mind. Rationally, I know my fear is unfounded. Lots of startled wildlife do make exactly that sound—squirrels, for instance. No cars pulled off when Karen did, and there are none parked anywhere around here. It makes no sense to imagine some person has been waiting in these woods, in the rain, on the off chance I'll do something I practically never do: walk up the driveway. But alone here in the dark, reason holds no sway for me. I race almost blindly the rest of the way up and straight to my door. Once inside, I turn on every light in the house and lean against the kitchen counter until I catch my breath. I'm safe, but the enjoyment and gratification of the evening has given way to a much less pleasant sensation. For the first time, this doesn't feel like entertainment, a mere abstraction. When I was running up the driveway, I felt scared.

CHAPTER
TWENTY-ONE

The next morning, I wake up to see Tessa swimming in the pool, and in the full light of day, the peace and serenity of the place is restored. I don't join her, but sip my coffee, relaxed as I watch her progress up and back, as smooth as a swan. Even now, though, I remember that awful sensation of danger—of being followed, even stalked—from the night before. It doesn't matter that it's my own mind playing tricks, working me up. I determine that I have done my duty by Margaret, having expended every effort to monitor and even push the investigation of her death as far as I can. The Iguana, the text strings, the piecing together of all the little bits of information our group has gleaned have been so fun I hate to see it all end, but the disquiet of last night is giving me pause. I'm no citizen sleuth; I'm just me, getting myself healthy—mind, body, and spirit—and figuring out what my true role in life is supposed to be. Detective work is Ridley's role, not mine.

I think I've made peace with my decision, but when Redd shows up for class, my resolve crumbles. He stays behind for the tea circle, and then to help clean up. Of course, he asks what I've been up to, so while we're in the back kitchen I tell him all about yesterday's get-together in the Nook, as well as Miller's visit to the open house.

"You guys have been busy! And even so, it seems like things are just getting more muddied instead of less so. The connections seem bizarre. But hey, the toughest puzzles are the best. It's got me hooked, too, I gotta admit—not like Miller though! Can you *believe* her?" He's grinning at me like we're sharing a big joke, but I'm not exactly sure what it is.

"She sure does like to be in the middle of the action! But I'm glad she visited the townhouse and met that Sharaya person," I say, because I don't want to just say nothing.

"Yep, that was a stroke of luck. But did you notice she sent that website out at *midnight* last night? She's on a rampage!"

"What website?"

"Lou's company—LumarGen. Didn't you see it?"

"No! She found his company's website? I didn't get anything."

I'm checking my phone, texts and emails, but there's nothing there. Redd pulls his phone out and starts to look through it, finds something, and shows me a link to LumarGen embedded in a text string, but I'm not on it. We've changed the name of our group and texted each other singly or in twos and threes so often that it's not surprising what has happened: some undoubtedly confused soul named Lillian got added by mistake.

What else have I, or frankly any of the others, missed? No wonder we're all so befuddled. I ask Redd to forward me the link, and almost the second he says, "No problem," my phone dings and it's there.

"Have you looked at it?" I ask him.

"Sure did, but it didn't mean a lot to me. I was a warrant officer in the army for most of my career. Ask me about boats, I might be able to tell you more. This stuff—whew. Can't even pronounce half of it."

This is news to me. I knew Redd was retired but didn't know what he'd done before. I didn't even know he'd served.

"Wow, Redd, that's great! Wait—did you say 'boats'? Isn't that navy?"

He laughs. "Everyone thinks that, and sure, the navy has plenty of boats. But believe it or not, once upon a time army had even more. Things have changed, but we still have a few left."

I've seen Redd in a T-shirt that says "BOAT ARMY." I meant to ask him about it but never did. Now it makes sense.

"Oh, cool." I smile back at him, but he's bustling around again, putting away the cups, wiping the counter, emptying the thermos. I'm helping mostly by keeping out of his way. Since he's busy, I go ahead and click on the link. My curiosity has reared its head, but I convince myself this is totally harmless. I'm not involving myself in anything, I'm being polite by taking a look at what Miller has taken the trouble to send.

The site is surprisingly artistic. At the top are pictures of flowers and plants waving in the wind, each one lasting a few seconds before fading into the next. Below that, in a stylish modern font, is an overview of the company followed by navigation links. I see what Redd means; it appears to be a private scientific research corporation, specializing in topics like "emerging history," "developmental progression," and "random variation transformation." Huh? There's also a link to a catalog of publications for sale, but their titles are even more obscure. I click on "schedule" and see a series of lectures, some featuring Lou himself and others featuring other (apparent) notables. It looks old though—nothing more recent than two years ago. In any case, the page includes pictures that look slick and snappy. There's one where people are laughing, so maybe these things are not as dry and boring as one might expect. Here's something interesting: I can click on the notable's name and get to a brief bio. Lou's includes a photo of a burly, smiling man in a hat and sweater sitting on an ancient-looking wall, some kind of tall spire behind him. I skim through and see that Dr. Luigi "Lou" DiSilvio is second-generation American, originally from Ohio. After the bachelor's degree from Michigan State and PhD from the University of Chicago, it describes his early work at NIH and then at the Stazione Sperimentale per l'Industria delle Bioingegneria in Pescara, Italy. There is no mention of a family, but it does say he now lives near Rome, where he is an adjunct professor at the University of Olgiata.

That's as far as I get before I look up to see that Redd is all done, and we head out the door together. If any of the others were here, it would be a perfect time for an Iguana meetup, but in fact even Redd has to get home. We wave goodbye, and he gets in his car as I ponder what to do next. Catching up with Redd felt good, and it occurs to me that I haven't seen Haisley in some time. It doesn't seem fair to leave her out of the loop, and she would normally have been here today with Redd. I decide to give her a call and make sure she's okay, see if maybe she's going to come tomorrow.

"Oh, hi, Lily. Sorry about the class. I skipped everything today. I have a cold or something, my throat is sore, and I figured I'd just stay home." Her voice does sound a little thick and nasal. But she doesn't sound, you know, as if she's on her deathbed. In fact, she goes on: "Actually, I'm kinda bored. You wouldn't like to come by, would you? My roommate, Jen, is gone, probably won't be back till late. I feel out of it and really want to hear the latest on the Margaret/Irene thing. I promise we can sit at least six feet apart."

I know she lives in the apartment complex just down from the studio's shopping center, and I have an idea.

"Would you like some soup? I'll bring us carryout from the Iguana; they have that delicious Mexican chicken soup with all the crunchy tortilla strips, remember?"

"*Yes!* Yes yes yes! I'd love some. Get the biggest size they have! You are awesome!"

I smile at that, happy to be able to brighten someone's day so easily. She tells me her apartment number, and I confirm, "Okay, see you in a few." I retrace my steps to cross the parking lot to the Iguana, and since it's carryout, I go to the bar to order. Star spots me, though, and comes over.

"All alone tonight? What happened to the rest of the crew?" Gosh, it's so nice to be recognized.

"One sick, the others flying in different directions." I hold up the bag containing the soup and continue, "I'm here to pick up a prescription for the patient."

Star laughs at that and wishes a speedy recovery. "You guys come back soon! I'll keep your table warm." It's so stupid, but I love the idea that we have a regular table.

Now it's on to Haisley's. The lobby is colorful and modern, and it gives off a fun, trendy vibe, which continues in the elevators and down the hallway. I like that all the doors are different colors, matching the fiesta stripes on the carpet. Haisley's is blue, and she opens it before I even ring the bell. A tiny dog greets me, jumping up excitedly and landing its little paws on my shin. I'm expecting to hear yapping, but instead it makes a barely audible "huff" sound, almost like it's clearing its throat.

"Huff! Huff huff!"

Haisley shoos it away, explaining, "We have a CCTV channel of the entrance, and I saw you come in. Howdy, howdy! That's Otto; he'll settle down in a minute." She takes the bag and opens it, inhaling the aroma and going "Aaaaah!"

I go in and am in awe. Wow, this is nice. It's night-and-day different from the depressing townhouse I was sharing as a student. It's bright and cheerful, urban chic with a touch of youthful elegance. The floors are ultra-wide luxury vinyl planks that look like beautiful old whitewashed boards. It's open-concept kitchen and living area, and for the most part those are also white. But there's a lot of color in the furnishings—the chairs, couch, curtains, and rugs. I can tell Haisley and Jen took some care with the decor. It's not that anything is expensive—I suspect I'm seeing quite a bit of Ikea in here— but even though nothing matches, it all goes together beautifully. There's nothing that's just ash and trash.

Haisley takes the bag into the kitchen, explaining that there are two matching master bedrooms, each with an en suite bathroom; Jen's is to the right, hers to the left. She's opening cabinets and drawers, getting bowls and spoons and cans of ginger ale. I wait and look around, taking it all in. Now I notice a cat—white with black patches on its ears, paws, and tail—watching me from its perch on a cat condo. Another one, a traditional tuxedo, hops down from the couch and makes for the sanctity of Jen's room.

"That's Dee Dee," Haisley says, pointing to the mostly white cat, "and that was Dexter. You've already met Otto. Oh, and over there is Putt Putt. They're all Jen's."

Sure enough, there is a turtle in a bowl sitting on one of the built-in shelves next to the window. We take our soups and drinks to the living room, where we settle into chairs across from each other, a coffee table in the middle.

"This is perfect," says Haisley, tasting a spoonful, and I nod in agreement. I love this soup too. It has lots of stuff in it, and it's spicy hot—just the thing to clear congested sinuses. We don't say much as we're eating, but when we both put our empty bowls on the table and sit back, I can see that Haisley is content. Her head lolls as she breathes deeply through her nose. Just then the most adorable bunny I've ever seen comes hopping over. It's huge for a rabbit, with enormous ears that flop to each side of its big bunny head like furry pigtails. It sniffs and hops and sniffs and hops until it gets to Haisley, who picks it up and puts it on her lap.

"This is Archie," she informs me with a huge smile. "He's mine!"

Archie settles on her lap, and in a blink he's fast asleep, Haisley stroking him gently. He is magnificent. I want one. I must say, this is quite an impressive menagerie they have in here—all the more so considering I noticed a sign by the lobby elevators admonishing, "No Pets."

"Now," Haisley continues, still stroking Archie but looking at me with a gleam in her eyes, "what's going on? Tell me all!"

I fill her in on the goings on and discoveries of the past few days. She's heard snippets of almost all of it, but not the details. She hangs on my description of Miller's conversation with Sharaya and chuckles knowingly about my barely contained giggle attacks. She even adds her own perfect imitation of Miller's accent and mannerisms, which has me in stitches. Finally I give her the scoop from the Nook, but I don't mention last night's scary race up the driveway or my resolve to drop the case. Sitting here in this snug living room, it's all fun again, and Haisley is even more intrigued now than Redd was. If she's not ready to leave it alone, how can I be? We end up talking about the website that Miller found, which, it turns out, we've been perusing from different points of interest. While I was focused on the descriptive sections, Haisley has looked through the research.

"What they mostly do is meta-analysis—that is, they collect together all the studies available on particular topics and provide an in-depth analysis of what all those things put together indicate. You know how sometimes you hear about some study that says something is really good for you, and then another one comes along and says actually it doesn't do anything for you at all? Lou's company looks at things like that and determines why the differences in outcomes exist, or what it all means together."

"Oh! Got it. Gosh, I didn't really look too much at the publications. Anything else jump out?"

"Not sure—a lot of the subject matter has to do with genetics, mostly plants and the effects of genetically modified organisms— you know, GMO foods and stuff. Seems like they were onto those really early. I can't see what that would have to do with anything, but you know, something did occur to me." Haisley stops, looks down at Archie, and starts stroking him again, maybe deciding whether what she's thinking is worth sharing.

"Hey," I say, "we're just talking here—doesn't matter if it's a long shot or what. Now that you brought it up, you can't just leave me hanging!"

She laughs and then shrugs, looking back up at me. "You're right—whatever! It's just that I noticed some of the publications acknowledge grants from the National Endowment for Scientific Development."

"Irene Li worked for NESD."

"Exactly. Of course, lots of people work there. And lots of researchers send in proposals for NESD funding, so it makes sense for Lou and Margaret ... but ... they could have met Irene that way."

"And that would mean they both knew her."

She's got me thinking. It's tenuous, but it's definitely possible that this is what links all three together. But so what? How could it lead to murder, especially after so many years? Haisley reads my mind.

"Yeah, I don't know, why would it matter? But maybe there's some patent or something that they all own ... maybe Lou wants to sell it? Or maybe they faked results and Margaret and Irene were going to come clean? That could be a motive for Lou to kill them both. Then again, why would they get together and decide to do that now?"

"You might be onto something." I'm rethinking the three of them as a unit rather than the girls vs. Lou. "What if all three of them got involved somehow, and now someone else is afraid that a study Lou and Margaret did, funded through Irene and the NESD, will either lose them a lot of money or land them in jail? Since Lou is the only one left, what if he's in danger now?"

"Huh. Yeah. That's definitely possible. Didn't Miller say something like that too? Maybe Lou really is the next target. Still seems weird about why now. It's been, what, like, fifteen years since Lou and Margaret divorced and Lou moved away. Would they really all three get together for this new fraud thing now? What would motivate them?"

"True. And why would Irene risk her own career like this? Ridley said it smacked of desperation. But what would she be so desperate about?"

"Maybe having a baby? How old was she?"

I think about this. What did Karen say? Age thirty-nine. Certainly a single woman nearing forty with no boyfriend might be desperate to have a baby. But what would that have to do with Margaret or Lou?

Haisley is also thinking. "What if it's like a surrogacy thing—Irene gets some other woman's baby planted in her womb, and she's supposed to give it back but doesn't want to?"

"At almost forty? Wouldn't they have chosen someone younger? And where do Margaret or Lou come in? And why go all the way to Italy? It's perfectly legal here."

"How about this—I got it! Maybe Lou got some *Italian* woman pregnant, and neither of them want the baby, so Lou has her give the fetus to Irene!"

"Ummm. This is getting a little far-fetched."

Haisley has gotten so excited that she wakes up Archie, who looks up at her and wiggles his nose. That must be bunny-speak for "Hey, I'm trying to sleep here," because she strokes him gently to settle him back down again. Watching them puts me into an instant state of Zen. Maybe I should get a pet.

"You're right, you're right," Haisley sighs. "This is getting crazy. Anyway, didn't you say that the police never found a link between Lou and Irene? So maybe this is just way off base. It's probably nothing to do with Lou. It might be some Italian mafia thing."

She's not joking, but her suggestion makes me smile. Haisley's mind works in mysterious ways.

"Let's go back a minute," I say. "The *Digest* article said the feds are still investigating whether there were other incidents. What if this isn't the first time? I wish we knew how to find out who at NESD approved Lou and Margaret's proposal for that earlier research piece."

"I think some kind of program administrator does that."

"That was Irene's title—program administrator."

"Huh."

We're looking at each other, on the same wavelength. There might really be a connection here, but we don't have the resources to find out. Before Haisley veered off into Al Capone la-la land, something niggled at me, but I can't quite make it out. Was it something she said? I think so, but it might have been something else. At any rate, we're not getting any further and Haisley is starting to look sleepy. She probably needs to rest.

Before I leave, I make use of her en suite bathroom and discover something rather poignant there. Sitting on the vanity is a box of disposable green contact lenses and a bottle of henna shampoo. She's giving nature a helping hand with her look. Haisley is very pretty, but I'm starting to see another side: she's also kind of kooky, and at heart she's a nerd, smart, self-conscious, apprehensive about fitting in. To me, it makes her all the more sympathetic, and it hits me that I'm very happy for both of us that she's in our circle, one of us now.

It's dark out when I walk back to the studio to get my bike. The memory of my frightened race up the driveway together with the warnings from Dr. Ben and Ridley are getting to me, because the thought of biking back in the dark seems suddenly scary, and I debate ordering an Uber. Then I'm scared that the Uber driver will turn out to be the killer, and he'll have me in his clutches. *Don't do this*, I tell myself. *It is irrational to think anyone out there is worried about you finding something. No one even knows you're looking.* I'll need my bike tomorrow to get to work anyway. I've got a good headlamp, back lights, and a neon reflective vest. I can go over twenty miles an hour with my electric motor—fast enough to get away from anyone on foot. I convince myself to bite the bullet and ride home.

Once I'm moving, it actually does feel good. The air is fresh and cool, and the familiarity of the route dispels most of my fear. I force myself to think about something other than Margaret and Irene, turning my mind instead to Haisley and my newfound insight, and how I'd missed this aspect of her personality for so long. I remember that evening at the Iguana when she told us she started using her middle name to be more like the "cool" girls. That was the evening we all really started to get to know each other, to become a group—regulars sitting at "our" table. We had such a nice time, Miller laughing at herself …

Bam! That niggle suddenly lights up for a second.

What was it? What was I thinking? I take my mind back slowly. Haisley's apartment ... Irene and NESD ... the Iguana ... Miller laughing ... Haisley ... Miller ... Irene. *Names.*

That's it.

------------------------------ CHAPTER ------------------------------

TWENTY-TWO

B ack home, I settle myself in my comfy chair, take a deep breath, and, channeling Nico, I don't think about it but dive right in and dial the number on the card.

After two rings, he answers, "Detective Ridley."

"Uh, hi. It's, ah, Lily Piper. I know it's late—actually, I wasn't really expecting you to pick up, but I thought of something, and, well, thought I should tell you." Damn, even Nico was smoother.

"Hi Lily, no problem, I'm just sitting here at home. It's fine; you've got my attention. What's your thought?"

His friendliness and interest calm me down, and I can speak normally again. "It's about how Lou may have known Irene. My friend Haisley and I had a look at his company's website, and she noticed that he has some early work that came out of an NESD grant."

"I see. Was Irene's name on it too?"

"No. Even so, I thought that while it would have been near the start of her career, she could have been the authorizing NESD administrator."

"It's a good thought, Lily, but you know, we looked quite comprehensively at email and paper correspondence, including from NESD, that dates all the way back to LumarGen's establishment and didn't find her name anywhere."

"That's what just occurred to me. She may have had another name." I tell him about Miller's real name being Uyen and how she picked an American-sounding name when she came here to make things easier. "Irene came from China. She may have been born with another, Chinese, name. I wonder if maybe Lou knew her by that name."

There is silence over the phone at first, and then he slowly says, "Oh ho! That's a very interesting idea. Something we hadn't thought about. I will most definitely get that checked first thing tomorrow. Now I'm very glad you called."

We say our good evenings and hang up, but of course I'm glowing again, on cloud nine. Even though I'm still full from dinner, I have to celebrate at least a little with a few handfuls of mini cookies.

I turn the TV on in the background and start playing games on my phone. Over an hour later, I'm still wide awake and tired of both, so I grab my laptop to have another look at LumarGen's site. I go back to the lecture schedule and notice that while it didn't show up when I checked the link on my phone, on the laptop a little drop-down menu appears in the browser where I can select a year. For some reason, the default is an earlier year in the series, not the current year. Poor web maintenance. I tut to myself as I wonder whether Lou or anyone else at LumarGen has even noticed. No matter, I select the current year and am rewarded with dates that make a lot more sense. There is a lecture every three weeks September through December, and Lou is featured for most of them. He gets around: Chicago, Boston, Pittsburgh, and Raleigh are all on the circuit, but the rest are in and around Washington, DC. In fact, the next one is this Friday evening at Lisner Auditorium. My Friday nights are not very lively; I could go. I stop myself immediately. *No way, no how. Clicking around the web, fine, but no more getting personally involved.* Anyway, just the title of the thing wears me out.

The next day, everyone is back in class. Karen and Miller are finishing up the early-afternoon session as Redd and Haisley show up for the late-afternoon one. There's no time for the Iguana, but we decide to dash across to Starbucks to take advantage of finally all being in the same place at the same time. We toast each other with lattes and cappuccinos and pull chairs from multiple outdoor tables so we can all cluster together at one. We're in a giddy sort of party mood, as if we're at a class reunion. Everyone talks at once, joking and razzing.

"Okay okay okay, guys, we've only got like ten minutes," exclaims Miller. "What's going on with the case? Does anyone have new information since yesterday morning?"

"I talked to Ridley last night," I say.

"What? Why? What happened?" they all more or less respond. Karen is looking at me with an expression that I can read as clear as day: "How could you not tell me?"

"I was going to tell you all but haven't really had a chance. Yesterday evening Haisley and I were talking about the website from Miller, and she noticed that some of LumarGen's early research was funded by an NESD grant."

"Hey, nice catch. I didn't even try to look at all those publications," Redd applauds.

"We were eating takeout from the Iguana," I continue.

"Their Mexican tortilla soup," interjects Haisley.

"Oh, I love that," moons Karen.

"I know! I had a stuffy nose, and it was so good!"

"Uh, guys, like, seven minutes now," Miller shushes them and turns back to me.

"Right, so, on the way home I started thinking about our happy hours and remembered how Miller got her name. It just seemed possible that Irene had done the same thing. I called Ridley to ask if they'd looked for Irene's Chinese name. Maybe Lou and Irene knew each other from NESD grants LumarGen got a long time ago and she was still using her old name." They're staring at me, quiet now, and I shrug. "He said they hadn't but he'd check today."

"Wow," says Karen.

"Darn. I should have thought of that!" says Miller. I savor their admiration for a brief moment, but we're running out of time, and I need to change the subject slightly.

"Hey, guys, some of us have to get back for the next session, but since everyone's here, I wanted to ask: according to the website schedule, Lou's doing a lecture tomorrow night at Lisner. Do any of you want to go?"

They're as curious about Lou as I am, but an abstruse lecture on a Friday night just doesn't have any appeal to any of them, not even Haisley. I don't blame them. I only put it out there because it's such a tantalizing opportunity to see Lou in the flesh, but from the safe distance of a crowded audience. I'm half relieved at their response, and half disappointed, realizing I do want to go but don't want to go alone.

Karen calls me later that evening, as I had a feeling she would. I am already thinking about checking to see whether she is online to chat when my phone rings.

"You called Ridley? Whoa! I don't think I'd have had the nerve! Did he say anything other than what you already told us?"

"Not really, no, but at least he didn't think it was stupid or that I was wasting his time. I really was pretty nervous about that. But he was intrigued, I could tell, and he did say he'd look into it. I haven't heard anything back from him—not that I necessarily will. Did you see Dr. Ben today? Did he say anything?"

"No, I worked from home today. I don't usually like working from home, there are so many distractions, but it was just easier. We scheduled someone to come in and clean our chimney for the first time ever since we've owned the house, but they couldn't say exactly when the sweep would show up. So no Dr. Ben. The first I heard anything was from you this afternoon. That was an amazing conjecture, by the way—I never would have thought of it. I'll bet they find something."

"Really? Thanks. I was going to tell you; I just figured I'd see you today and was planning to fill you in then. It's funny, I just had this light bulb go off, probably because I was reminiscing about our wonderful Iguana congregations right after Haisley said LumarGen got NESD money way back when." I tell her about applying Nico's just-do-it attitude to overcome my nervousness in phoning Ridley, and then spluttering over my opening, and we both laugh. "I really was kind of hoping Ridley would let me know if he found out anything. Of course, he hasn't. And maybe there's nothing to find after all."

"Always trust your intuition. Now *my* intuition tells me you're on to something. I'm going back in to work tomorrow and will try to accidentally bump into Dr. Ben. If there's any news, I'll let you know."

I tell her thanks, and we're about to hang up when she calls out, "Oh, wait a minute! What did you decide about the Lisner thing? Are you going?"

"I haven't really decided yet. Maybe. Can you do me one favor?"

I feel her smiling down the phone as she says, "Sure, what?"

"Don't mention this to Dr. Ben if you see him. I don't want him—or Ridley—to think I'm doing anything ... I don't know, risky or whatever."

"You got it. I won't say a word. It could be a little risky at that though. Be careful."

"It's a big auditorium. Don't worry."

Now we do end the call. What made me say "maybe?" I'll be all alone, it'll be boring, I won't learn anything about Margaret or Irene, and just this morning I swore myself off all this. Ridley would be horrified; even Dr. Ben would be concerned. Do I dare chance one more *final* final foray, just to put my fascination with this whole inquiry to bed once and for all?

Maybe.

CHAPTER
TWENTY-THREE

Tessa is taking the kids to a puppet show at Montgomery Mall, so I ask her for a lift to the metro. I've already told her about the news articles, and since she knows Karen and Miller now, I tell her about our open house discussion and the revelation from Sharaya about Irene's trip to Italy, while the kids chatter and sing in the back. I mention it seems strange to me that a woman she worked with in the past would know so much about Irene's life, while her closest colleagues now didn't seem to know much at all, but Tessa disagrees.

"I've noticed that when it comes to work friendships in big companies where people spend their whole careers, the friends you have right now might be different from the ones you had, say, ten years ago—not necessarily because there was a falling out or anything, but just because of simple geography. People move around to different positions and offices. If that's what happened here, Irene's current colleagues might not even know who Sharaya is, but she and Irene could have kept in touch, maybe gone out to lunch on occasion or bumped into each other getting coffee. In fact, Irene may have talked more freely if the relationship was purely friendship now, no longer constrained by some sense of professionalism."

I guess that does make sense, but there's no time to discuss it further, as we're at the entryway and I need to get out. "Bye, Lily!" I hear the kids shouting as I head toward the escalator for the long descent. Rumor has it that the Bethesda station was built to be used as a bomb shelter if ever need be. I don't know if that's true, but it is a very, very long ride down to the tracks. It's crowded, and I end up standing the entire way, switching trains at Metro Center and ultimately surfacing at Foggy Bottom. It feels good to be downtown on a Friday night, and I enjoy the short walk to Lisner, sharing the sidewalk with groups of students and tourists and even—rarity of rarities!—actual DC residents.

The auditorium doors aren't open yet, but there are already people milling around the hallway, waiting to get in. With nothing better to do, I join them, playing games on my phone to pass the time. It suddenly starts buzzing (as I have put it on vibrate in anticipation of the seminar), and I almost ignore it because it's not a contact. But there's something familiar about the number, so just before it kicks over to voice mail, I decide to take it.

"Hello?"

"Ms. Piper? Lily? This is Detective Ridley. Do you have a minute?"

Oh, hurray! I almost can't believe he's actually calling. More people have arrived, and there's a faint buzz of conversation around me, but it's not too loud and I don't want to risk asking him to call back; I'm dying to hear what he's found out.

"Hi! Yes, sure do. Is this about Irene and Lou?"

"It is indeed. I figured I owed you at least a call back about that last tip of yours, which turned out to be a good one."

"Oh gosh, thank you. I've been wondering."

I can practically feel his slight smile down the line.

"I'm sure you have been. Fair enough, you were right. Irene Li came here as an intern for NESD before ultimately being hired by them full-time. NESD sponsored her visa and green card, but they identified her through their global scholarship program, and she started working with them virtually while still a university student in China. So her original email was under her name at the time: Li Xiuying. When she entered the US, though, her official name immediately became Irene, so her citizenship certificate, passport, social security—all her records—are under that name, and that was the only one we checked. Anyway, it took some work, especially since NESD's email naming convention has changed over the years, but we were able to ascertain that the user's address that now starts 'irene.li' ultimately resolves back to her original username, which was xiuyil—and an email address beginning xiuyil does show up in very old LumarGen correspondence to both Lou and Margaret. She was so junior back then, there was no record of her being connected to any grant authorization, which is why our investigation didn't uncover any link. But in her support role, she was on the cc for some of the back-and-forth between LumarGen and both the program administrator and the technical overseer for the first project NESD ever funded for the company."

"Oh, wow! That's amazing! So they all did know each other. Can you tell me anything more—like, was that project real, or was it a scam too?" I'm talking softly into the phone, but no one around seems to be paying the least bit of attention, and the noise level is just enough now that I doubt anyone can hear me anyway. The doors have opened, and we're all slowly making our way toward them. I hang back with the last stragglers, giving Ridley as much time as he needs.

"Very much a real project. The research was a success, and LumarGen gained a patent that they leveraged not only to keep the company viable but to grow it."

"Cool. So, ah, what comes next?"

Ridley doesn't just smile; he actually chuckles and says, "What comes next is we thank you—thank you!—and we take it from here, while you go back to your armchair and your yoga studio."

"But what about …"

"Lily, I'm serious. Stay away from anything to do with this case until we wrap it all up. Got that? Desperate people are dangerous people, so keep away from anyone connected to Margaret or Irene—I mean anyone: Nico, Geoff Turner, Aunt Alice, Lou DiSilvio, their colleagues, the mailman. Your zeal worries me."

"Got it, got it. Thank you for the call, and I really do appreciate your concern," I tell him.

"Okay, then. My wife just walked in the door, so I'd better go. Take care, Lily, and remember: keep away from the DiSilvios."

"Thanks again! Bye."

We hang up, and the first thing that strikes me is Ridley's incredibly poor timing. I'm sitting in the middle of a row that is now almost filled. The auditorium is growing quiet, and Lou is going to begin at any minute. As I hesitate, unable to decide whether to get up now and leave or just stay, the lights start to dim. I resign myself to sitting through it, no matter how dull it gets. I promise myself that if there's an intermission, I can leave and that will be that. Then Lou himself walks onto the stage, a fairly ordinary looking, five-foot-nineish man with thinning hair. He seems younger than Margaret—maybe early sixties. He's definitely burly, like in his bio picture, with the neck and shoulders of a tree trunk, but smiling, with twinkly eyes and a spring in his step. He is eminently likable, and I almost can't help smiling back. Lou casually places a bottle of water on the podium, grins out at us, and says into the microphone, "Good evening, everyone; thanks for coming. I think we can get started."

He is fabulous.

I'm on the edge of my seat the entire time. Technically, I suppose it's a slideshow, but not like any I've ever seen before. Easily on the level of a Hollywood production, this has gorgeous photography, superb animations, and beautiful musical soundtracks. Lou is a born entertainer. He explains intricate concepts and theories in a way that I can grasp, and he adds plenty of humor perfectly on cue. The topic has to do with how things change over time, sometimes over millennia and sometimes overnight, and how those changes impact the world, and us, right now. Lou describes the intricacy of gathering and analyzing millions of tiny items of data to parse together changes that have taken place since time began. He inserts just the right clips from old movies like *Jurassic Park, The*

Butterfly Effect, and *Back to the Future* to keep things playful while demonstrating his points. Even so, this is no lightweight overview; he delves deep into the science of mitochondria, epigenetics, and molecular chemistry, among other things.

"... thousands of generations, stretching across time and circumstances that are so unfamiliar one to the other that there appears to be nothing that connects them at all," he expounds, "but it's there. One thing leads to another; over eons, they have an impact. Sometimes we can discover what happened and how, but mostly it goes by unknown to humankind. You may have children or grandchildren. You may think about the influence you have on them; maybe you wonder in what way you had a lasting impact on their lives. Certainly, some of them will remember you for a generation or two, or maybe three. But what about your impact on the second or third *thousandth* generation after you? That is unknowable and well-nigh unimaginable. We cannot conceive of the circumstances of a person's life so many years distant from ours, neither what his or her daily irritations will comprise, nor what types of big dreams those descendants may have. But we know that one day, as time ticks by drop by drop, those descendants will come, and they will embody in some way those things that we started and left for them."

He talks about using trends from the past to make predictions but ends with acknowledging that while many changes are predictable, many are complete surprises to us. We must take care, he warns us, not to be so arrogant as to think we mere humans can manage it all. The more prudent way forward in some cases, he suggests, is for us to step back and let nature take its course.

It seems he can answer any question with amazing erudition and lucidity, somehow making us laugh all the while. There is a whiteboard on stage for him to use, and as he writes, it gets projected onto the big screen. At one point he's talking and drawing, and as the pictures reveal themselves, it leaves us howling so loud and so long he has to stop the lecture until we all settle down again. He is masterful, and I don't want it to end. When it does, we give him a standing ovation.

The audience starts getting up, and a lot of people are going down to the dais to talk to Lou and ask more questions. I can't move; I sit gaga in my seat and review it all again in my mind. Karen and the gang would have loved this, and I can't wait till we're at our table in the Iguana and I can tell them all about it. I'm so excited, and I don't want to forget the really good stuff, so I hunt in my purse for a pen and something to write on. I still have my paper ticket, which I printed out at home. That'll do. I start scribbling, and every time I put something down, it reminds me of something else. I'm barely aware of time passing until I look up and see that Lou is saying goodbye to the last questioner. He also looks up, sees me, and smiles.

"Hi there," he says. "Did you enjoy it?"

There's no way I can just get up and walk out now, not saying anything. I stand up and climb down to the stage.

"I sure did," I tell him honestly. "That was incredible."

His smile gets bigger as he says, "Thank you! Thank you. Glad to hear it. And are you a student? Or a scientist yourself?"

I smile back. "Nope. I'm a yoga instructor."

"Well! I must say, that's a new one on me, and I thought I'd seen it all. What's your name?"

"Lily. Lily Piper," I tell him, trying to sound mature and confident.

"It's nice to meet you, Lily. I'd be very interested to hear what brings a yoga instructor to an event like this. Tell you what: Giustina's is right outside; would you care to join me for a cup of coffee?"

How do I get myself into these things? The situation is becoming surreal. I ponder Ridley's phone call. Then I consider the fact that I haven't experienced DC nightlife since my junior year in college. And Lou is utterly charming. It's just a cup of coffee, in a very public place. I can handle it.

"I'd love to."

We go out to the sidewalk, and as promised, Giustina's is just steps away. It's an ultracontemporary Euro café and pasticceria, obviously popular, as even this late it's all lit up and crowded. This is cool. I don't feel nervous in the least; I feel invigorated. I'm having fun. Lou offers to get us drinks while I try to find a table.

"What would you like?" he asks.

"Anything. Whatever's good. Just order me what you're having," I reply with a smile. It really doesn't matter to me; I've rarely met a coffee or tea that I didn't like.

"Okey doke!"

Lou gets in the order line, and I thread my way through the café. This place is hopping, but I find an empty table for two behind the wall of the creamer station. I can't believe I'm about to sit down with Lou DiSilvio, but it doesn't feel remotely dangerous. There are so many people around, and not to sound too spy-thriller about it, but I've already scoped out three separate escape routes should I need one. Lou comes over with a smile and a tray, from which he deposits two plates, each holding a beautiful fruit tart, and two see-through mugs of coffee.

"They're Americanos," he says. "I hope that's okay."

"Sure," I reply. "This is so nice of you." For some reason I'm surprised. I think I expected something a little more ... Italian. But no problem, I can tell just looking at the coffee that it's going to be good. Right now it's scalding, so I put it aside to cool a bit. I'm at a loss, wondering what I can possibly say, but Lou makes it easy. He starts off with simple stuff.

"Tell me about yourself, Lily. Are you from here, or a transplant? And do you have family?" Lou asks.

"I grew up around here, went to the University of Maryland for a few years. My parents still live nearby, but no family of my own yet. How about you? Your bio says you live in Italy. Do you have family there?"

"I do. I have two girls, eleven and thirteen. Alas, they live with their mother in the east, near San Marino, while I'm outside Rome, in the west. I don't get to see them nearly as much as I'd like."

I'm taken aback. I was expecting him to say something about Nico, perhaps, or tell me there was no one, which is ridiculous, really. He and Margaret split over fifteen years ago. It would have been stranger if he *hadn't* started a new family in Italy. I try to look blasé, but he notices something in my expression.

"You're surprised?"

"Oh, no, not really," I say, trying to laugh it off. "Only that your family is still so young."

I guess it's the right answer, because Lou seems pleased as he waves his fork at me and says, "Ah! Flattery will get you everywhere! I can see I'll have to be careful around you!"

We finish our tarts, and he takes a sip of coffee. As he sets it down, he asks, "So you're not a student as well as a yoga practitioner? Tell me, truly, what would your interest be in attending something like this? I really am very curious."

I reply that I was studying biology at UMD when I got into a terrible accident that forced me to drop out and take the next year to recuperate, and that's when I got into yoga. It's the super curtailed version of my recent past, but I don't want him to think I'm just an uneducated punk.

"Oh my! I'm sorry. So now you're thinking of returning to college? Is that it?"

This is an absolutely extraordinary opportunity. Just two weeks ago I heard about Lou and his work, and wondered about his perspective on it. It was pure whimsy then, no way ever to know the answer. But here he is, right in front of me, and now is the chance to ask him those questions. It must be fate or something, and I decide to go for it. As I did that day in the cafeteria with Dr. Ben, I describe the philosophy behind Eye of Horus yoga and the way we concentrate on physical movement to reach the mind and beyond, to know the spirit and the soul.

"The thing is, in biology we focused on the individual elements that compose a human being, which of course is critical, and foundational. But now I'm always on the lookout for scientists who study those parts in a bigger context—people who are interested in whether there might be an extra, nonphysiological element too. I heard about your talks (okay, a bit of an exaggeration) and wanted to come and see for myself." Now I look over at Lou and am utterly sincere when I tell him, "And I wasn't disappointed. If anything, it was almost too much to take in; I feel like I want to watch a rerun! It's like you're trying to tackle the big questions by diving deep into the infinitesimal. Is that true?"

"Beautifully put! You're absolutely right. I would have to say it is." Lou settles himself comfortably, pensively. We end up having a long, wonderful discussion that includes some of the things Dr. Ben and I discussed. We talk about what makes us human. I'm enthralled. Lou is an excellent listener, attentive, adding just the right words at the right times. He seems to be as engrossed as I am and encourages me to voice my thoughts.

I ask him about his work on the human genome, the building blocks of humankind, and throw in something like, "It seems like DNA is everything, but maybe it's not. I've read about cats that have been cloned, but they don't look anything like each other, you know? A gray tabby's clone might turn out calico, for instance, and they have completely different personalities. I wonder if that's an indicator that we're more than just our piece parts."

"My goodness, you have done some reading—and some thinking. Maybe we should get you out there on stage."

I know he's kidding, but I soak up his praise and keep going: more ideas, more examples. I'm on a roll. But I notice that he's talking less and less, and now I'm wondering whether I'm embarrassing myself. He's a world-renowned authority in multiple scientific fields, and I must be kidding myself thinking my ideas are brilliant and new. Yikes. My Americano has cooled, and I take a few sips to stop myself and give Lou a chance to say more, but he doesn't. He's just contemplating me quietly, sipping his own coffee. His gaze is starting to make me feel a little uncomfortable. I need a few moments to regain my composure, so I excuse myself for a second to get some cream and sugar. When I stand up, my purse, which I've hung over my chair, threatens to slide down to the floor now that the pressure of my back is no longer gluing it in place. Almost unconsciously, I grab it and sling it over my shoulder, which turns out to be a fortuitous move.

I go around our table to the front of the creamer station, and my heart skips a beat. From my new vantage point, I can see a uniformed police officer standing just inside the café, scanning the tables. *Shit.* Deep breath. This is Washington, DC; there are a hundred reasons why a cop might walk into a coffee shop. Unfortunately, at this moment, I can think of only one: he's here for Lou.

Seeing the policeman, who is possibly looking to arrest Lou—or maybe he's here to request that DNA sample—it hits home to me that I'm very much in the wrong place at the wrong time. The thrill of the evening evaporates, and all I want to do is get out of here. Ridley warned me to stay away, and the last thing I want is to get caught up in this scenario. It's terribly rude to abandon someone who has just bought you dessert, but I don't care. Bit by bit, I slide myself over to the pastry display and inch past the queue of people until I can get out the door undetected. Then I take off for the metro as fast as I can go.

C H A P T E R
TWENTY-FOUR

I toss and turn all night; what little sleep I do get is interrupted by vaguely disturbing dreams. In the morning, I lie there thinking over and over, *How could I? How could I be so stupid? What was I thinking? So, so stupid. Why do I do these things? That was so stupid.* I can't help myself; I just let the dark, self-flagellating thoughts flood in, washing over me. As it gets later and the sun shines brightly through the window, I finally make an attempt to take things in hand. I tell myself that I was overtaken by the spectacle of it all, Lou's charisma, and all the other attendees, who were likely brilliant themselves but still fawning over him like kids vying to be teacher's pet. Lou was a rock star, and I got caught up in the sense of reflected glory. Lou inviting *me* for coffee, the excitement of being in the city at night, discussing my favorite topic. It can happen to anyone. *But you told him all about yourself! You told him your name! Stupid! Why are you always so stupid?* Before this goes any further, I stop myself. *Hey, now, wait a minute. When you introduce yourself to someone, it's a perfectly normal thing to give your real name. It's not stupid; it's natural. So what if he knows my name? If that cop was really there for him, he's got bigger things on his mind and has probably forgotten all about me by now. If not, well, so his "date" did a runner, no big deal. He's still probably forgotten all about me by now.*

I take a deep breath and consider the evening in a more reasonable light. I went to a lecture with a thousand other people. Yes, I went for coffee with Lou, but to him I'm just a random member of said thousand. I was never in any danger, and I'm not in danger now. I might be a bit of a fool, but I'm not stupid. The self-talk eventually starts to have the desired effect of pulling me out of the worst of my despondency, and I start to think about having breakfast.

Then, at eight thirty, Karen calls. It's not exactly the crack of dawn, but it's awfully early for a Saturday, and I answer with a horrible sense of foreboding.

"Good morning," I say into the phone. "What's haps?"

"Hi, Lily, I hope I didn't wake you up."

"Nope, I was just thinking about what to have for breakfast. You must be an early bird. Or did something happen?" I ask, although really I know she wouldn't call at this hour just to shoot the breeze.

"Yeah, you could say so. I feel like my head is going to explode, but I made myself wait until a halfway decent hour to call you. You won't believe this."

"What? What happened? Is it Lou? Did somebody else …?" I trail off, but my first thought is that someone else got killed.

I can't see her, but I have a feeling Karen is shaking her head as she says, "No, it's not what you're thinking. Let me back up. I went to take a shower this morning around seven, and when I got out, I saw that I had two missed calls: one from the NICU, and one from Dr. Ben."

"Whoa. Okay."

"Yeah, so I figured something big was up. The NICU left a message—baby Victoria didn't make it. She died late last night."

"Oh, I'm sorry. That's such a shame. Poor little thing, I really thought she'd be going home with Andrew Li and his family."

"Well, I was hoping that would happen too, but it's been touch-and-go for her ever since she was born. Her lungs were too underdeveloped, and oh, other things. She just needed a little more time in the womb than she got. It is sad. I can't help feeling like if Irene were alive, she'd be totally devastated."

"I know what you mean. She would be. Is that why Dr. Ben was calling too?"

"So, okay, about Dr. Ben. No, this was something else. Remember the paternity test?"

"Yeah—did they compel Lou to take one? Was Victoria his?" I think back to the policeman scanning the tables last night.

"I don't know. I think they got the warrant, but that's not the one I mean. It's the original test that they did with Tom Peary. Remember Dr. Ben said there was an anomaly? Well, it happened again. So the hospital had four different techs take four different samples and send them to four different labs. All the results came back the same."

I feel like she's stringing this out but can't imagine why. Dr. Ben seemed pretty certain Tom Peary wasn't the father when we were all together in the Nook, and according to Karen they haven't yet got the results of any testing on Lou. So why the hushed excitement in her voice? Whatever is causing it, it's contagious, and I practically whisper back, "And? Who's the father?"

"That's the thing. There isn't one. Baby Victoria's DNA is a one hundred percent exact match to Irene's. Dr. Ben says the odds of that occurring in a normal birth are so many gazillions to one that it doesn't bear considering. There's really only one thing this can mean. She's her clone."

"What? Oh. My. God. No way. That's impossible. Isn't that impossible? I didn't think that had ever been done before—at least not on a human! They're really sure? That would be ... that's, well, just incredible!" I really can't believe it. Of all the things I might have been worried Karen was going to tell me during this phone call, that didn't even make the list. Talk about a sudden right turn into the truly bizarre.

"I know! Each of the labs just thinks there's an error, but of course Dr. Ben knows that it's no error. Because you're right: there's no known case of a human clone. Apparently there have been some claims before, but so far they've just been hoaxes or at least unproven." Karen stops for breath, and I dive in again.

"So … is that the crime someone is trying to cover up? I mean, it must be illegal, right?"

"Actually, it's not illegal, but it's definitely considered unethical; it's pretty much taboo. Any scientist who cloned a human would basically be blackballed by the respected scientific community. Dr. Ben thinks this might well be what Lou was trying to hide when Ridley questioned him, not murder or some financial scam."

"Why Lou, exactly? Does he think it's Lou's company? But … Irene went to Italy … his university?" I'm spluttering, thinking too quickly to spit the words out.

"I don't know about any of that, but who else if not Lou? You're right, though, there could be someone we don't know about. I haven't really thought this through; I just wanted to let you know about baby Victoria. I knew it would blow your mind as much as mine!"

"I'm so glad you did; my mind is *totally* blown!"

As amazing as this news is, Karen has no other details, so there isn't much else to say. We're about to hang up when Karen asks, "Speaking of Lou, did you go to his talk last night?"

Oh boy, cue the *How could I be so stupid* refrain. More out of embarrassment than anything else, I hedge a little in my response.

"Yeah, I went. There were a ton of people there; the place was almost full."

"That's good. I mean, there's no way he would recognize you or know who you were, but still, it feels too close for comfort now. I'm glad you're home safe."

"I'm fine. It was some show, but I'll tell everyone about it next time we're at the Iguana. Let me know if you hear anything more, okay?"

"You got it!"

Now we do hang up, and I sit on my comfy chair with my knees drawn into my chest and take deep breaths. My mind is on fire, and everything starts to click. *Who else is there*, Karen said. I grab my laptop and go back to Lou's LumarGen bio, rereading the name of the research station in Italy where he worked before the university.

I google it, and while there's a lot of scientific gobbledygook, that's not my focus right now. I'm looking for Lou and Margaret's names, to see if they're still associated with it. I don't find them, but the director, Dr. Sergio Zannelli, appears to be a person of some notoriety in Italy. There are a lot of news links to his name—mostly on tabloidy-looking sites, although the most recent news describes his arrest and incarceration for racketeering. *Racketeering.* I think of Haisley and her mafia scenario. I'd mentally tossed that one onto the crazy pile, but she turned out to be kinda sorta close. That part is by the by though; it's the tabloids that hold my interest. What did people do before everything in the media could be translated into English at the press of a button? That's a question for another day. I skim through, noting that over the years there have been a lot of rumors out there about what goes on in Zannelli's lab. Designer drugs, money laundering, result tampering—the criminal list is long enough, but I find what I'm looking for buried in the more lurid gossip: alien autopsies, mass hypnosis, psychokinesis, human cloning.

What if?

Lou got quiet right after that remark about the cloned cats. Margaret and Lou worked together on the human genome at NIH; what if they went to Italy and worked together at Zannelli's lab? What if they did successfully clone a human? Nico. Dear God, what if Nico is a clone? If Irene knew about it, and wanted a baby of her own, what if she convinced Margaret to get her into that lab to create another clone?

It fits, I tell myself, getting goose bumps. It explains the trip to Italy, the money going in part to Margaret to broker the engagement and the other part going to that European bank account—not Irene's or Lou's, but Zannelli's. I think back to Lou's lecture and his dire warnings not to mess with the natural world too much, his concern for long-term repercussions we can't yet even imagine. Maybe he's had second thoughts about cloning. Lou could have discovered Margaret and Irene's scam—a desperate gambit to get a big sum of money!—the same way Ridley did, through the snail mail correspondence that automatically went to LumarGen's office. Maybe Margaret confesses and he kills her out of anger, or maybe he kills her to keep her from ever helping anyone else. With Zannelli in jail, she might be the last person other than him who knows how they did it. And Irene? Maybe he kills Irene to stop her having the clone, not realizing the baby was already here, born so very prematurely.

It all fits. It's Lou.

My phone suddenly goes off, startling me, and this time it's my mom. I don't really want to talk to her, as she has that ultramom radar where she can tell just by the way I say "Hello" that something is amiss. If she asks what's wrong, I'm afraid I'll just fall apart and blurt out the whole story, and then she will be very, very worried about me. And I don't want to cause her more worry. She'll never replace the gray hair that came from my accident and its aftermath, and now she's coping with my dad. My mom is a youthful fifty-five, with a high-powered engineering job and a lot of verve. My dad is twenty-seven years older than she is, and not so lucky. He is very much in decline. They moved together to an assisted living facility in Laurel because he needs so much care now. It's a nice place, and they both like it there, but the whole situation is no picnic. As much as possible these days, I do what I can to convince her that her daughter is well, healed, and happy. Sitting frozen in my chair, I hesitate but just can't bring myself to ignore the call, so I decide to answer it but not say anything about all this until I'm in a better frame of mind. I try to convey youthful bubbliness as I press the button.

"Hi, Mom."

"Hey there. Is this a good time?"

"Sure! What's going on?"

We chat about general things for a while, like my dad and Tessa's family. It feels good to have this nice, normal conversation, and I think I've gotten away without setting off her radar when she stops me cold.

"I wanted to ask you about something. Did you go to someone's funeral recently? Margaret Crawford?"

"Uh ... well, sort of. I mean, I did. How do you know about that?"

"I got a strange phone call this morning. Was she someone you knew well? I don't remember you ever mentioning her."

"Wait, first tell me about the call. You said it was strange? Who was it? What did they say?"

"Not much, I thought it was a mix-up at first. It was a man who said he was Margaret Crawford's husband, and he wanted to thank me for sending the flowers when his wife passed away. Like I say, I thought he'd called the wrong person and said so. But he seemed so sure, and then he clarified that he meant my daughter Lily brought the flowers, but that she'd said they were from me because I knew Margaret from Oakton Montessori."

I feel sick, almost dizzy. Lou called my mom. That means he looked me up, he knows something, he's trying to find me. What the hell? It feels cold in the room, and I pull my blanket over me. For a second, I think I might even be about to faint, because my mom's voice sounds kind of far away, so I concentrate hard to hear what she's saying.

"It threw me for a loop, because I couldn't think of anyone I knew by that name and I didn't think you even remembered Oakton, but, then I thought maybe somehow you did."

"Remember Oakton ... What do you mean?"

"Well, we did put you in Oakton for a semester, but you weren't even two years old. That's why I was surprised you could have remembered. As soon as Mrs. Reilly started her daycare right in our neighborhood, we switched you there. It was cheaper and much more convenient."

This is unbelievable. I went to the same Montessori as Nico? I do the math in my head, figuring out the year I turned two and trying to remember the date in Nico's class photo, but I can't. Wouldn't that be something. I realize my Mom is still talking, so I quickly tune back in.

"Anyway, it all seemed so odd, but he knew your name, so I thought I'd better ask you. Do you know what this is about?"

"Hang on a sec, Mom, the kettle's boiling." I put my phone on mute for a few seconds because I need to take a breath and gather my thoughts. How did he find them? Somehow he knew my backstory. Did he talk to Nico? To Alice? Doesn't matter now; he's on to me. *Don't panic*, I tell myself. My mom and dad are not in danger. Their community is gated, and no one can just walk into their building unless his or her name is on a precoordinated list. It's not them Lou wants; it's me. *Okay, take it from there.*

"Sorry about that," I say into the phone. "It was making so much noise I had to turn it off. So, uh, yeah, the Margaret thing. I was supposed to be with Karen—you know, the friend I've told you about? One of the patients at her hospital died, so I, ah, said I'd go to the funeral with her. But when I went, Karen wasn't there, and I felt kind of dumb showing up for a stranger's funeral, so I just made that up about you and her being friends through the school, because her son went there. I really went to Oakton too? That's amazing. I don't remember that at all." I try a little laugh, keeping things light.

"Oh, Lily, honestly. You don't have to make things so complicated. You could so easily just have said you were from the hospital and left it at that. I couldn't decide if this was some kind of crank or if I'm starting to lose it myself. I've been racking my brains trying to remember a Margaret Crawford!" She sounds sort of annoyed at first, but by the end she's laughing too. The relief of clearing away the confusion dulled her Lily radar for once, so there's no need for me to explain further or tell her about last night. At least not yet.

"So how did you end the call with that guy?" I ask casually.

"I don't know; it felt so awkward. I just told him I was sorry for his loss and left it at that. Please warn me the next time you use me as part of some zany cover story."

I smile down the phone and promise that I will absolutely warn her next time, and I am relieved to sense that she's back to her old self, thinking this is more funny than anything else now. I'm curious enough to ask her more about Oakton and whether she remembers any of the other moms or kids or anything, but she doesn't. All she remembers is that some colleague of my dad's recommended it highly so they decided to give it a try, but with both of them working it was hard to keep to the stringent drop-off and pickup times. There isn't much more to say, and Mom needs to go, so we hang up with Mom sighing a little about how long ago all that was.

I pull my blanket more tightly around me. He must have talked to Nico. Why didn't I think of that before? I assumed they were no longer in contact, because Nico only mentioned Aunt Alice. But then, I only asked about Aunt Alice. *Damn, damn, damn.* I need to calm down, to stop obsessing for a few minutes, so I decide to finally make myself that breakfast. Tea, not coffee—something soothing. I dig through my canister and find some sachets of lavender mint. Perfect. Next up: buttered toast with jam. What could be more stress reducing than tea and toast? No TV—I don't want to listen to the news just now. Instead I put on some rainy day music and settle myself cross-legged on my comfy chair, with my repast balanced on top of a pillow. I eat slowly, mindfully, forcing myself to concentrate on the food and nothing else. It does seem to help, and when I'm done, I walk through this new turn of events with more circumspection.

Sure, Lou called my mom because he wondered about this Lily person showing up at his talk and finding out this selfsame Lily had also been to see Nico. But if the Montessori story held—and from what my mom said, it's just possible that it did, assuming Nico garbled it a little, which is very believable—then maybe it's not that strange. Nico could have mentioned that his famous father gives talks, so I decided to go to one of them. Perfectly reasonable. It's even possible that the talk with my mom diffused Lou's concerns, if he came away thinking my original story was true. It's not *im*possible.

Lou isn't looking to come kill me; he's probably just wondering why I ran off last night. Shoot, maybe he's worried something happened to me. That makes much more sense, and I finish my breakfast in a more positive frame of mind.

Since he did call my mom, I guess that means Lou isn't in police custody, and at first this starts me worrying again, but then I think maybe he's not in custody because he's not guilty. *No jumping to conclusions, remember, Lily?* I have to stop dwelling on this, so I decide to see what Tessa is up to. I throw on some clothes, walk across the pool deck to knock on the kitchen door, and open it, calling out, "Anyone home?" There's a muffled answer that I take as leave to come in. Once inside the kitchen, I hear Tessa's voice much more clearly calling, "Hi, Lily! I'm in the basement. Come on down!"

Tessa is sitting on the floor, surrounded by all kinds of things, most but not all baby-related: pieces of furniture, toys on springs and wheels for baby to scoot and bounce, bottles and binkies and similar paraphernalia. She is currently occupied with bags of itty bitty clothes, which she is sorting by size and gender.

"Hi," she says again. "Perfect timing! We've decided we have too much stuff in here that we don't need anymore, so we're going to do a big donation run. I'm sorting and making lists. Want to help?"

"Sounds fun!" I say, and I mean it. This is just what the doctor ordered. I step carefully over Brie, who is sprawled on the floor, playing on her kiddie tablet. She smiled broadly and called "Hi, Lily!" when I first appeared, but she never quite moved her eyes off the screen. Now she is oblivious. I settle next to Tessa and grab a bag, and we work companionably, although not terribly productively, for a few hours. I debate telling Tessa all about Victoria, the lecture last night—everything—but I remind myself I'm here to distract myself from all that. Unless she asks, I decide, I'm not going to bring it up. As with my mom, I play it super bubbly, just ordinary old me enjoying a quiet weekend without a care in the world. I exclaim over the especially adorable outfits that we come across and hold up for each other to see, and even though I'm not as into it as I'm making out, it really is nice being here with Tessa, seeing her enjoy the nostalgia brought on by memories of her babies wearing all these cute things. As time ticks by, my anxiety from the morning fades considerably.

The whole peaceful scene is shattered when we hear a wail from above and a bawling Charlie comes running downstairs screaming, "Mommy! Mommy!"

It takes Tessa a second to figure out what he's trying to tell us, but I got it immediately: a man came into the kitchen and took Julie. I know it's got to be Lou. I've been worrying all morning he'll come after me. But Julie? Never did it occur to me that he might come after the kids. What is he thinking? Could he possibly think she's mine? Kidnap Julie to keep me quiet? I'm outraged more than anything, and my protective instincts rise to a fever pitch as Tessa and I race up the stairs. I can't even imagine what's going through her head. Frank has appeared from somewhere, having heard Charlie. It's Lou all right; he's visible through the window, making fast down the driveway.

Frank shouts, "Lily, just keep him in sight! I'm getting my gun."

He takes the stairs up three at a time, and I'm out the door. Tessa is dialing 911 as she follows me out a few steps, but she has to stop. She's holding a now hysterical Brie, with saucer-eyed Charlie and Christopher clinging to her on either side.

"Oh my God! Frank! Hurry!"

I can't actually see Julie, but I can still see Lou, who made it all the way down the drive and is now jogging through the trees. I go after them, losing sight for a moment as I round the big stone pillars at the driveway entrance. Trees are thick along the C&O canal, but even so, it isn't the Amazon jungle, where you have to slice a path with a machete. Once you're in the woods, you can see quite a distance through the trunks. I'm still in full protector mode, determined to save Julie, but I'm also pretty scared and don't want to confront Lou until Frank gets here. So when I spy his blue jacket well away and to my left, I slow a little, hiding myself behind trees while keeping him in sight. He's stopped moving, and there's still no Julie. I'm wondering what to do next, as I don't see Frank but don't want to call to him and startle Lou, who remains motionless. *Is he lost?* I risk moving a little closer. There are plenty of leaves on the ground, but it rained early this morning, so they're wet and don't make a rustle. Lou doesn't turn around, and I go still closer. Alarm bells are now going off in my head, and I feel sick even before I confirm what I'd started to suspect about fifty yards back. It's not Lou. It's a blue coat that some hiker has left hanging on a rock. I look around and don't see Lou. *Shit.*

"Lily!" I hear Frank calling. "Lily! It's okay! We've got Julie!"

"Lily!" Julie's own little voice now. "Come back! I'm here!"

Oh, thank God. I've left my phone at the house, so I shout back that I'm on my way. It's difficult walking where I am, so I decide to head down toward the hiking path and then go along that until I find an easier way back up. This turns out to be farther away and much steeper than I realized, and the wet leaves that were my friends when I wanted quiet are now making it slippery. It's slow going, but I'm pretty sure the path is just ahead. I'm watching my feet as I make my way, and don't see Lou until the last minute. He sees me, too, and my heart starts pounding.

"Wait, Lily ... look, I just wanted to talk to you."

There's something about him, maybe his tone or his expression, that makes me almost believe him, but I don't feel like discussing it out here all alone in the woods. He comes toward me, and I pick up my pace to get away. Ridley's dire warning about staying away from the DiSilvios rings in my ears. I don't think there is a word for the bubbling of emotions when you are out of your mind with fear and running for your life while your situation turns absurdly comic. As soon as I try to run, I slip. Then Lou slips—he's in the same boat. We're both a little out of control because of the wet leaves and the extreme steepness of the bank. I get up and slip again. He's doing the same. I slip, he slips, we both keep slipping and catching ourselves. It's ridiculous—and terrifying.

Shouting for Frank—I hope he can still hear me—I realize I've overshot the trail and ended up right near the edge of the rocky face some ten feet above the river. Looking down, I think, *This is it, I* have *to get my footing and climb back to the path as fast as I can.* There's a big root jutting out from the leaves, and I step on this for leverage, lunging forward to clutch the trunk of a skinny tree that I can use to haul myself up. Lou is too close, though, and he grabs me.

Well, there is panic, and then there is something beyond panic. When Lou grabs me, my mind buzzes and then goes perfectly clear, and it's true what they say: time slows way down. I have only a split second, but it's enough to think, and to plan. He is bigger, heavier, and stronger than I am. But we're right over the water, and I am a swimmer; I am acclimated to cold water, and if it comes to it, I bet I can hold my breath longer than he can. Instead of trying to get away, I hold tight to Lou and push my legs with all my might, heaving both of us over the edge. Whatever Lou was expecting, it wasn't this. I'd had visions of us wrestling in the water, like in the movies, with Lou bursting up to attack again if I ever managed to get free. It wasn't like that at all. For one thing, the Potomac isn't very deep. When we went in, we hit bottom. That and the frigidity of the water instantly shocked Lou helpless. When I pop my own head up, I never see him again. While I was better prepared than Lou, I'm still terribly discombobulated. The current whisks me off, and the cold water makes my hands hurt and gives me brain freeze. But I eventually come to myself, and I remember that this is manageable. I swim hard against the current for ten strokes, then bicycle my legs to lift my head and hands up out of the water to let them warm. I swim another ten strokes, lift to warm, and manage fifteen strokes this time. Then I can do twenty, and then one more set of strokes, and there I am, back at the shore. Frank must have heard me after all, and I guess he had his phone with him, because a park ranger appears almost immediately. He helps me out, and gives me his warm, dry jacket to replace my sodden sweatshirt. I take some time to rest and catch my breath, but I assure him that I'm okay. He radios in to someone to say he's found me and I'm not hurt. When I'm ready, he leads me to a wooden staircase that takes us up where we can see his ranger car parked a short distance away.

TWENTY-FIVE

Lou made it out. It would have been ironic if he'd drowned, but he managed to get ahold of some branches and just hang on there. The police found him even before my ranger got to me. They arrested him and took him to the hospital to be checked out. Detective Dan Ridley went in to question him, and by this point Lou was out of fight. He told Ridley absolutely everything. The police also got statements from Frank, Tessa, the kids, and, of course, from me. Ridley put the story all together and relayed most of it to Dr. Ben, who fortunately has a kind and thoughtful heart. He knew we'd all be out of our minds with curiosity, so he called me to see if it would be okay to drop by—"Of course!"—and late that evening he, Karen, and I are sitting with Tessa and Frank in their family room, drinking tea. We finally get the scoop on the rest of the story. As I listen to Dr. Ben, I can't help feeling a little thrill of pride at how much of this I had worked out for myself.

Drs. Luigi DiSilvio and Margaret Crawford met at work and bonded over their sheer, overpowering ambition to make a big splash in the scientific world. They were both extremely successful but never made it to the upper stratosphere to which they aspired—no mega patents, no mega prizes, no morning talk shows. As Margaret got older, she became increasingly obsessed with having a baby. Lou also wanted a family, but he wanted a breakthrough more. When he met Sergio Zannelli through an international research collaboration program, the stars seemed to align. Zannelli had a lab in Italy and some keen backers. Margaret was a willing test subject. They could create the world's first, perfect, human clone. But things went a little wrong. It took a long time to get an embryo to take, and when one did, the baby—Nico—was born five weeks prematurely, and with some problems.

"Is that because he is a clone?" Detective Ridley asked during the interview, intrigued despite himself at this irrelevant (to the crime) piece of the puzzle.

"I have no idea," Lou responded with a sad shrug. "There's no reason for that to be true. There are so many possible causes; these things happen with babies of ordinary birth all the time. Nico was a sample of one, so it's impossible to say."

At any rate, they waited and watched, and it became clear that Nico's issues were quite severe, that he would be compromised his whole life. None of the scientists wanted to publish this result as the glorious outcome of their work. Margaret wanted to protect Nico at all costs. Lou went through a crisis of conscience.

He told Detective Ridley, "It just hit me hard that we don't know what we're doing, we have no idea where this could go. This is *humanity*, and we could do damage that we can't even imagine. We *need* gene diversity, we need to have differences so we don't all succumb to the same problem, whether that's a disease or some other malformation. I went through months of soul-searching and years of regret. We should not have played with this kind of fire. No one should. But if it ever happened again, and I believed it would one day, I didn't want it to happen based on any work that I did. I don't want to be the one that lit that match."

At first Lou and Margaret stayed together but dropped their human genetics research. They returned to the States and started up their own company, performing metaresearch on plant genetics and publishing their analyses. They came up with an idea related to the development of what we now commonly call GMOs and applied for and received a grant from NESD, which is how they met Irene, who was a new, young program analyst at the time. The project had some success, but the things that once held Lou and Margaret together were no longer there. Margaret took to parenthood with a vengeance, but Lou had a hard time with it.

"Nico was just a little baby, our son—my son—and I loved him. I will always love him," Lou told Ridley. "But Nico is also my clone, and together he and Margaret were a constant reminder of the travesty I had committed, with all its potential implications. It's not Nico's fault—not at all; he is totally innocent, and he doesn't even know anything about all this. I blame myself, but I also blamed Margaret, because she had been as gung ho as I was. We couldn't stay together; we got so we couldn't stand each other. I went back to Italy because I know the language and still had contacts, and took up a position at one of the smaller universities there. Margaret stayed here with Nico and moved in another career direction. She took over the deed to the house; I bought out her share of the company."

Margaret and Irene, Lou told Ridley, remained close throughout their careers. They bonded over similarities that defied age and culture, two very ambitious, perfectionist professional women who dared to want a perfect family as well. It wasn't that they saw each other all that much—quite the contrary, they weren't part of each other's social circles at all, and years could go by with no contact. But either one could call the other at a moment's notice and pick up right where they left off. One of those soul-mates-for-life kind of deals.

Even from afar, Lou, it turned out, was a more hands-on manager of his now solely owned company than Margaret realized. When he discovered the NESD grant fraud, he was absolutely furious. She had put him and LumarGen in danger of facing charges, and he had a horrible suspicion Margaret and Irene were going to use the money for Irene to have a clone. He would never let that happen. He confronted Margaret, who refused to admit anything. When their argument escalated, she got scared, so much so that she ran away from him into the guest bathroom. Before she could close the door, he was there, and at this point, he told Ridley, he went haywire. He grabbed her to make her talk, and when she fought him, he just got angrier. In a rage, he stuck her head under the tub spout. He wanted to scare her, to force her to tell him what she and Irene had done, and didn't realize she couldn't breathe at all.

"I was so mad. I wanted her to suffer, and I wanted to make her talk. But not to kill her. That was never in my head, never my intention. I know Nico needs her, and I would never have taken her from him. Never, never, never."

He apparently looked right at Ridley as he said this, emphatically shaking his head all the while. When Margaret was quiet for too long, Lou realized what he'd done. Terrified what would happen, what would come out in a police inquiry, he tucked Margaret into bed and left the house. Once again, he miscalculated.

"I didn't think about who would find her," Lou told Ridley, tears forming in his eyes, "Certainly, the possibility of it being Nico didn't enter my head. I just wanted time to pass before she was discovered."

"Dan told me that rang pretty true for him," Dr. Ben is saying. "But of course, it begged the next question: if it was true, why would he turn around and kill Irene?"

"I didn't," Lou told Dan. "I mean, I did need to see her, because now she was the only one left who could tell me what they'd done. I knew she'd bought the old house, so that's where I went. I had no idea she'd just had a baby. I just wanted to surprise her into talking, so I went around back to see if she'd left the basement sliders open, which she had, and got in that way. I ran up the stairs and found her on the sofa, watching TV. She was surprised, all right. I'll never forget the look on her face. She leapt up, and then she just … she just froze and then crumpled. I couldn't wake her up. I couldn't feel a pulse. I tried to resuscitate her, but nothing worked. She was gone. I panicked. I propped her back up on the sofa and left the way I'd come."

"So she really did have a heart attack?" asks Karen.

"Essentially, yes. Giving birth is fraught with a lot of peril. Sometimes there are things we can detect in advance and then take precautions, and sometimes things just happen. It's entirely possible she would have died without Lou ever entering the picture. More likely, the shock of seeing him was too much and that was the trigger. That's something no autopsy can tell us, though, so we'll never know. Lou's story did answer one question that has been bothering me—there were hairline cracks in her ribs. Performing CPR can absolutely crack or even break someone's ribs, and that's almost certainly what happened here."

We sit quietly for a minute, taking this in. I'm remembering that day in the woods.

"He came after me," I say slowly, pensive. "I was sure he was there to kill me too, but he did say he just wanted to talk." I repeat Lou's words to me and describe how, even then, I'd sort of believed him.

Dr. Ben looks at me and sighs and shakes his head. "In hindsight, this is a comedy of errors, but you could so easily have been in a lot of danger."

Comedy of errors? Karen and I glance at each other quizzically and then back at Dr. Ben, who is now looking at me a little grimly.

"Dan thought he'd made it clear to you that involving yourself with Nico's family was a bad idea. But there Lou sits, recounting a conversation he happened to have with a young woman, a certain Ms. Lily Piper, who showed up at one of his public lectures *and then sat down with him for coffee.*"

What could I say? Of course, he's right. My only defense, sort of, is that I wasn't trying to investigate anything at that point. *I was just curious to see Nico's father / Margaret's ex-husband up on stage, and then he invited me ...* I sound lame to myself.

"Mmm hmm. I see." Dr. Ben rolls his eyes up and sighs again, but when he looks back at me, he's at least smiling. "Well, Lily, whatever you talked about, Lou ended up with the distinct impression that you might be either some kind of investigative journalist or working with the police. He started to wonder if you might be recording your conversation, trying to goad him into admitting something either about Margaret or about the truth of Nico's birth. He didn't know which it was, and was desperate to find out what you knew and what you wanted."

I'm thunderstruck. I close my eyes and then open them again, looking first at Dr. Ben and then around at everyone else. It begs a comment, but I don't know what to say.

"Oh."

"Yes, 'oh.' A man who just caused the deaths of two woman—whether he meant to or not—could well have been considering what he'd need to do to keep you quiet too. Fortunately, it never got that far."

Dr. Ben tells us that Lou, afraid that he might be arrested soon and that this may be his last chance to see Nico, went early in the morning to visit his son for the first time in a very long time. Lo and behold, Nico talks about his new friend Lily Piper, whose story is that her mother knew Margaret from Oakton Montessori School. Lou did some checking, and whatever he found out—"for some reason" Dr. Ben injects, clearly still puzzled about this—it tempered his concern.

"But your address was in the book you signed, sitting on Nico's counter right there in front of him, and he had to know for sure, so he decided to confront you face-to-face."

It is almost funny. Lou was doing exactly what I was doing: telling himself how irrational his fears were, how it makes much more sense that my showing up at Lisner and our conversation at Giustina's was just a coincidence brought on by the timing of Margaret's funeral. I make an unlikely private eye and an even more unlikely cop. So much more probable that I really am a friend of a friend of Nico's who did, in fact, look up his dad and decide to attend the lecture. If he'd just found me and I'd played dumb, maybe he would have gone away none the wiser ... but then we would have remained none the wiser too, forever wondering what really happened. *Besides ...*

"So why kidnap Julie?" Karen asks, beating me to it.

Now Dr. Ben chuckles. "More misunderstanding. Lily wrote down Tessa's house address as her own, so that's where he went, expecting you"—here he nods at me—"to live alone. True to form, he did the same thing that he did with Irene: went around back to see if a door was open so he could startle you into talking, and got into the mudroom. Julie told the police that she was in the kitchen and saw a scary man coming toward her, so she ran outside in terror and hid behind the towel drying rack. Lou says he never saw Julie; he heard noises and realized there were multiple people in the house, so he took off. By happenstance he left through the same door that she did. Charlie was playing a game in the living room. He got a glimpse of first Julie and, right after her, this strange man going out the door, and he came to the conclusion the man had taken her."

Oh, man. Wow. So that's what happened. Tessa and Frank already know that part, since they've heard it from both kids already. But Karen and I are doing similar versions of clasping our hands to our heads, shaking them and exclaiming something along the lines of "Aaaaah!"

"Okay, okay," I say. "That's his story, but what about when we were stumbling around in the woods? Why did he grab me like that?"

Dr. Ben is having himself a good laugh now. "Because," he says, "he saw you lurch and thought you were about to fall off a cliff. He was trying to save you."

Now we all stare at him the same way—open-mouthed.

"Oh yeah," says Dr. Ben, "That was some maneuver you pulled. Lou was more surprised than he'd ever been in his life."

Everyone's grinning now, shaking their heads with more mutterings of the "oh my God" ilk.

"Good move though." Frank winks at me. "I mean, had he been trying to kill you."

Tessa throws a pillow at him and gets up to go toward the kitchen. "Tea isn't doing it for me tonight," she says. "Who else wants a glass of wine?"

CHAPTER
TWENTY-SIX

Lou ultimately pled guilty to manslaughter for Margaret Crawford. He begged the police not to make public the facts of baby Victoria's conception. "Please don't let that be in the headlines," he implored them, believing the story would spur on any others out there who have considered trying to clone a human, who just need confirmation that it can be done to go forth and attempt it themselves. And it did stay quiet. Without a trial, there was no requirement to bring it to light and prove it was real, no need to make it public record at all. Incredibly, the only thing about Margaret or Irene that made it into the press was related to the NESD fraud story. Lou went to jail, but he won't be in forever. When he gets out, he intends to divide his time more evenly, seeing his girls regularly in Italy but also being here, helping to look after Nico.

Nico, in the meantime, continues his routine at Sherwood Independent Living, going on outings with Geoff and the League, and texting his contacts whenever the spirit moves him. His trust keeps him solvent, and Aunt Alice flies down every few months to make sure he's okay. None of them have any idea about the extraordinary facts of his birth, and as far as any of us who do know are concerned, they never will. Why invite a circus? Margaret worked hard to protect him, so he could live his life peacefully and on his own terms. We're all in agreement on that score: Ridley and Dr. Ben, Tessa and Frank, Karen, all the Whatevers from the Iguana (damn, we really need a better name), our lips will keep forever mum. Of course, even if we wanted to tell the world, we have no proof. Lou and Nico together are the only ones with the key to that particular vault.

In high school, I once had an English assignment to write an essay starting with the words "To live is to be ..." I had to finish the sentence and then explain it. I've thought about that phrase many times over in the years since then; I use it as a gauge of how I think things are going and how I'm feeling. My endings have run the gamut: To live is to be challenged, disappointed, miserable, disillusioned, hopeful, determined, confused. Of late I've been thinking that to live is to be surprised—surprised when things actually go as you expect, and surprised when they don't; surprised by things that happen and by things that don't; surprised by others; surprised by yourself. If you had asked me on that first day, when we heard that someone had murdered Margaret Crawford, how I would feel about her death and about all the different characters I've come in contact with since then, I would never have imagined it would be what I feel now. Back then I was an avenger, hell-bent on upholding the innocent and pouring down retribution on the perpetrator. I still feel sorry for Margaret—sorry that she died in such a horrible way. I also feel sorry for Irene, who died too soon. But I'm a little conflicted about them too. They are innocent in some ways and not in others. They conspired and committed a serious crime. And Lou doesn't seem purely evil; he has done horrible things, but he also has deep regret, and not everything he is or does is bad. Nico loves him; he can't wait to have his dad back on the scene. I didn't expect to feel sympathy. I didn't expect that someone else's tragedy would fire me up and bring me back to life. I didn't expect to make friends, all at once, out of a disparate troupe of studio regulars. Now I don't know what to expect next—other than that, as I continue on, I will probably keep on being surprised.

For me, of course, the biggest thing looming once the case is closed is the cold water challenge. The plus side of my little adventure (misadventure?) is that I gained confidence in open water swimming.

I know I can do it. Thank you, Lou, for that. So I'm super excited the morning of the big day as I pack towels, goggles, and extra clothes into a gym bag. Yes, honestly, I'm still disappointed Tessa won't be there. It's so much more fun with two, talking together on the way, giving each other courage at the start, and, best of all, celebrating together after we're done. I will miss that. But there will be other opportunities, I'm sure. For now, I feel ready, and I really want to go. I walk over to the main house to collect Tessa's car keys, and she greets me with a big, mischievous smile.

"You have some visitors."

Visitors? What does she mean? She opens the door, and there on the driveway is Karen's big SUV. It's not just Karen; Haisley, Redd, and Miller are there too. I can't believe it! I go running out, and they're laughing, turning around so I can see their T-shirts. They're all wearing the same one—it's dark blue, with an exact replica of the sign on the wall of Tessa and Frank's house: red letters surround a growling red bear face, and it reads "MATTAPONI BEARS SWIM TEAM." Karen hands me one, and Tessa unzips her jacket and I see that she's wearing one too. My heart swells; I'm so touched.

"You guys! You guys are the best! What *is* this?" It's stupid, but I'm overwhelmed.

"We're coming with you!" says Karen. "All for one, and one for all!"

I look around in disbelief. "Oh my God, you guys. No way! You didn't have to do this. You know you don't have to. You're all really coming?"

They crack up at that, and Miller and Haisley speak at the same time.

"Oh, yeah we do! We gotta see this!" (Miller)

"Of *course* we are! We wouldn't miss it!" (Haisley)

I look over at Redd, who deadpans, "I didn't want to come. But Miller said they needed a token black man."

I know I'll cry if I try to say anything, so instead I give him a big hug. The others come over, and we're all hugging. We break apart with big smiles but a little choked up too. I look closer at Haisley, who has a piece of masking tape on her shirt right above the word "BEARS." On it she has written "PANDA" in thick red magic marker. She grins at me, and I shake my head, grinning back. *Oh, Haisley, you and your pandas.*

"Okay, everyone," says Tessa, "You'd better get going; you don't want to be late!"

We pile into the SUV. Karen lowers the windows so we can wave at Tessa and call out our best wishes for Julie and her recital. Then we're on the road, music blaring, talking over each other, laughing and joking. I feel so happy. We are a team, and we have a name. It's written in italics across the backs of our T-shirts: *"Go Bears!"*

ACKNOWLEDGMENTS

Very special thanks to my husband, Ron Loiselle, for so many reasons there isn't space enough on this page to list them all. Truly, were it not for Ron, this novel would never have been written. Also, my heartfelt gratitude to the inimitable Barbara and Charlie Huffman, for their friendship, endless support, and enthusiasm. Thank you to all their kids and grandkids too; unbeknownst to them, they supplied so much in the way of examples and fodder for ideas. And thank you to Kathleen "Kathi" Britske, friend and fellow laker, for reading my very first draft from front to back and providing invaluable feedback. Finally, I really must acknowledge my siblings, Albert Clepper and Charlotte Osborne, along with the Linde "kids," Michael, Sarah, and Anita. If they ever read this book, they will know why.

To the citizenry of Bethesda, Maryland, I apologize for playing a bit fast and loose with its geography; some of the places in this book do exist, and some are complete fabrications. Since this is a work of fiction, I was aiming for realist*ic* rather than absolute reality, but it might be jarring if you know the place well. Be that as it may, your fine city has been an inspiration to me and an ideal setting to provide Lily and her friends a wealth of opportunity, and for that, we thank you.

Did you enjoy this book?

Keep an eye out for book two of the Eye of Horus series!

Lily and her friends are back, again unintentionally embroiled in a mystery. This time it is one that hits a little too close to home.

ABOUT THE AUTHOR

Born in Washington, DC, Anne Loiselle grew up in Bethesda, Maryland. She headed to Scotland for college, where she received both bachelor's and master's degrees in Russian from the University of St. Andrews, and then worked in Russia for several years. After moving back to the DC area, she completed another master's degree at George Mason University and had a career as a defense and intelligence contractor. Now she lives with her husband in the foothills of the Blue Ridge mountains in Virginia and is fully focused on writing.

Find out more about Anne and read her blog, *The Full Writer Experience*, on her website at www.anneloiselleauthor.com.